THE
BOHEMIAN GIRL

Frances Vernon

MICHAEL JOSEPH
LONDON

MICHAEL JOSEPH LTD
Penguin Books Ltd, 27 Wrights Lane, London W8 5TZ (Publishing and Editorial)
and Harmondsworth, Middlesex, England (Distribution and Warehouse)
Viking Penguin Inc., 40 West 23rd Street, New York, New York 10010, USA
Penguin Books Australia Ltd, Ringwood, Victoria, Australia
Penguin Books Canada Ltd, 2801 John Street, Markham,
Ontario, Canada L3R 1B4
Penguin Books (NZ) Ltd, 182–190 Wairau Road, Auckland 10, New Zealand

First published in Great Britain 1988

Typeset in 10½ on 12½ Garamond
by Cambrian Typesetters, Frimley, Surrey
Printed and bound in Great Britain by
Butler & Tanner Ltd, Frome and London

British Library Cataloguing in Publication Data
Vernon, Frances
The Bohemian Girl.
I. Title
823'.914[F]   PR6072.E6/
ISBN 0-7181-2933-4

To Kingstone and Johnny,
just to annoy, with love.

CONTENTS

PART ONE: The Hon. Diana Blentham
1880–1896

PART TWO: Mrs Michael Molloy
1896–1901

THE BLENTHAMS OF DUNSTANTON PARK

Sir Roderick Blentham, b.1542, d.1607

Son of a poor attorney. One of the most
trusted agents of Sir Francis Walsingham,
and a handsome charming man, he was
knighted by Queen Elizabeth and made
Ranger of a Royal Forest.
His son, Edward Blentham Esq, acquired
Dunstanton Park by marriage.

Charles Roderick,
4th Baron Blentham, b.1830, d.1897
= 1862, Angelina Caroline, dau. Admiral Venables

Maud Victoria b.1863, d.1913	Edward Charles b.1864, d.1919	Roderick Harold b.1868, d.1940	Violet Angelina b.1872, d.1899	Diana Mary b.1874, d.1912
	= 1891 Kitty Dupree [large family]	= 1899 Cicely Vane, dau. Major Vane, Indian Army	= 1895 Sir Walter Montrose, Bt	= 1896 Michael Molloy

Alice Maria
b.1897, d.1958

= 1916
Anatole Brécu

Finola Leonie
b.1916

= 1944
Gerard Parnell

Part One
THE HON. DIANA BLENTHAM
1880–1896

CHAPTER 1

A CHILDREN'S PICNIC,
CHESHIRE 1880

'Nurse says your father is connected with Trade,' said Diana. She had an audience of three younger children, who were picking at the remains of potted shrimps and ice-cream.

'He's not, and I'll pull your hair if you say it again,' said Thomas.

'Nurse says your father is – '

Thomas jerked a straggling piece of hair, but not hard enough really to hurt her.

'I was *going* to say something else!' said Diana. 'And now I shan't tell you what.' She grinned at him, showing a gap in her teeth, when he had expected her to cry.

At that moment, Thomas's fat governess came up.

'I saw, Thomas. I saw that you're incapable of behaving like a little gentleman even for an hour.'

'He *could* be a gentleman, I s'pose,' said Diana, with her head on one side.

Miss Taplow hesitated, looked at the child, then said: 'Apologise to Diana, Thomas.'

'I shan't.' The governess slapped his face, and Thomas turned white.

'You need not stay,' she told him, and pressed her hands to her forehead as he ran off in the direction of the grown-ups' picnic, on the other side of the tall Gothick folly which all had been taken to admire. Miss Taplow slowly followed him, and the nannies, who were guarding the food baskets under an elder tree, looked after her with pursed lips before they started to criticise her: not because of what she had done to Thomas, but because she was a governess and not a nanny.

3

It was a very hot day, and party discipline had grown lax. At first, the twenty or so children had been arranged in neat circles, and food had been brought to them by the various nurses, and one under-footman from the house. Now, most had had enough to eat and were sitting in idle and irregular positions, while the nannies talked among themselves with their highest collar-buttons undone.

Diana Blentham sat cross-legged on the grass, yawning to herself with one black stocking down. There was a ginger-beer stain on her pink-and-white-striped front, and the bunched back of her skirt was very badly creased. She noticed, as she glanced round, that two of the smaller girls near her were beginning to grow fractious, but their mood did not affect her: she was, as usual, contented but a little bored. She was pleased that Thomas Pagett had pulled her hair, for she liked unusual attentions: she turned her head and saw that he had not come back. Everyone else was occupied in some uninteresting way.

Diana pulled up her stocking, but did not fasten it in place. She got up and walked slowly, in order to attract no attention from the nurses, round the huge clump of rhododendrons which gave the children shade. Before the picnic began she had observed an opening between two lower branches, which had intrigued her, for the rhododendrons at her own home in Kent were not much larger than rose-bushes.

She found the slender gap, pushed aside the branches, and suddenly found herself perfectly enclosed in an open space like a hot and dusty room. Diana stood up, raised her head to the blaze of sky, and hitched her stocking up again. She stuck her finger in her mouth and looked quickly about her.

Stiff leaves and brown flowers with long withered stamens littered most of the ground, and the four low twisting roots were pale as dry earth. When she saw these, Diana realised that the rhododendron was not one miraculously large plant, but several, each of which grew in a different direction. She saw another space ahead, and decided to go further on, and pull apart more barriers.

Diana was six years old, and she had never done anything

4

so tomboyish as this before. Her own enjoyment of dirt and difficulty surprised her, and she thought of herself as Snow White, deserted in the forest by the huntsman who had just refrained from murdering her. Presently she came to what seemed the last of the dull little glades; she could hear the chink of china and grown-up conversation.

Diana sat down on a low branch and looked through the screen of leaves at the main picnic. At that moment, she saw Thomas's sister Miss Sophie Pagett dart forward with her arm through a young man's, pause, and quickly kiss him. Diana blew out her cheeks to stop a giggle, then frowned: for on her way up to the folly she had seen Sophie Pagett flirting in a very fast way with the local rector. Nurse had even remarked on it.

When the couple passed, Diana leant further forward, and caught a glimpse of her parents. They were standing in the sun, quite some way away, and seemed to be worriedly debating.

She drew back, and began gently to rock up and down on her branch. Then she straddled it, and found that an improvement. The rough thin wood felt strangely pleasant, there between her legs, and she rocked more vigorously, until a piece of broken twig scratched, too hard, at the bare stretch of thigh between her loosened stocking and pushed-up knicker leg. She thought, meanwhile, of kisses, and of rescuing some handsome man from death.

Diana saw the stocky, freckled Thomas Pagett kneeling to her right. She stopped rocking altogether.

'What are *you* doing here?' he said.

'Riding!'

'No you're not.'

They spoke in whispers, because the grown-ups were so near. Thomas got to his feet and came closer. His Norfolks, Diana saw, did not show the dirt as her frock did.

'You *are* in a pickle,' he said in a slightly affected voice, as though he were acting.

'Why should I be? I wasn't disobedient,' said Diana. 'I wasn't actually told I *couldn't* – do it.'

'But you know you shouldn't. That's disobedience just the same.'

'No it's not. Disobedience is different, actually. And what about you? I bet you *were* told you couldn't.'

Thomas ignored this. His eyes were on her bare stretch of pink thigh: he had no brothers or sisters of his own age, and had never seen another person who was not fully covered in his life.

'This belongs to me,' he said suddenly.

'What does?'

'This place. All of it.'

'It belongs to your father. Don't tell stories.'

'It will belong to me. I've got a right to be here.'

'You're a very rude little boy!' said Diana.

Then she heard her nurse's voice, not very close, saying: 'I don't know *where* she can have got to for the life of me. Didie!'

'And you're a stupid girl!'

Just as she remembered that her leg was exposed, and took her hand off the branch to pull down her skirt, Thomas moved quickly as a cat and pinched her naked flesh, far harder than he had pulled her hair.

'Ow!'

'I'll do it again,' he said, and did it.

'Miss – Diana!' came from far away.

Diana scratched Thomas's face, then scrambled off her branch, hampered by her petticoats, and said in a high voice: 'Coming, Nurse!' Nurse would not be able to hear that.

'Coward!' said Thomas. His face was red and his eyes were glittering. 'I'll kiss you, if, if –'

'I'm going,' said Diana. She made for the other side of the clearing, and Thomas moved awkwardly towards her.

They had been making too much noise. Suddenly, both heard a charming and very close voice.

'Gracious, whatever *is* going on in there? James, is it rabbits? Do see!'

Thomas and Diana stood still, their hearts beating foolishly, as the leaves rustled and parted and the moustached Captain

Tremaine, who had kissed Sophie Pagett five minutes before, poked his face through.

'I say! By Jove, I wish *I* could get into the rhododendrons with a girl, young Thomas!'

'I'm not a girl!' Diana said. She was crying, and did not know quite what she meant, except that Captain Tremaine had humiliated her.

'Well, come out then, there's a good girl,' the captain said good-humouredly.

'Is it Thomas in there?' said Sophie Pagett. 'Oh dear, he *is* a bore.'

Diana stumbled out past the captain, who held the branches apart for her.

'Goodness,' said Sophie when she landed.

'Nurse was calling, and I'm going to find her!' Diana said.

The captain said: 'Well, we'll both find her then. Come on.'

He picked Diana up as though she were a toy, and sat her on his arm, with a brief wink at Sophie. When he put his hands on her, Diana was too surprised to speak, but a moment later Captain Tremaine saw that she was looking rather sick, and that her lips were working like a baby's. Sophie Pagett looked up inquiringly from under her parasol, then turned to speak to another young lady.

'I say, no need to cry! Come on – a-gallopy, gallopy, gallopy – ' Captain Tremaine ran over the lumpy ground up towards the folly, and jolted Diana badly: yet while being jolted, she relaxed. Her tears dried quickly in the heat.

'*Didie!*' said Nurse, who came hurrying up as soon as she saw the young man with a child in his arms. 'Oh, you naughty girl! Are you all right then? I never saw such a mess. Thank you, sir,' she added.

'Here's a prodigal child,' said the captain, setting her down. 'Been making hay while the sun shines in the rhododendrons with young Thomas. Still, she's going to be a regular beauty, ain't she?' He thought Diana might be in more trouble than she deserved, and so he said this to Nurse although he did not, in fact, think she would be a beauty at all. Addressing Diana herself, he said: 'A *Professional* Beauty! I say, won't you like having your photograph in all the shop windows? I shouldn't wonder if you sold as many copies as Mrs Langtry!' He looked at Nurse, who was herself attractive in a snub-nosed way. She did not laugh, and he raised his monocle. 'The Jersey Lily, you know, Nurse!'

'You can't sell copies of yourself!' snapped Diana. 'You've only *got* one self.'

Nurse scolded Diana well as she led her firmly away from the remains of the picnic to a modest dip in the ground behind a grove of rowan trees. There she began to tidy the child, pulling up her grubby skirt to deal with the fallen stocking and loose knicker-leg. She searched for needle and thread in her pocket.

'I'm sure I don't know what can have come over you, Didie. Naughty as Violet may be, with her pulling faces and all, *she's* never thought of doing just such a thing, I'm sure.' Violet was eight, and Nurse loved her although she was neither as pretty nor as intelligent as Diana. 'Old Mr Jenkins used to say, when I was nursery maid, before you came even, that Miss Maud was always wanting to be a little boy, forever climbing trees she was at your age, and ever so mischievous, and now she's giving your Ma funny turns with all her nonsense about I don't know what, and her going to be presented to the Queen, too, not six months from now! I hope *you* won't – ' Nurse stopped, and stared at Diana's leg.

'What is it?' said Diana, who had quite calmed down during Nurse's lecture.

Nurse looked up. 'Sit down please, Miss Diana.'

'Don't call me that,' she said. The unease and tearful fright which had first surprised her when Captain Tremaine appeared in the bushes came over her again.

'I'll call you what I like *when* I like. Now – ' Nurse pushed back Diana's skirts as far as they would go, and pointed to two fat scarlet pinch-marks on her thigh. 'What are these? How did you come by them?'

There was a pause.

8

'T-Thomas pinched me – I hate him! Oh, don't be like that, *don't*! *Why* are you like that, it's *stupid*!'

'He was alone with you? In the bushes? I thought the Captain was – Miss Diana, don't cry.' Nurse's voice was very low. 'Did you pinch him – anywhere? Tell me now!'

'I scratched his face!' cried Diana. 'And I'm not sorry!'

'You scratched his face, did you?' Nurse let out a little breath. 'Now, Didie, I see you're upset, and I want you to stop crying. See? Now listen to me. Thomas did something very wrong – very wrong – though you're both of you too young to know why. But you knew it was wrong in a way, didn't you? Isn't that why you're crying?'

'Yes!' said Diana. She had wanted to pinch him, equally hard, but his rough tweeds had left no flesh exposed for her to pinch.

'It was horrid, wasn't it, when he did it?'

'Yes!' It had certainly been painful for a moment, and she had been very angry.

'Well, it's high time Master Thomas went to school!' Nurse said. She continued: 'Didie, if a little boy pinches you in a bad place again – which I trust he won't never have the chance to, not if you keep your stockings up like a lady should! – don't scratch his face. You scream, loud as you can.'

'But why? I thought it was naughty to scratch people, and –'

'Not when – oh, dear me, if only you wasn't a child! Didie, it's not so bad as all that, not now, but when you're a little older – as old as Miss Maud – you'll never be allowed to be alone with a big boy. A young man I mean. You know that, don't you?'

Diana's eldest sister Maud was seventeen.

'In case he pinches me?'

'Yes.'

'Even if – suppose I wanted him to pinch me, Nurse?'

Nurse took hold of her shoulders. 'That's what would be wrong! Oh, dear, Didie, you mustn't want a – boy to pinch you till you're married. And you won't get married if you let him pinch you before! You *mustn't* ever want him to, it's not what the good Lord intended. And remember it hurts, miss!'

She looked down. 'I shouldn't be telling you all this, you're sharp enough as it is, Lord knows, and you'll be asking questions. Don't you ask of your Ma, or you'll be losing me my place!'

'Oh!'

'Now, it's nothing, I'm talking foolishness. But don't. Didie, I'm just warning you as I shouldn't.' Nurse paused. 'I had a little sister, who'd dead now, and she came to a bad end – a very bad end – through letting people pinch her in an unseemly sort of way.'

'But *how*?' Though Nurse was puzzling her, obviously not explaining something because she was a child, Diana felt oddly grown-up: because of the expression on Nurse's face.

Nurse got to her feet, and with her lips pursed together picked a spray of rowan berries. Her little sister, made pregnant by the son of the house in which she had had her first situation, had become a Haymarket prostitute and died of a mangled abortion four years later.

'But *how*?' said Diana, whining. 'What d'you mean, Nurse?'

Nurse was daintily examining the berries, thinking now of certain ladies of the Prince of Wales's set, to whom Lady Blentham, Diana's mother, would only give a distant bow in passing, and a two-fingered handshake if it could not be avoided. They led lives as morally adventurous as her sister Rose's; though less full of variety, Nurse supposed. She knew that such ladies could not regard Lady Blentham as quite their social equal, and her bows and cold handshakes, which they precisely returned, amused them very much.

'Nurse, am *I* going to come to a bad end?' said Diana. 'Is that what you mean?' She realised that she must not ask more about Nurse's sister, and she was not, in any case, a very curious girl in general.

Nurse knelt down at once and put her arm round the child.

'You? My little Didie? You keep your stockings up, and you'll be a duchess, a *respectable* duchess, with a house in Park Lane and a big place in the country, and diamonds and carriages and I don't know what besides, and Nurse'll be your housekeeper! Now, is that what you call a bad end?'

Diana giggled as Nurse cuddled her, and looked up into the shade of the rowan umbrella, waggling her latest loose tooth. 'I sh'd like to be a duchess,' she said when Nurse removed her fingers from her mouth. 'And I'm sure I'm old enough to be one *now*.'

'Well, I should think it's good enough to be plain the Honourable Diana for the present – and Nurse's good girl too, I hope, which is more important!'

Diana looked up at the sunshot green leaves, and the orange clusters of berries which looked both jewel-like and edible, but decided she was too sleepy and comfortable to reach for them just yet.

'Virtue is the true nobility!' said Nurse, and pinched Diana's elbow.

CHAPTER 2

THE BLENTHAMS
AT DUNSTANTON

One morning early in 1886, when his younger daughters were at their lessons upstairs, Lord Blentham stood at his study window and watched his wife, wrapped in furs, descend from her carriage and enter the house. He went to the hall to meet her.

Dunstanton Park, in a flat part of north Kent near Strood and Rochester, was a dark brick Tudor manor house to which a white portico had later been added by Inigo Jones. The linen-fold panelled hall, and the gallery above it, were the only sizeable rooms in the building, and the house was cold from September to May.

Lady Blentham always ignored the cold. Her husband saw her take off her gloves, little bonnet and furs without a shiver, and hand them to the butler while she gave orders about that evening's small dinner-party. She was in mourning for a cousin, and wore thin grey cashmere with jet ornaments, and an Alexandra fringe.

'Well, Charles?' she said. 'The crocuses are coming up very prettily, all down the drive.'

'How was old Nellie?'

'Oh, not at all well I fear. Nothing else of course was to be expected. That niece of hers – Harriet – was with her.'

Lady Blentham paused, and Lord Blentham expressed surprise, and added, 'Pretty girl, that.'

'Charles, you sound like a *masher*. Well, she admitted she left her place before her year was up, but I think service has improved her, nonetheless – she said thank you very nicely when I gave her my mother's receipt for embrocation, and remembered to curtsey, too!' She smiled.

'Good, good.' They went into a little family sitting-room which opened off the hall and was full of photographs and china and fashionable thick-leaved plants.

'Charles, is there something on your mind?'

Lady Blentham was a thin pale beauty who always dressed in excellent taste; her husband was plain and fat, and wore out-of-date Dundreary whiskers which his wife persuaded him slightly to trim. They were fine golden-red whiskers, though he was fifty-six and the remaining hair on his head was grey.

'Well, Angelina, I've had some news, got some news for you, and I'm afraid you won't be – altogether pleased. Though . . .'

She opened her eyes as he waited.

'Is it Maud?' she said. 'Don't tell me that very odd young man has written to ask you for her?'

'No, no, nothing to do with poor Maud. *I* couldn't see that the fellow was smitten with her, I must say, my dear.'

Lady Blentham sighed. 'A pity. In her case, any husband would be better than none. There are times when I fear – well, what is your news, Charles?'

Lord Blentham put his shoulders back, and looked her in the eyes. 'My dear, I learnt this morning – got a letter, from Granville in fact – that it's perfectly true. Gladstone does mean to introduce a Home Rule Bill.'

There was silence for a while, and Lady Blentham's thoughts turned away from her eldest daughter. She remembered how often Mr and Mrs Gladstone had stayed with her father, Admiral Venables, when she was a girl. She also thought of how Lord Blentham had failed to become a Cabinet Minister in either of Mr Gladstone's previous governments: though it was true he had been Under Secretary of State at the War Office in 1869. That seemed a very long time ago.

'To introduce one? It will be the end of the Liberal Party,' said Lady Blentham, sitting down on her bustle and gripping the arms of her chair. Her husband coughed and she added, quite humbly, with a smile: 'Home Rule for Ireland! Well,

Papa would have said that Mr Gladstone knows best, I dare say, and who am I to think it will destroy the Party and ruin the country? Of course, dear Mr Gladstone is a very old man now, but my dear Charles, whoever would have thought it?'

'Hartington . . . '

'Oh, Lord Hartington!' She waved a hand. 'Yes, I know you told me he said something to you at the club, *en passant*, but how was I to take it seriously?'

'I would never have expected it of Gladstone myself, before this winter,' said Lord Blentham, rather coldly, because he would have liked Angelina to be a little proud of his close acquaintance with Lord Hartington, deputy leader of the Party to which she felt loyal. 'But I will say, Angelina, I think he's right. My own fear is that he may be ousted from the leadership because of this devotion to – principle. Things have come to a pretty pass in the Commons, I can tell you.'

Lady Blentham's mouth trembled. She was not a virago, and she did not speak in an intimidating voice. 'Charles,' she said, 'do you *believe* in Home Rule?'

'Well, yes, Angelina! Yes, I think it's the only solution.'

She got up from her chair and looked at him. 'I have always been prepared to be guided by your judgement, Charles. Now – in all the years of our marriage, you never even told me – your real views on Ireland?'

'Oh, I haven't been a Home Ruler quite since we were married, Angelina,' said Lord Blentham, looking at the fire. He was smiling. 'But now Gladstone is prepared to introduce a bill, I thought I'd . . . '

The butler came in to announce that luncheon was ready, and that Miss Maud was in the dining-room. The Blenthams did not discuss politics in front of their daughter, who called herself a socialist but, as they told her, was quite ignorant of the realities of government. Maud herself happened to mention women's political rights, and her mother said: 'Women can have nothing to do with such things, my darling,' without telling her about Mr Gladstone's conversion. Lord Blentham took no notice.

✻   ✻   ✻

When luncheon was over, Lady Blentham went up to the
·schoolroom to see Violet and Diana. Half way up the big
stairs she paused, and fingered the oak gryphon at the top of
the newel-post. Her expression was grave. As she studied the
little gargoyle, Lady Blentham regretted the hypocrisy of her
remark to Maud about politics being quite outside the
feminine sphere. She tied a knot in her handkerchief to remind
herself to mention that fault in her prayers, and went on up
towards the landing, still thinking hard.

Lady Blentham thought she had not been merely hypocriti-
cal, but cowardly, and she sighed. Cowardice had prevented
her explaining to Maud in front of Charles that a political
hostess, a statesman's wife or mother, had far more influence
on events than a woman with a vote. Her husband would have
raised his eyebrows if she had dropped such a hint – but he
had not noticed her duplicity with Maud, which was of course
improper only on a high religious level. It was impossible
always to tell girls the truth.

Walking quickly along the corridor, she wondered whether
Mr Gladstone (for whose sake she had always been a Liberal)
would require all future members of his government to be
convinced Home Rulers, and thus whether Charles would at
last have a seat in Cabinet. Lady Blentham was still angry with
both her husband and the Prime Minister; and she was so sure
of the wrongness of Home Rule that she did not feel remorse.
Charles would deserve it, she thought, if he had a very
difficult time in the next government . . . she wondered how
he had guessed in the first place that she, who had always been
affectionate and submissive, would care so very much about
this latest disaster in the world. She would no more openly
argue about men's business with her husband than she
would dispute his right to share her bed and do as he liked
there.

Lady Blentham opened the schoolroom door, and looked
in. It was the middle of a French lesson, and her daughters
were reciting a poem they had learnt. When they saw their
mother, Violet and Diana pushed back their chairs and came
over to kiss her; so naturally that she thought they would

always be a comfort to her, unlike Maud, and her two sons Edward and Roderick. The girls were not often quite so easy with her, though she had always considered herself an indulgent parent.

'Well, Mrs Mackay, I suppose I shouldn't interrupt their lesson!' she said happily to the governess. 'But I haven't seen you since Tuesday, have I, girls?' Now, she thought, looking at the two of them, this is my proper sphere.

'You neglect us,' said Diana, smiling.

'Hush, my baby. Mamma is very busy, with – ' she hesitated, for she had been about to mention Mr Gladstone and their father.

'With what?'

'Now, no questions.' She tapped Diana's cheek, and saw the next moment that, at twelve, Diana had picked up her father's habit of raising her eyebrows.

'This is *such* a nice interruption, Mamma,' said Violet, diverting Lady Blentham's attention. Violet was no taller than her little sister, but fatter, with her father's too-curly hair, wide mouth and blunt nose. Her eyes were large and dark and lively, and might attract a husband in four years' time. 'Mrs Mackay is *so* strict and French is so *particularly* dull!' She winked and pouted at the governess, who flushed, because Violet's gesture looked so affectionate. The Blentham girls were sharper and more tiring than any she had taught before, though their mother thought them quite normal.

'Is she very badly behaved?' said Angelina to Mrs Mackay.

'Yes, Lady Blentham, she is!'

'Sometimes,' said Violet, clasping her hands before her. 'Only sometimes.'

'Yes, that's quite true,' said Diana seriously. 'Only occasionally.'

Lady Blentham turned and looked at the two girls, who were steadily regarding her in a way which made her realise that perhaps they were not children. She put an arm briefly round each one.

'My dears,' she said, 'I think you're both inclined to be rather impertinent. Tomorrow – we must have a little talk.'

16

She continued, when they did not respond: 'I shall be driving into Rochester to call on Mrs Denison. Mrs Mackay, can you spare them to me for an afternoon?'

'Certainly, Lady Blentham.'

'Work hard at your French, girls,' she said as she prepared to go. They went back to the table and sat idly down. In the doorway, Lady Blentham turned, and Violet and Diana looked at her in surprise.

The fringed jet brooch at her collar jangled, and her face looked tired in the full cold light. 'I shall tell Annie not to light a fire in here tomorrow morning,' she told the governess with sudden severity. 'It can be lit at tea-time. It's nearly March – nearly spring, and the girls can very well do without a fire during the day.'

'Mamma, it's *cold*!' said Violet. 'It's winter.'

'Violet, you must learn not to answer back. You must not expect to be pampered, either of you.' She left, and shut the door behind her.

Lying on her stomach, Diana warmed her chilblained fingers at the fire until they hurt. Violet wriggled deeper into her armchair, and spread her hair over its back. She gave a hollow groan to attract her sister's attention, but Diana only smiled and looked down at the book which lay open before her. Outside the window, it was dark.

'Di–*die*,' said Violet at last.

'What?'

'Don't be fusty. Talk to me.'

'About what?'

'Anything. Oh, I'm so bored.' Violet jumped up and went to the table, where the remains of tea lay waiting for the third housemaid to take them away. She inspected them, and put a piece of dry bun in her mouth.

Diana closed her book, rolled over, and looked up at the cracks in the schoolroom ceiling. She was particularly fond of the one shaped like a bonnet with an ostrich plume.

The schoolroom was on the second floor, directly under the roof of the house. Together with Mrs Mackay's bed-sitting-room, and the girls' own bedrooms, it looked out over the drive, at the lawn and cedar trees, while the old nurseries and the servants' quarters were on the same floor in the two short wings which poked out at the back. Nothing in the schoolroom had been changed since Diana could remember.

The walls were dim cream, decorated with maps of English counties and the world; the Turkey rug was full of holes and stained with ink, and the hard armchairs were like those in the servants' hall. Over the little iron fireplace, there hung a pen-and-ink drawing of a tiger shoot in India, in which the bearers looked very small, and the Englishmen too large for their elephants, though the elephants were nearly as tall as the palm trees. It had been done by the girls' eldest brother Edward before he went to school, and the wounded tiger in the foreground, Diana thought, was particularly unrealistic. There were other drawings on the fireplace wall, but there were very few books in the schoolroom.

'I wish Mamma would leave us alone,' said Violet.

Diana sat up. 'Do you? Vio, d'you *love* her?'

'Of course I do! Goodness, what funny questions you ask.'

'I don't think *I* do.'

'*Didie.*'

'Not as I love – some people. How could I? It's common sense.'

'Oh, of course one couldn't be as fond of her as one is of Nurse, for example.' Violet sat down in the armchair again. 'But I do admit,' she said, pulling a face, 'that Mamma is a vast improvement on Fusty Mac.'

' "When I was a ga-irl in Sco-atland," ' said Diana, and they both began to laugh, ' "one of the greet Clan Menzies, there was noo such thing as a fire, Diana Blentham. Fire hadn't even been inv-*ented* then. *I* was verra hardy, when *I* was a gairl, one of the greet clan Menzies! *Raw* herrings for breakfast on the Sabbath, Diana Blentham, and . . . !" '

'Oh, poor old widow!' said Violet, still giggling. 'She must feel *persecuted*. I must try and be kind to her, really I must.'

'No, I suppose I do love Mamma,' said Diana suddenly. 'I *admire* her.' Diana herself wished to be influential, self-sufficient, and much admired.

Violet did not take her sister's remark very seriously. 'But you love me most, don't you?'

'Mm.' Diana smiled. Violet came over, and thumped her on the collar-bone.

'You love me most. Say it.'

'You're so *undignified*, Vio.'

'Say it.'

'Yes, Vio.'

'Say it?'

'I love you mostest.'

'So do *I*,' said Violet, thumping her again and then sitting up straight. 'I say, Didie, d'you think I'm very young for my age?'

'No,' said Diana, surprised.

'I'm not as clever as you are,' said Violet, 'and so I suppose I naturally feel – roughly the same age. It's hard to think I'll be coming out two whole years before you.' She looked up over the table at the black window.

'I don't want to come out,' Diana told her, and she meant it. 'Though it'll be nice to get rid of Fusty Mac.'

Violet said: 'Oh Didie, you *are* young.'

'In many ways, I'm rather old for my age,' said Diana.

They were quiet for a while, and Diana opened her book again. The housemaid came in, and took away the tea-things. When she had gone, Violet said in a deep but casual voice: 'Didie, have you ever wondered how babies – are made? I don't imagine you know!' She clapped her hands as though swatting a fly.

'They grow inside a woman once she's married,' said Diana, looking up. 'Just as puppies grow inside dogs.' She had gathered this, because the Blenthams kept several male and female terriers, and because did not believe in telling children direct lies on any subject at all, but only in misleading them when necessary.

'Even if the dogs aren't – mm – properly married?' Though

19

she did not know quite why, Violet began to giggle again. 'The *bitches* aren't married, with a white veil and all that – I wonder. . . . Of course I know that, but Didie, how do they *get* inside one? How d'you think? And where do they come *out*, come to that, one does think a great big *baby* . . .'

'I don't know. Does it matter?' It then occurred to Diana that, of course, men had something to do with it. Quickly she remembered the boy Thomas Pagett, who had pinched her thigh five years ago at Lynmore Hall, and she remembered Nurse's odd distress. She flushed, wondered why she had never thought about the matter before; then decided it did not really interest her.

'The woman's husband must have something to do with it,' said Violet, making her sister start. 'Look, do you think Mamma would tell us if we asked her?'

'No,' said Diana.

'Why not?'

'I don't quite know.'

Diana found secret pleasure in her own body and she hoped that, when she married and shared a bedroom, the man would not disturb her: that was all, she thought, and she tried to dismiss the question from her mind. There was something very insecure about that deep private pleasure. Though no one had ever discovered it, or told her so, Diana knew that it was wrong, a squalid thing, which ought to make her unhappy. 'I don't want to have children,' she said.

'*Don't* you?' Violet, who had been resting her head on her arms, lifted her face and looked at her sister. 'Oh, I want as many as possible!'

'No, I don't want any,' said Diana. 'I don't want to marry at all. I'll be an old maid and I'll manage perfectly well on my own.'

The door opened, and Maud, who was twenty-two, came into the room.

Maud had inherited Lady Blentham's looks, but no one described her as a beauty, which was most unfair. Her sight was very weak, and thick spectacles concealed her eyes, which were not large, but very clear, framed with blonde lashes, and

20

blue as Canterbury bells. She was far too thin, and her soft complexion was so anaemic as to look grey in a bad light. She had a true Grecian nose which ran straight down from her forehead, a pale clear-cut mouth and a fine oval face; but her defects prevented these being easily noticed. Only her hair attracted the attention it deserved, for she was the one true, rich blonde in the family. Edward was flaxen-haired like his mother, Roderick and Violet were brown, and Diana's hair was too red in some lights and too dark in others to be called blonde except by very generous people. Mrs Mackay called it ginger.

'Hello', said Violet and Diana together. They rarely saw their elder sister.

'Hello, children. I came up because I suppose you don't know yet – that Bateman is going to be married?'

Nurse's name was Alice Bateman, and now that she acted as Maud's lady's-maid, and took care of their clothes too when the family was not in London, Violet and Diana were supposed to call her by her surname.

'Queen Anne's dead,' said Diana, and Maud looked coldly at her.

Violet giggled at Diana, and said: 'But she's been going to be married for ages, Maud. She got engaged on Didie's eighth birthday – I remember it very well.'

'I meant that she's going to be married next month. Her uncle died and left her a legacy – enough to get married on at last, or so she told me.' Maud smiled. 'We must wish her happy.'

There was a pause. 'I don't *believe* it!' said Diana at length. She had been very upset when Nurse first announced she was going to be married; but the engagement had gone on so long she had thought the wedding would never take place.

'Well, I suppose it must be true,' said Violet. 'So she'll be leaving?'

'Yes, of course. I came to tell you because – ' Maud hesitated – 'because it would be very bad if either of you reproached her for going. I realise that you're both very much attached to her, but you won't, will you?'

'She ought to have told us herself,' said Diana. 'And why did she tell *you*?'

Maud flushed. 'She was going to tell you. She doesn't know that I've come. Diana, you mustn't make a – a scene when Bateman does tell you! Thank goodness I did come up! There's no reason for her to feel tied to us! She's well over thirty – it's time she was married – do you expect her to put you before her husband?'

'Yes,' said Diana.

'Didie doesn't mean that seriously,' said Violet.

'I do,' said Diana. Tears dropped out of her eyes, and her ears were bright red as she looked down at the floor. Nurse's betrothed was second gardener at a house in the Midlands; and Nurse had always said that he meant to set up on his own as a market-gardener as soon as he was able. Now they had a little capital, they would go to live in Worcestershire, and Diana would be lucky to see Nurse once a year. 'There is reason for her to feel tied to us,' she said.

'There is none. She's a servant. Do you expect to buy her – her *soul* with wages, as well as her labour?' Maud said this very loudly, because in her parents' presence she found it very difficult to express herself just as she wished.

'Oh, Maud, *really*,' said Violet, and added: 'she wasn't your nurse, but do try to understand how – Didie must feel.'

'Surely you're both too old to care in this way?' said Maud.

Violet went to put her arm round Diana. She cleared her throat, hugging her sister, and in order to divert herself as well as Diana from unhappiness, said: 'Maud, before you came in, Didie and I were talking about – how babies are made. We're neither of us quite sure. Can you possibly tell us?'

Maud put her hand on the doorknob, and one corner of her mouth twitched. 'The doctor brings them in his black bag, Violet. Surely you knew that!'

'Maud! Here, you're making fun of us! No, do please tell us.'

'As far as I know,' said Maud calmly, 'that is the truth.' She knew exactly as much as her sisters did, and her curiosity about the subject was far greater. But it seemed to her that discovering the whole truth about the matter was quite as difficult as permanently improving the condition of England's poor. There were no books to explain, references in forbidden novels were very odd, and no one, of course, could be asked. It occurred to Maud then that she might ask Bateman, and she blushed thickly under her spectacles. 'Remember what I said!' she told them, and left.

'*Well!*' said Violet, putting her hands on her hips.

After supper, Nurse came herself to tell the girls about her coming marriage. Violet wept pleasurably through her congratulations, whereas Diana was perfectly polite, saying that Maud had already informed them of the happy event. She did not cry at all. Nurse told them that she would always be fond of them both, and remember them; and Diana reminded herself that in any case she had seen comparatively little of Nurse, of Bateman, during the past five years. There was no reason for her to be unhappy.

Lady Blentham had an uneasy night. At first, she could not sleep at all for worrying about Charles and Home Rule and Mr Gladstone's mental health. When she did fall asleep, she had several confused dreams, in one of which all three of her daughters ran away to Ireland in a train bound for Vienna, and Alice Bateman announced that she was a cousin of Lady Londonderry's. Recently, Angelina had begun to suspect that, when the girls were little, Bateman had not been quite the strict well-trained nurse she had appeared in public.

She woke very early, as usual, in a cold bedroom, and when she rang the bell her letters were brought up to her with her toast and tea. Lady Blentham was surprised to see one addressed in her son Roderick's hand, and she tried to feel love. At present, for no particular reason, Angelina felt that all children in the world were merely a source of trouble.

Roderick as a child had been plain, stolid, generally obedient, but obstinate sometimes. He had always been intended for the Church, and had accepted the idea until two years ago, when he had simply announced that he did not want to take orders, and would not do so. His virtue, thought Lady

Blentham as she slit the envelope, was that he was sincerely fond both of her and of his little sisters. Roderick was now eighteen, and handsome in a heavy, youthful way in spite of being rather pimply.

My dear Mater, he had written from Harrow,

> *I expect you will be surprised to receive this letter from me. I know I do not write often enough; this is one of my faults which I intend to reform.*

Lady Blentham sat further up in bed and pulled her pillows into shape behind her, before returning to the letter.

> *In fact, I mean to reform in every way possible. I know, Mater, that ever since I made the First XI, I have been very arrogant, especially with regard to the more serious matters in life. At school, it is sometimes very difficult to concentrate on the more serious side. Certain things in that line are just not done, but that, of course, is very wrong.*
>
> *I can confess now that, a year ago, I actually had real doubts about the Christian faith, it was not simply that I no longer wished to go into the Church. But when one is in the Sixth, and one realises one will soon have left school, one starts to think rather, about the future. The chief thing is that now, after talking matters over with Morrison (the Head of House and a splendid chap, though rather an Evangelical – but most of the men here are simply unregenerate, heathens to a boy, absolutely as though there were no Chapel, and so I suppose he cannot be criticised too much for being Low), I know that I should like of all things to be ordained when I have taken my degree. I remember all you said to me on the subject last holidays, and although I did not appear to pay proper attention to you, Mater, I know, Morrison made me see that Church is the thing and you were right. The only thing that matters, in fact.*

All this is very difficult to write, Mater. I know of course that I am unworthy, but I mean seriously to try. I have committed a great many sins at Harrow, some very bad, especially of late, and I long in some way to make up for them.

You will be pleased, I know, to hear that I have spent very little money this term. I still have the £5 Aunt Emmeline gave me at Christmas (bless her for her generosity) and so I require absolutely nothing in that line. I shall never be extravagant again.

I hope that you and my father will consider me fit to take Holy Orders; I mean to make myself fit. Please give my love to Violet and little Didie, and I remain,

Your affectionate son,
R. H. Blentham

P.S. Do you suppose it would be appropriate if, in view of your religious opinions, with which I entirely agree, I were to be entered at Keble rather than Magdalen as my father intended originally?

P.P.S. Forgive so many postscripts, but I must excuse the use of the purple sealing-wax and Jennerson Major's seal. I have most unfortunately lost my own, and it would never do to leave this about unsealed for my fag to find.

Lady Blentham read this twice. She expected very little of a boy still at school except good-natured obedience, and Roderick's awkward words seemed to her as full of proper feeling as a sermon by the late Dr Pusey.

Angelina felt her faith in children restored by grace; but she was a little puzzled, for though she thought Roderick as sinful as most boys, she knew that only some great and peculiar sin could have prompted his conscience in this way, and she could not quite think what that might be.

After a two-days' interval for reflection, she took her son's letter down to the library and showed it to Lord Blentham, saying that it had arrived that morning. He was pleased enough with it after a short discussion.

'I hope he won't become too – earnest, but I agree, Angelina, it's a very proper letter and it's a good thing to have him settled. I never thought he'd do for the Army or the Navy, and what else is there? Though the Church isn't what it used to be. He's not clever enough for the Bar.'

'One son in the Army is quite enough,' agreed Lady Blentham, ignoring the implication that a stupid man would do well enough for the Church. 'But there is something which puzzles me rather, Charles.'

'Yes, my dear?'

She hesitated. 'Roderick is reserved, and has never been – eloquent, shall I say. But he writes now almost as though he had done something – very wrong. I am worried, Charles.'

Charles looked at the last postscript, and folded the letter up. 'Oh yes, I should think he's done something pretty wrong.'

'But what possible opportunity could he have for doing something – sinful, at Harrow? A public school! A few illicit trips to London – even the occasional glass of beer – could not be considered absolutely *immoral*, Charles. And what worse could there be – for a boy of his age? Edward is in no way repentant of *his* sins!'

Lord Blentham studied her beautiful face. His own was rather grim. 'Don't worry, Angelina. It's nothing which could concern you, now he's – repented, as you would say.'

'You – guess what it is, and will not tell me?'

'No, my dear. Some things – really are men's business. I don't mean politics, to be sure!'

Lady Blentham told her husband that no doubt he was right, and quickly left the room, holding up her skirt on one side as though the well-polished floor were dirty. She could no more think what Roderick's sin might be than her daughters could guess how babies were made.

CHAPTER 3

MISS KITTY DUPREE
OF THE SAVOY THEATRE

'My darling,' said Lady Blentham, tapping her daughter's cheek, and Diana sucked in her lips with pleasure. She was seventeen now, and her mother's delicate hints at her beauty, her affection and encouragement, were Diana's only compensations for being still with her governess while Violet, at nineteen, was in her second Season.

Angelina continued, looking out into the rainy street: 'I wonder, Diana, what Violet can want? What could *any* girl want more? Such a very nice young man, and so eligible in every way. Don't you agree with me, my dear?' She turned. 'I'm sure *you* would be able to feel affection for him, if you were old enough, wouldn't you?'

The two women were in Diana's little pink bedroom at the Blenthams' house in Queen Anne's Gate, and Lady Blentham had just made her first worried confidence to her youngest daughter, in the form of a gentle lecture.

'He does seem very kind, Mamma, but if Violet doesn't love him – you've told us before that it's very wrong and vulgar to marry for money, or position, or all that.'

'Of course it is! Of course. But – oh, Diana.'

'If only he weren't a Viscount, and *we* weren't rather poor.'

'Diana!'

'I'm sorry, Mamma, but I know it's a great expense, bringing us all out, and if Violet doesn't marry soon my – my own coming out next year will be a pretty heavy financial burden. I know we have this house now, since Grandmamma died, so there's no rent to pay, but with two of us to dress, and hire horses for, and – it mounts up wickedly, I *know*.'

'Don't think that I shall put it off,' said Lady Blentham, looking at her daughter's golden-brown, red-flecked hair, which waved all over her face, back and shoulders.

'I'm glad – I was afraid you might be thinking of it.' Diana looked away to hide her hot relief.

'Your feelings are very understandable,' said Angelina, 'but I hope that if it *were* necessary to put off your coming out another year, Diana, you would bear such a trial with Christian fortitude?' She spoke kindly. 'And Diana, please, in future, don't talk quite so frankly about money – not in front of other people.'

'It's so dull, when I *know* I'm old enough!' stammered Diana. 'So dull always having to be silent when I *am* allowed downstairs, and having to dine alone with Mademoiselle, and go to museums and practise my Italian and my French and my wretched music! It was all right before Violet came out, but now it's so different! Mamma, please – can't I just put my hair up and wear proper dresses, down to the floor? Even that would be – ' She faltered at last.

Angelina was not angry, though she said: 'Diana, Diana, control yourself.'

'Mamma, I'm so afraid my looks will go before next year!' Thoroughly emboldened, she went on: 'You know Maud used to be a beauty, still is in a way, but . . . '

'Don't be vain,' smiled Angelina. 'Besides, I don't think that's at all likely.' She too was very much afraid of Diana's suddenly losing her looks before it was time for her to be shown, but she knew she must comfort her daughter and not betray this. She continued: 'I'm afraid I can't allow you to put your hair up, Diana, because I didn't let either Maud or Violet do so before she turned eighteen. You must know that I can't grant such a privilege to you – however much I would like to.'

Diana looked down at the bed and clasped her hands tightly. She had had no idea, when she was younger, that she could care so passionately about anything.

'You will *soon* be grown-up, my darling,' said Angelina.

'Soon!' When Diana considered that little more than a year

ago she had been glad to be an inky schoolgirl, trying to write poems and enjoying muddy walks, she felt not too young for adult society but that she was a spinster as aged as Maud.

'You may find,' said her mother, noting her disbelief, 'that being grown-up is not quite such a pleasure as you think it will be now.'

Diana jumped off the bed and tried to laugh. 'That's what Violet says, more or less. Oh, of course, in her *first* season she did quite enjoy being a young lady, but now *she's* forever saying what a bore it is, Society, and looking at me as if I don't understand life at all, and *I'm* forever saying what a bore it is in the schoolroom, and hasn't she forgotten, and *she* doesn't understand. We smile cynically at each other,' said Diana.

'My dear, you're amusing, but you ought *not* to talk cynically,' said Lady Blentham, who thought all her children except Diana a little unintelligent. 'Do you know, *I* find Society a bore, just as Violet does? Though not because I'm lazy, I hope! Except, in – certain circles, there are so many different amusements, so very many people whom of course one dislikes – and yet such a lack of real variety! And then, Diana – listen to me, my love – Society is constantly becoming more *hollow* as they say – even immoral. Which I dislike very much.' She paused, thinking of last year's scandals, and of how she herself seemed to be the only woman in London who truly abhorred bad behaviour.

'Immoral?' said Diana.

'For example, my dear, when I was a girl, there was no question of receiving callers, or giving dinner-parties, on a Sunday. Certainly no question of jaunts to Richmond!'

'Oh, I see,' said Diana, thinking of the O'Shea divorce case last year, which had precipitated a quarrel between her parents about whether or not the Irish leader's being a co-respondent proved that Home Rule was intrinsically wicked. Violet had overheard something of that quarrel, the first true violent argument of the Blenthams' married life: and when reporting it to Diana she had cried horribly over the whole affair.

'Now, my love, I'm sure your headache is better. Come

down to the morning-room and join us,' said Angelina.

It was a Sunday afternoon, and there would be no callers, or entertainment of any kind: thus it was quite permissible for Diana to be downstairs. Lord Blentham would be present, for he refrained from going to one of his clubs on a Sunday. The girls would spend their time reading and sewing and playing illicit Patience; while Lady Blentham generally looked at *The Christian Year* or *Idylls of the King*, and mused over the past and coming weeks of well-managed events.

Diana followed her mother downstairs and there, just as she had expected, she found Maud reading *Fabian Essays*, which had already occupied her for two months, her father asleep, and Violet fidgeting over a new novel from Mudies'. Lady Blentham did not reach for *The Christian Year*, but took a hank of wool from the bottom drawer of her bureau and asked Diana to hold it while she wound it into a ball.

They sat in silence for a while, all looking more or less unhappy, listening to the ticking of the grandmother clock and the tiny click of driven rain upon the glass in the windows. Then they heard noise in the hall, a door banging, the butler's murmur, and the loud voice of Edward. The Blenthams revived.

Edward Blentham was twenty-seven, and at the beginning of this London Season he had horrified his family by quitting the Army three weeks after gaining his captaincy in the Coldstream Guards. He now lived alone in very expensive rooms off St James's Street, and his parents were worried both by his extravagance and by the inefficient taste he had always shown for literature and the arts. Like Maud, he had inherited Lady Blentham's fine-boned beauty, but like her also, he could not make others see that he was a strikingly handsome person. He was fair and slender, with an aquiline nose, a brief moustache, a sharp expression, light-blue eyes and quickly-moving lips and eyebrows. His complexion was slightly ruddy, like his father's, and in secret, he blamed this defect on army life.

'Well, Mater! Father – hullo, girls,' Edward said, walking into the room and pulling Diana's hair-ribbon. He wore a morning coat, and his very well-brushed hair had been faintly disturbed by the removal of his hat.

'This is a surprise, Edward,' said Lady Blentham, continuing to wind her wool. 'Surely you have more amusing things to do than visit us on a Sunday afternoon?'

'Nothin' at all, Mater.' When Edward was a child, Angelina had so adored him that she had feared herself guilty of idolatry.

'It *is* nice to see you,' said Violet.

Lord Blentham woke ostentatiously, got to his feet, and went to stand with his back to the fire. He eyed his son, who two days ago had broken an appointment to meet him at Brooks's for a glass of madeira and a little chat, and said: 'Very nice, I must say, Edward.'

'As a matter of fact,' said Edward, spreading his coat-tails and sitting down behind a miniature palm-tree, 'I thought it best to come today, as I knew you'd all be at home, no Sunday callers. I've got some *rather* important news, don't you know.'

'Edward . . . ' Lady Blentham smiled, for she was suddenly hopeful, though she could not quite think why or for what. 'What is it, good news? Perhaps you mean to travel?'

Edward twirled his knobbly cane, and put his head on one side to gaze at it, so that his collar cracked. He had always been a man of fashion, ever since he left school. 'Fact is, I came to tell you that I got married quite recently. I thought you ought to know.'

There was silence for several moments, until one of the terriers began to yap and had to be shushed by Maud. Violet was the first to speak.

'Teddy dear, who *to*? To whom, I mean? You can't really be married! Goodness, why didn't you have us as bridesmaids? I *do* think it's unkind!'

'Be quiet, Violet!' said Angelina. She looked at her husband, then said: 'Girls, I think you had better leave us. You'll learn about – this marriage of your brother's in due course, I don't doubt, but he ought not to have made such an announcement in front of you. Your father and I must decide

31

what is to be done.' She stopped, and fixed her eyes on them.

Maud, Violet and Diana slowly prepared to leave, and they all looked equally resentful. Diana thought that if she were Maud's age, she would not submit to Mamma's pieces of arbitrary tyranny no matter how much she loved her.

Suddenly, their father said: 'I don't see why they should. If Edward's married, it's a great pity they can't be bridesmaids at the wedding, but his marriage does concern them, after all, and we've no reason yet to believe it's a scandalous affair, Angelina!'

Angelina sat back in her chair, glanced at Diana, and shook her head at her daughters with a sad, angry smile.

'Just so, Pater,' said Edward, adjusting his monocle.

'Well, Edward, who is this fortunate young woman?' said Charles, with his hands behind his back, swaying gently back and forth in front of the fire in a way he usually considered to be rather pompous, a habit suitable for a certain type of judge, a comfortable tradesman, or an ambitious politician from the middle class.

'Well, her name *used* to be Kitty Dupree,' said Edward.

'Oh. . . Miss Kitty Dupree? An actress, ain't she? At the Gaiety at one time, I believe?' He spoke very quietly. Though his son did not know it, Charles enjoyed the Gaiety burlesques, and had even met the theatre's manager, John Hollingshead, and liked him.

Edward jumped. 'She did start off at the Gaiety, perfectly correct, Pater, but latterly, don't you know, she's been with D'Oyly Carte, at the Savoy – sang in nearly every one of theirs since *Iolanthe*. And she was dashed good as one of the three little maids in *The Mikado*. You took Maud to see that, I think, Mater,' he finished with perfect blandness.

Lady Blentham was sitting absolutely still.

'She's been on the stage since she was quite a child, of course.' Edward paused. 'She's only been retired a matter of a few months, in fact. Always supported herself jolly well!'

'And since her retirement?' said his father. 'How old is Miss Dupree, by the by?'

'Mrs Edward, don't you know. We've been married since then. Awful long time, I know.' Edward lit a cigarette with a slightly awkward hand. Kitty Blentham was four years older than himself. 'But as she says, we can't keep the thing a secret forever, and this seemed as good a time as any to break the news, what? She's a charmin' girl, absolutely sound – full of old-fashioned ideas, Mater, simply refused to come here without your invitation – '

'Edward,' said Angelina, 'put out that cigarette! How dare you try to smoke in here? How often have I said that in my house men will use the dining-room – *after* dinner?' Everyone stared at her and murmured.

'I *say*, Mater!' said Edward.

Lady Blentham rose from her chair and said something: then suddenly and peacefully fainted, as she had not done since she was a girl at boarding-school with her waist laced down day and night to eighteen inches. Lord Blentham grabbed her, Violet cried: 'Mam*ma*!', and both she and Maud slapped her wrists and unbuttoned her collar. Maud's face ran with slow, unstoppable tears.

Edward turned his face from the scene and, with his eyes closed, murmured to himself one of Kitty's favourite songs from *Princess Ida*:

> Politics we bar
> They are not our bent
> On the whole we are
> Not intelligent.

He beat time and bit his lip, longing for his mother to come to her senses, and wondering whether her swoon was put on.

Diana, who had run out to call for Lady Blentham's maid and smelling salts, came back into the morning-room. 'I suppose you think you're very brave, Teddy,' she said quietly to her brother. She looked a little over-excited, and ashamed.

'Actually, I s'pose I do.' They looked at each other with dislike; then Diana smiled.

'I don't think it's awfully brave to tell Mamma in front of us. I expect Papa will want to see you alone?'

33

'Didie, you're a very impertinent, tiresome little girl,' said Edward, removing his monocle and replacing it.

'Well,' she whispered in a hurry, seeing that her mother was coming round, 'no doubt it's very – very romantic to marry an actress!'

Maud, still crying silently, left the room unnoticed.

Kitty Dupree, the Hon. Mrs Edward Blentham, was wide-hipped and full-bosomed, but so short and small-boned and dark that it had been easy to mistake her for a real Japanese when she was playing Pitti-Sing in *The Mikado*. Her real name was Ellen Rosenthal; but she was only one quarter Jewish, for her paternal grandfather had married a Gentile, and his son's wife, Kitty's mother, had been of French descent. Edward Blentham had never believed that his wife's stage name was her true one, though at first she had told him it was. He had not minded her lying to him when he first knew her, for the truth about her origin did not really interest him. He was only concerned with the fact that she was a very pretty, clever little woman who loved him.

When she told him some of the truth about her background, saying that her mother was a Huguenot, whose silk-weaving family had once owned one of the best houses in Folegate Street, Spitalfields, and that, though her father was a tailor, one of her great-great-grandfathers had been a professor at the university of Heidelberg, Edward did not believe her. He smiled indulgently at her, and preferred to think that she was a pure London urchin, even though she did not talk like one. Edward imagined that he would spread many different rumours about Kitty round London, when his marriage was known. Her own story would do for one, but he would tell some of his more liberal-theoried friends that she was a workhouse child, others that she was part Lascar, and more that she was the natural daughter of some distantly hinted-at eminent man.

Kitty did not introduce Edward to any of her relations, most of whom disapproved of her being on the stage and thought that only trouble could come of her marriage to a peer's son, if her marriage was a true one at all and he was not a deceiver. She knew that her people would have to be dropped, and Edward quite agreed with her.

Sometimes Kitty herself could not wholly believe in her marriage. This was partly because it was of course so extraordinary that she, Nellie Rosenthal, truly was to be a baroness and the mistress of Dunstanton Park, and partly because, after fifteen years, she had found a man who was not only a peer, who would marry her, but a darling boy whom she could adore. There was a third and slightly less agreeable reason for her irrational doubt: Kitty had spent these first six months of her marriage living more like a mistress than a wife.

She did not share Edward's rooms off St James's Street, but lived in a rented house in Brompton Square which was considerably drearier than most kept mistresses' establishments. It was the financial strain of keeping two places in London on a bachelor's allowance which, a few days ago, had enabled Kitty to persuade her husband that it was time, at last, for his family to know.

Kitty studied her face in the bedroom mirror and narrowed her eyes, as she waited for Edward's return from Queen Anne's Gate, and imagined the Blenthams all together. She was wearing a silk dressing-gown over elaborate stays, and as she brushed her hair she sang, with the impertinent air of doubt her husband loved:

> Hearts *just* as pure and fair
> May beat in Belgrave Square
> As in the lowly air
> Of Seven Dials.

Then she stuck her tongue out at the mirror and said: 'Ya!' Such vulgarities did not come quite naturally to her, but they were amusing.

Kitty's face was often called amusing, enchanting, impish, but above all lovely. Edward said she looked quite deliciously the girl of the period. She had little parted lips, discreetly noticeable white teeth, very big tilted hazel eyes, and waving hair which was almost black. Her nose was retroussé, her chin pointed, and her only fault was a slightly sallow complexion which a dab of rouge could entirely cure. She photographed very well, and she favoured big elaborate dresses, ostrich feathers and furs, for such things made her look like a wonderfully promising girl-child, although she was thirty-one.

Suddenly as she was twisting her hair up, a flicker of evening sunlight made Kitty lean forward and examine her face in detail. There was a tiny, soft crack between her nostril and the corner of her mouth: another two under her eyes. She looked up fearfully at the photograph of herself in white lace which had once been publicly for sale. It had been taken nine years ago at a high point in her career, before she quarrelled with the manager of the Gaiety Theatre. Kitty tried to think that she had not aged at all; then remembered that she was very good for her age in spite of her little lines of character, and that she was married and retired besides.

Just as she was thinking that one day she might miss the stage, which was by no means so immoral as Lady Blentham thought, else she would never have become an actress in the first place, Edward opened the door.

He startled Kitty, and when she looked up, she thought he looked ridiculously startled too. 'Well, Teddy my love?' she said. 'How was it, then?'

'Dear little Kitty,' he said, 'dear little girl.' Edward sat down on the bed, removed his monocle, and sighed. His face was pale.

Kitty watched him for a few moments, then said: 'Well, before we talk, you can help me dress. That's what I'm going to wear tonight, and you can button me down the back.'

'How soothin' you are,' said Edward, as he rose to obey her. 'But I don't think I can face the thought of Frascati's tonight. Besides,' he added dully, 'it ain't time just yet to dress, is it?'

'What, as bad as that?' said Kitty, seeing his expression. She paused. 'Well, good Lord! Come, Teddy, didn't we agree to celebrate your *telling* them, whatever the outcome? A brave stand, my boy! Our first appearance as a couple!'

36

'Jolly good,' said Edward, raising loving eyes. He smiled, and reached out for her.

Kitty pulled her peignoir round her and went to sit firmly beside him on the bed. 'So they *are* coming the ugly?'

'Oh, awful. Mater fainted and then refused to say a word. Absolutely. Just said she wouldn't know you, or bow to you, etc, etc.' Edward began to look a little better. 'The fact is, darlin' one, nothing and no one can remove her deepest native prejudice that *every* actress is a lady of the night! Mrs Siddons of sacred memory? A courtesan, don't you know! Our own Miss Terry? Worse and worse!'

Kitty hissed. She said after a moment, 'I suppose of course she's too much of a *lady* to say such things aloud?'

'What, in front of the girls? My darling!'

'I was never such a bloody fool as to get caught by any man that way,' said Kitty, very quietly. 'Presents and promises!' This was not true. She had been seduced at the age of eighteen.

'Darling, I know. You're a *clever* girl and, as Cornwallis says, you *do* deserve your coronet.' Cornwallis was Edward's closest friend; he had been at Oxford with him, but instead of leaving after two years to become a Guards officer had become a literary man and the master of a little literary circle. Long ago, Cornwallis had admired Edward for going into the Army out of boredom with juvenile Oxford.

'Don't talk to me like that,' Kitty said.

'Love!' he cried. 'Oh darling, not offended? I say!'

'No,' she said, 'not really, if you're sorry.' She looked at him and waited.

'*Awfully* sorry. Never sorrier.'

Kitty patted his knee. 'Well then, what about your Papa?'

'He says he'll raise my allowance to fourteen hundred a year.' This was an increase of five hundred pounds. 'And pay my debts, you know.'

'Nice old gentleman!' said Kitty, surprised. She wondered for a moment, then added: 'Teddy, did you tell him alone first of all?'

'I ought to have done,' said Edward. 'But it was so awfully hard to resist the temptation to announce the news in front of

Mater and the girls! When Mater left the room – awfully dramatic – he took me into the study. Felt like a schoolboy.'

'H'm. Wouldn't it have been better to have told him straight off, and left him to – break the news to your mother?'

'Yes, I know, darling.'

'Oh, you are a foolish boy. What did he say besides?'

Edward moved further up the bed and Kitty, though she was usually more passionate than he, hoped he would not want to make love just yet. 'Kitty, I don't know how we're to manage on fourteen hundred. The old man knows damn' well I've spent more than that per annum ever since I was at Oxford! Don't mean he hasn't been good about paying up once in a while, but now – Kitty, what are we going to do?'

'Well, for a start you'll give up those lodgings of yours. That'll be a considerable economy. And then don't worry: I'll contrive somehow. Lord, Teddy, when I was a kid my dad thought himself lucky if the shop brought in a hundred and fifty pounds a year, and there was six of us! I know a good deal about keeping house. Now then, what else did he say, darling? We can talk about the money later.'

Edward sat gazing round the bedroom and holding his wife's hand. He thought of how, already, she had improved upon the heavy and old-fashioned decoration of this furnished house, with its dark papers and curtains, overstuffed balloon-backed chairs and billiard-cloth carpets. Kitty had bought small things in odd places for surprisingly little money, had somehow quite changed the house's general effect: she was wholly perfect. As she looked at her distant grey reflection in the dressing-table mirror, Edward laid his head on Kitty's lap. 'Darling.'

'Come now, Teddy-love. Tell Kitty.'

'I tried to explain what sort of a girl you are – anyway, he said he was satisfied that I wasn't such a fool as to be caught by one who was, well, bad, darling. But he didn't like it.'

'And why not? It's happened before, our sort of marriage. And may I ask what sort of catch *you* are for a girl, Mr Blentham, compared to His Royal Highness the Duke of Cambridge?'

'Such an amusing girl you are,' said Edward. 'Love.'

'Well, what else did he say?'

'Well, darling, he pointed out that I wasn't under age, and he said of course he wouldn't attempt to do as Clancarty did with poor little Dunlo last year. Dashed good of him, wasn't it!' said Edward into her lap. 'Doesn't want more scandal than is strictly necessary. Besides, my love, he never liked Clancarty.'

'Yes,' said Kitty. 'And I'll have him know that I'm not such a namby-pamby creature as Belle Bilton, with her bastard kid, and her self-pity, and marrying Lord Dunlo *while* living with that other poor chap! Oh, I don't deny she was innocent of adultery proper – I'm glad they gave her flowers at the Empire, I'm sure. But talk about a girl with no character!'

'Yes, darling love.'

'And now she'll be moping herself to death in Ireland. Well, I've no intention of doing that, Teddy-love. We're going to be in Society. Are we not, sir?'

' 'Course we are!'

'Pity your Mater didn't *quite* commit herself to presenting me at court, ain't it?' said Kitty, putting her hands on her hips and raising one eyebrow up to her hairline.

'A damn' shame.'

'Yes, well, we shan't let it trouble us.'

Edward raised his head from her lap. 'You'll win her round, Kitty, in time. She's a grand old girl in her way, don't you know, and less of a snob than many women.' He cleared his throat. 'Fact is, the only thing she can't stand is what she calls impropriety. Once she knows you're not that way inclined – '

'That I wasn't your mistress before I married you?' said Kitty, swinging round from the waist. 'But who'll make her believe that? Or anyone believe it – though we could hardly have lived more respectably, I made sure enough of that! Look at this house, let to Deans and whatnot – I'm not sure it wouldn't have been better for us to have made a splash from the start.'

'They'll have to believe it,' said Edward.

'There's one economy we're not going to make,' said Kitty,

getting up from the bed. 'No more hired broughams and hansoms, Teddy. We're going to Long Acre tomorrow to buy a carriage – a victoria – and you can go to Tattersalls' for a nice pair of tits. You and I are going to drive in the Park, my boy, morning and evening, I'll learn to ride, and first thing of all, you can send the notice of our marriage to the newspapers. After which I'll start leaving cards. And now,' she said, 'you can help me dress, as I said, and then get yourself ready for Frascati's!'

'Dear Kitty, I do so love you,' said Edward after a slight hesitation, in which both stood quite still, and looked at each other. He turned away, put his monocle in his eye, and whisked Kitty's evening dress off the bedroom screen.

Lady Blentham's vision of Kitty's physical appearance was remarkably accurate. She guessed at the large breasts, black hair, little features and big dark eyes, but in her imagination the actress was not a small creature, but as tall as her son. She could not quite decide whether Kitty would have some influence over Edward or would, one day, be a whining overweight crying at her husband's every subtle snub.

Diana, who had gone to visit her mother in her boudoir after Edward's quitting the house, and had been allowed to stay, watched Angelina making little dabs at her blotter with a dry pen. She herself was sitting as upright as her mother, with her hands folded in her lap. They had barely spoken and did not intend to speak; Diana because she did not know where it would be tactful to begin, and Lady Blentham because the subject of actresses and Edward could not be discussed with a girl. If Diana tried to talk about it, she would have to be silenced. In spite of this, the two women did not want to separate, and they continued to sit in silence, thinking about Kitty.

Diana's picture of Edward's wife did not resemble Angelina's. She imagined her to be fair and slim and graceful, with a light foreign accent and deep grey eyes. The question of whether Edward was to rule Kitty, or the other way about, did not occur to her: she thought only of how brilliantly charming the woman must be to marry above her station at her age. Diana wanted quite fiercely to meet and impress her, but she knew she would not for years, unless her mother gave way.

Idly, but almost seriously, she considered becoming an actress herself. It must really be possible to run away and go on the stage, as Kitty Dupree must have done. She was learning, she thought: it was not, after all, like going to another planet. Diana's lips formed the words, 'I would be good at it', but not enough sound came out to distract Angelina.

For years, Diana had happily imagined herself running off to sea disguised as a boy, or fighting in an old-fashioned battle without guns, or becoming a second Miss Nightingale; and her picture of herself as a very dashing actress had been much like these other visions: shining, but suitable only for bedtime. She had never seen any play but an undistinguished matinee performance of *Macbeth*, of which she had not understood the whole though the roll of the words had inspired her to write several poems. The real theatre had seemed a rather dull place in a way; for she had heard too many rumours of the stage's being golden, wicked, and gay, to be altogether pleased with acted Shakespeare.

Now someone from that other theatre-world, which it seemed did really exist, had stepped into her family; and the thought could only elate her. Smiling awkwardly at her mother's back, grateful to Angelina for allowing her to be there, Diana enjoyed a realistic fantasy of finding out where Kitty lived with Edward, of slipping out of the house, taking a hansom and going to call on her alone. 'I will,' she whispered.

Angelina turned. 'Did you say anything, Diana?'

'No, Mamma!'

Angelina thought of asking her to go and do something suitable, but she was so much distressed at the moment that no occupation for Diana came quickly to mind.

She remembered the scandal there had been last year, when Lord Dunlo had married an actress and his father Lord Clancarty had hired detectives to try and prove that the woman was not only fallen before marriage, but an adulteress

41

as well. No one had admired his behaviour: Angelina herself had thought him vulgar and tyrannical. Her hand trembled, as she wildly imagined being vulgar, hiring detectives herself.

She had read a few detective stories by Arthur Conan Doyle in the *Strand Magazine*, and rather enjoyed them in spite of her proud out-of-date suspicion of all that was made up. Now she pictured herself going to Mr Sherlock Holmes in Baker Street. She saw herself explaining that she did not want to bring any case, or do anything at all: that she only wanted to know perfectly, exactly, whether the actress was in fact technically virtuous, for that would make a very great difference to the Blenthams and Society. Female unchastity did not so much shock Angelina as fill her with shivering rage. She knew she ought not to abominate others' vice quite so intensely, and she made resentful apologies for her intensity in church.

Flushed at the thought of her own nonsensical fantasy about detectives, Lady Blentham turned to Diana and said: 'Thank you for sitting with me, Diana. Now – do go back to Mademoiselle, please darling! I'm sure she's in the blue room, and will provide you with something to do.'

Diana jumped up and murmured a cross, 'Very well, Mamma.'

Her mother did not correct her, and when the door shut behind her daughter with rude slowness, she got up herself, went through to the bedroom and looked down at her wide stiff bed. Suddenly, as she stood there, Angelina no longer felt tired or cursed by the world. She had work to do in crushing a scandal. She would not crush a person, that would be unkind.

Diana's irritation and disappointment lasted only till she reached the top of the main stairs and sat down. She had no intention of going to the improvised schoolroom where Mademoiselle lived: she hoped none of the maids would discover her here, and make a sympathetic nuisance of herself. Diana glanced at the roof-window above her, and noticed that the rain was over, and that dark but very clear yellow sunlight was striking through the filthy glass. Her face was warmed by it.

Although she so longed to come out into Society and cease to be an innocent, Diana had until today thought she was weary of life itself, sceptical of all she was told though she had little material with which to fight it. Now, Diana thought, it was rather nice to discover that one was still truly young, and had ideals, ambitions, curiosity and enthusiasm for unconventional things; and she even wondered how many other possessing states of mind might turn out to be as unreal as the cynicism of clever sixteen.

CHAPTER 4

AT THE QUEEN'S DRAWING-ROOM,
AND IN ROTTEN ROW

Diana was standing in a crowd of other debutantes and chaperones, some twelve feet past the top of the stairs. For the second time since her arrival at Buckingham Palace, she allowed herself to look about her instead of merely peering ahead, and she turned her face carefully to avoid disarranging her headdress. She could see nothing but women dressed exactly as she was, shafts of unflattering daylight, and details of decoration much like that of a new hotel. Diana took a deep breath, and looked down at her corsage.

She wore an evening dress of cream silk so deep in colour it was almost yellow, with short puffed sleeves, a low neck, and a trimming of seed pearls. A three-yard-long train lay over her arm, and a white veil hung down her back, pinned to her head by three little ostrich plumes. Her dress was new, but the feathers, train and veil had been worn both by Violet and by Maud.

Diana had not lost her looks in the past year, as she and Lady Blentham had once feared she would, but she was a handsome girl rather than a beauty. She was five feet nine inches tall, with wide rounded shoulders, a deep bosom, a long waist, and legs and arms like well-turned columns. During the last few months, she had grown an inch and had put on weight, though her mother had frowned on this.

Her long sloping neck was perfect, and so was the classical nose which she had inherited from her mother, but Diana's other beauties were more original. Her eyes were oval and full-lidded, and their irises were a rare, deep auburn brown, rimmed with a line of black. When she smiled, the outer corners of her eyes dipped downwards in two odd little wrinkles. She had straight, rather thick black eyebrows which contrasted with her ruddy hair. Her mouth was wide, full and red, too heavy for fashion, and beneath it there was a round cleft chin. She had a white skin with correctly-coloured cheeks, but across the bridge of her nose there were several tiny freckles which nothing could remove. She was sometimes criticised for being a very big girl, Junoesque, statuesque, and decidedly the goddess type, which was an excellent thing in a woman of thirty, but not in a girl of eighteen. Diana did not object to being large as she would have done to being a little slender thing; although occasionally she lacked dancing-partners because shorter men did not like to be seen standing up with her.

'What's the time?' said a small skinny girl with freckles like Diana's, to her twin sister who was examining a mark on her train.

'However should I know, Sylvia? Oh, heavens, do *look* at this. I told you you stepped on it when we were getting into the coach!'

Her sister was not disturbed. 'Do you suppose it's too late for the Queen?'

'Oh, it can't be more than half-past two,' said Diana, who knew them both slightly.

They turned to her in surprise, then the smaller twin said quite confidingly: 'I do so hope the Queen *won't* have retired by the time we do get to the Presence Room, or the Throne Room, or whatever it is one calls it! Don't you? Whatever is the point of going through all this, and then not being presented to the Queen herself?'

'Well, in a way, I rather hope it *is* the Princess,' said Diana, 'because then we'll simply have to curtsey. I've been dreading having to be kissed by the Queen for weeks. I am so big, you see, I'll have to bend down to her, and it will look very odd. I suppose!' Talking about it made her feel nervous: she had not been very nervous before.

'Oh, yes,' said the small girl. 'Oh, that doesn't apply to us, we only have to kiss her hand, don't we, Mabel?'

'I suppose your mother's presenting you, Miss Blentham?' said the twin with a black mark on her train.

'Yes. Is yours not?'

The girl looked at the ceiling. 'Oh yes. You see, although our cousin Lady Mount Colber has the entrée at Court, she's been unwell lately, and couldn't present us although she was to have done so.'

Her sister said: 'Yes, we were so looking forward to driving down Constitution Hill! Now I'll have to marry a Cabinet Minister, or something, if I want to do that!'

'I'm sorry she's not well,' said Diana. 'I think I was introduced to her only the other day.'

'Oh, Mrs Lyon, I've lost my ticket, my card!' another girl behind her whispered frantically. 'I'm *sure* I've lost it!'

'You gave it to me, my dear, here it is. Now *put it in your glove*, your left glove – remember you'll have to remove your right.'

Lady Blentham, who had been separated from her daughter by the careful pushing of the crowd, pressed gently past this couple and rejoined her. 'It isn't altogether elegant, is it, Mamma?' murmured Diana.

'No, Diana. Hush,' Angelina replied, smiling, as they shifted forward into another one of the anterooms, guided by fussing male courtiers.

Both were thirsty, but otherwise not too uncomfortable. Lady Blentham had insisted on their drinking nothing before setting out from Queen Anne's Gate: the journey down the Mall had taken over an hour, they had been waiting in the Palace a long time already, and it would be hours more before they were at home and able to use a commode.

Diana walked forward, with her train at last spread out behind her, thinking of the moment when she would have to step back on it. It was the Queen sitting there, a tiny fat black-and-white old figure with the blue ribbon spread across her bosom and a veil on her head as in all the prints made of her since the Prince Consort's death. Diana felt her diaphragm thumping inside her and her cheeks turning red. The Lord Chamberlain's

46

announcement of her name was still sounding in her ears.

Diana carried on. She had not, she thought, expected the Queen to look so ancient and so sad and bored, and yet so like her portraits. The Princess of Wales was beside her, the Prince of Wales was standing some way away, laughing in the way everyone said was rather German, and there was another royal lady, whom her mother had whispered was Princess Louise, Duchess of Argyll. Courtiers were everywhere and none seemed to be watching.

The Queen smiled just as Diana manoeuvred into position before her, then put her face close to the girl's and murmured something. Then Diana, still very hot, stepped backwards, did not trip, curtseyed to the other members of the Royal Family, and received a broad compliment from the Prince of Wales which angered Lady Blentham.

In the supper-room, where there were in fact no refreshments, only a crowd of over-relaxed people, Diana turned to her mother and opened her mouth. 'You did very well, darling,' said Angelina, before her daughter could speak.

'Oh,' said Diana, looking round. 'It's supposed to be the climax of one's life, isn't it, of one's Season, at all events – rather like getting married. I supposed it was rather like that.' She rubbed her cheek hard with her gloved knuckles. 'Better than a ball in many ways. I – '

Diana at times had a deliberate awareness of herself and her surroundings, which her mother said was unusual in a girl of her age. She wondered now whether she would ever have a daughter to present at Court, and what Court would be like in twenty years or so. She thought, quite unnecessarily, for it was so obviously true, that now this ritual was over she could never go back to the idle peace of the schoolroom. Because she was thoroughly free of the boredom of the schoolroom, adult parties would never be so interesting to her again as they had been these past few months. Holding her eyes wide, Diana thought suddenly that she must now think of something else to do, but she did not know what.

'Don't scrub your face like that, Diana. You don't want it to smell of cleaning-petrol, surely?'

'It's been kissed, Mamma.'

Angelina frowned. 'My dear, I never expected *you* to be so ill-at-ease.'

'No. It's – I had a very odd – vision, of a kind, when I was curtseying just now. I thought I was *you*, and that one of those men behind her – must be the Prince Consort. He wasn't yet dead, was he, when you were presented?'

Lady Blentham was quite pleased with this fancy of her daughter's.

'No. I came out in eighteen fifty-eight, as you know. I can tell you that it was very much more difficult when one had to manage a crinoline, as well as a train!'

Diana smiled with her mother.

Friends came up to them, and separated them, and Diana had to listen to other girls' descriptions of their fears and imaginings and what had actually happened. One very silly young woman, whose particularly strict mother was out of earshot, then mentioned the Prince of Wales' appearance at the Drawing-Room, and spoke in a whisper about his involvement in the recent Tranby Croft scandal.

Her attempt to shock raised Diana's spirits to a point of high gaiety. She changed the subject in an obvious manner and, to illustrate a point about lawn tennis, took one of the plumes out of head-dress and threw it in the air. She watched it tumble down among the upturned pink faces of nice girls who, laughing, thought she must be very odd. Diana wondered then why she had done it but reflected that at least Lady Blentham had not seen, and would probably never know.

Violet peered up at the chestnuts overhanging Rotten Row, and wished that she were as beautiful as Diana. Her thick nose, too-curly hair and plumpness had not improved with time, but people said she had a very sweet, lively expression. 'Didie, *why* am I not as pretty as you, do you suppose?' she said, and smiled.

Diana, who was sitting with her back to the horses, smiled too. 'It's God's will, Vio.'

Violet pulled her lower lip down, and Lady Blentham said: 'You're two very naughty girls, and you've scarcely changed since you were in the schoolroom in many ways. Diana, do put up your parasol, your freckles will be made far worse by this dreadful sun.'

The Blenthams' old landau slowed down, and the coachman eased it between two other, larger carriages while the girls and their mother exchanged compliments about their last meeting with those whom they passed. Lady Blentham, as they came out again into a narrow strip of free ground, thought suddenly that she would be happy if none of her girls ever married.

She had always preferred her daughters to her sons, and had more toleration of their faults and mistakes; for she did not pretend to understand men and made no allowances for them. They were expected to be better creatures, and she had contempt for women who pretended men were merely children. Even Maud, Angelina reflected, had now quite settled down, had only the mildest interest in socialism and slumming, and was a useful unmarried daughter of whom it was possible to be very fond. Once, she had thought Maud needed a husband, or that she herself needed a husband for her; now she could not imagine such a thing. For years, she thought, as Lady Hartington bowed to her and smiled at her but did not stop, she had imagined it would be a disaster if her girls did not find husbands: now, seeing Diana and Violet once more as close as they had been before Violet's growing up separated them, she knew how mistaken she had been.

'I think we should turn back soon, girls,' Angelina said, 'or we won't be in time to dress. By the by, I should like both of you to wear your pink muslins tonight – if you have no particular objection.'

'Very well, Mamma,' said Violet. Diana had been planning to wear her pink muslin in any case, and she said nothing.

Only her sons were unsatisfactory, thought Lady Blentham, as the carriage came to a halt again and two young men, less handsome than either Edward or Roderick, rode up to it and were polite to her before turning their attention to the girls and threatening her plan for having three good spinster daughters. Roderick was now ordained, acting as a curate in Northumberland while waiting for the living at Melton Balbridge in Dorset to fall in. Edward still lived with his wife in Brompton Square, and rarely visited his parents; but Lady Blentham had been forced not to add to the rather mild scandal of his marriage by refusing entirely to recognise Kitty, who had now produced a son. Angelina had made herself realise that it was her own well-known old-fashioned ideas and stiff principles which had made people gossip as much as they had. Thus she spoke to her daughter-in-law in public, and invited her to her very largest and dullest parties; and her anger with her grew colder and more deep, even though she now believed the actress was not in fact a whore. She used the word in a secret, terrible way.

Just as she was thinking about Kitty, who often refused her invitations, Angelina heard Diana say: 'Yes, it is enjoyable isn't it? *Le monde où l'on s'amuse!* Sometimes I imagine what would happen if an anarchist appeared one evening and started throwing bombs among us. Do you think it would put a stop to the Season?'

'My dear!' said Angelina, as Violet laughed.

'I wish it *would*,' she said with an eye on her mother.

'I'd rescue you, Miss Diana,' said one of the young men, refusing to be impressed. 'That's all I can promise you would happen in that event.'

Diana closed her eyes and inclined her head.

'I think we must be making our way home, Mr St John – I suppose you'll be at Mrs Jameson-Fraser's reception tonight?' said Angelina.

'Yes, indeed!'

The landaulet lurched round after a few more courtesies and turned back towards Grosvenor Gate. Lady Blentham spoke to Diana about her nonsensical way of talking and Violet relaxed in her seat, wiggled her toes, and watched her calm sister before she grew bored.

'I say, Mamma,' she said, interrupting. 'Isn't that – Edward's wife, over there, with Cousin Theresa? Goodness,

they're talking nineteen to the dozen, or it looks like it.' She
nodded to the right, for she had never been allowed to point,
and Angelina, after slight pause, said: 'Yes, certainly it is.'

'What an awfully smart phaeton she's got, I must say!' said
Violet.

'Don't use that word, Violet, it's very vulgar.'

'Smart?'

'Yes.'

Diana was blushing, but staring straight ahead at Kitty.
Whenever she caught sight of her brother's wife she coloured,
remembering the afternoon nearly a year ago on which she
had gone to visit her, alone. Although she had been
frightened, she had enjoyed leaving Queen Anne's Gate
unobserved and, after some trouble, hailing a four-wheeler
instead of the hansom cab of her imagination. But when she
reached Brompton Square and was taken in to Kitty, Kitty
had come near to scolding Diana for going out without either
permission or a chaperone, and had told her that, though she
was pleased by her kindness in coming to call, she must never
do it again. Kitty had promised, unprompted, not to tell Lady
Blentham about her adventure, and had had a servant fetch a
cab to the door without offering Diana even a cup of tea. It
had not been the conduct to be expected of an actress, and
Diana had cried on the way home. It was the memory of her
childishness which made her blush now, and refuse to look
away.

Lady Blentham made up her mind. They could not, she
decided, claim not to have seen Kitty's phaeton, especially
when Cousin Theresa was with her, and she coldly asked the
coachman to stop. Kitty had been watching their slow
progress with amusement for the past five minutes.

'Why, Lady Blentham!' she said. 'How nice to see you.
May I present – oh, how silly, I'm sure I don't need to
introduce you – ain't you Lady Blentham's cousin, Theresa?'

'No, you don't need to introduce us,' said Angelina. 'I hope
I see you well? Theresa, this is a surprise! Shall you be in
London for long?' She saw the girls nod at Kitty and exchange
satisfactory murmured greetings.

'Just a few more weeks,' said Cousin Theresa. 'As a matter of fact, after that you won't be seeing me for a *long* time. Jimmy's regiment is being sent out to India. I rather look forward to it.'

'Well, I hope you find it meets your expectation. For how long do you expect to be stationed there?' said Lady Blentham, who had never really liked her young first cousin once removed. She was a younger, plainer version of Kitty.

'Three or five years. How nice it is to see you grown-up, Diana,' she said, making Diana start. 'Last time I saw you you can't have been more than thirteen. And I was at Girton. You told me you were going to be a poet – and didn't need an education.'

'Yes,' said Diana, smiling, remembering that Cousin Theresa had laughed at her then.

'A poet?' said Kitty. 'Gracious me! Does Arthur Cornwallis know – Edward's friend, Mr Cornwallis? He'd be interested, I'm sure.'

'I've outgrown that sort of folly,' said Diana quietly, looking into her eyes.

'Theresa,' said Lady Blentham, 'you must come to call on us soon. I'll send you a card for my next dinner-party – not a very formal affair, you know! I think we must be going – so sorry. Goodbye, Mrs Blentham – give my love to my grandson, and Edward, of course.'

'Goodbye, Lady Blentham!' said Kitty, and laughed.

The landaulet rolled out of the big park gates and from her position at the horses' back Diana could see Kitty's head and Cousin Theresa's dipping and turning in the phaeton for quite a long time. It seemed to her that Kitty often looked in her direction, but that was not possible; she would take no interest in Edward's little debutante sister.

'Mamma,' she said suddenly as they entered Piccadilly. 'If I told you that I should like to go to Cambridge, to Girton or Somerville, what would you say?'

'Somerville College is at Oxford, my dear, not Cambridge.'

CHAPTER 5

SEVERAL MEN,
AND AN EDUCATION

No one doubted that Diana was clever enough to go to Girton or Newnham: those who wished to discourage her said she was too clever. No one said the women were less intelligent than men, or that women's colleges were an abomination and a waste of time; or that a young lady must occupy herself with Society and frivolity, and nothing besides, in order to be attractive to men. The Blenthams firmly denied that truth, and laughed at Diana a little.

They considered that a severe and formal education was not necessary for a strikingly intelligent young woman who, when she was at Dunstanton, had plenty of time to make use of her grandfather's excellent library. Although Lady Blentham forbade the girls to read some of the novels which Violet liked and did read, either because they were rubbish or because like *Tess of the d'Urbervilles* they said too much about men and women, she saw no harm in serious works, except the medical dictionary and the newspapers. Even the Authorised Version was allowed: much of it was incomprehensible.

Angelina encouraged Diana's longing for knowledge, and told her to read Gibbon and Macaulay, Addison and Steele, Carlyle and Ruskin and even Walter Pater, and von Ranke's *History of the Popes*. She liked to discuss all these with her daughter; and when she was fully satisfied that Diana was in earnest about wishing to read seriously, she told her as she never had before that some novels were positively good.

Diana was bored by her sister's favourite Ouida and Marie Corelli, but she enjoyed the works of Jane Austen, some of

Dickens, and the Barsetshire and Palliser novels to which her mother introduced her. She learnt a good deal about life and men from her reading, and she was very grateful to Lady Blentham for allowing her to acquire some kind of education now that she had left the schoolroom, but she was not content. Throughout that winter, spent at Dunstanton but for a few house-parties in hunting country, she campaigned to be allowed to try for a place at Cambridge.

'I'm proud of your brains, Diana,' her father told her one day when they were hacking down a wide flat road, where rotten leaves lay cold in the ditches at the side. 'Pity you're not a boy, or I daresay you think so at the moment, but I believe there are all kinds of lectures and so forth that a girl can go to in London. At that place in Harley Street, and some other college, Bedford is it – all kinds of places. We'll see in the spring, shall we? Rather fewer visits to the milliner, and a few more lectures – a considerable economy,' he said. '*I* don't mind your cutting a few At Homes and morning calls, and neither I suppose will your mother.'

'Papa, I do so want to go to Girton. It's not unknown! Cousin Theresa went.'

'Your cousin Theresa's mamma was a queer sort of woman, Didie, as your mother must have told you, and as for her father – well, you're old enough to know that all those girls' lives were made damned difficult by the scandal. What's more, I don't believe Theresa enjoyed herself at Girton. Lucky she found Jimmy,' he said.

'She must have *learned* a great deal,' muttered Diana. 'And been able to *talk* about it, properly!'

'Nonsense, my dear, you know nothing about it. Don't shuffle about like that, d'you want to give the poor brute a sore back? No, Diana – er – the ordinary sort of chap doesn't learn anything at Cambridge, unless he's a parson, I suppose.' He smiled a little. 'It can't be so very different from Oxford. And all I learnt when I was at the House was how to drink three bottles of claret in an evening and – well, I made a few speeches at the Union, true enough, and that was good practice for the Commons.' Charles had been Member for

Maidstone West before his father died. 'One learns, you know, *after* one's finished one's so-called education.'

Tears began to slop down Diana's face, making her angry and hot. When she took off her hat, they were partly washed away by the icy drips which fell from the black twigs above them. She was crying a little because she had heard the same things so many times, and was beginning to believe them to be true.

'Now, where are Violet and Roderick? Put your hat on, Diana, why did you take it off?'

'They went on ahead, Papa, they wanted to gallop.' She lifted her eyes, and made out the faint shape of Dunstanton through the full white January fog. Her father was relieved to see the house, where this conversation would end.

'Roderick's got a damned bad seat. Violet's the best of you, so far as that's concerned – though you too are very good.'

'Yes, Papa. Thank you.'

'Didie, you aren't unhappy, I trust?' he said with difficulty, as she replaced her tight little hat.

'No Papa. Just so very bored.' She thought: why am I really so keen to go to Cambridge?

'I'm afraid all intelligent women are bored. Your mother for instance. One marries a woman with a good mind, but one can't discuss intellectual matters with her after one's been married to her for a few months. Somehow marriage and conversation don't quite go together.' He paused. 'You'll have to get used to it, my dear.' Charles spoke with absolute seriousness for the first time.

Lord Blentham could see no real harm in female suffrage, and sometimes thought that women's brains were wasted, though nothing could be done about this. When drunk enough, he would say that his wife would have made a good Prime Minister, but that on the whole he was thankful she could not be. He had often been unfaithful to Angelina since their marriage, and he was proud of how for thirty years he had evaded her skilful plans for his advancement in politics and for his conversion to Toryism. She had sincerely and silently desired that for a long time, because if Charles deserted the Liberal Party, she could then abandon her pretence of Gladstonian convictions, and obey her husband by making herself useful to the Primrose League. He knew all this, though she had said nothing.

Charles was sufficiently fond of Angelina to be sorry that he was a disappointment to her but he reminded himself that, when they married, he too had had high ambitions and could not have been expected to know that in fact one junior ministry would be enough to satisfy him by the time he reached early middle age. He also liked to remind himself that, as a young man, he had married Angelina for love of both her mind and her beauty, rather than for her ten thousand pounds or her connection with Mr Gladstone. Because of this she ought, he believed, to be grateful for the physical attentions he still paid her, and had paid her with vigour in the past. He supposed she was grateful in spite of her delicacy: Angelina was nearly as good as she meant to be.

Like his wife, Lord Blentham preferred his daughters to his sons though he knew them far less well. He had been fiercely strict with the boys when they were young, because it was so important that they should not turn out unsatisfactory in any way. Though Edward and Roderick had not turned out very well, the girls were good enough, and could be fully enjoyed now they were grown-up: even their little follies could be a minor source of pleasure, for he was a tolerant man. Charles supposed that his sons were good enough too, in their separate ways, but both of them had irritated him ever since they were born. They were his responsibility, as the girls were not.

Charles and Angelina had come an unspoken agreement some time age that Diana, their youngest, was their favourite child. They voiced their agreement that all the other children more or less lacked brains, though Maud and Edward tried to be clever; and they talked a good deal about Diana's innocent wish to go to Girton, which they need never gratify.

It was an easy and rather wrongful pleasure to have a young favourite, Charles thought; and he promised himself as they rode up to the house that, even if Diana's brains led her to some grave lapse in good behaviour, he would not be too hard upon her. She never had been truly naughty, even as a tiny girl: only alert and rather self-assured.

In the stable yard, he helped her to dismount; and told her that she was a lucky girl, because apart from anything else she had a figure which other girls must envy. Roderick came out of one of the loose-boxes at that moment, with his greatcoat buttoned up to hide his clerical collar. He heard Charles's remark and saw Diana flush.

'Yes, you're what one used to call a strapping wench, Didie!' he said, hitting his boot with his riding crop.

'Not a very suitable expression to use in front of your little sister, eh, Roderick,' said his father, quite idly. 'And hardly very suitable for a man of the cloth, either.'

Roderick gave him a slightly pouting frown. 'I daresay,' he admitted. 'Have I offended you, Diana?'

'Yes, bo – yes, you have. Strapping wench!' She smiled, and swallowed. Her cheeks were still very red. 'You know Roddy, you oughtn't to have gone into the Church. Why did you? I know you'd have made a splendid sort of Parson Woodforde, a hundred years ago, but now we're so strict about religion, *surely* you must hate it? You know how Mamma disapproves of clergymen hunting – so does everybody!'

'Mamma's a regular Lady Lufton – as you were saying just the other day,' said Roderick, still pouting slightly, and watching his father. Diana had persuaded him to try *Framley Parsonage*, but he was not fond of novels and found it easy to write sermons against them. 'Besides, people nowadays are hardly strict *enough* about religion. There's far too much Rationalism and other rubbish about.' He saw that Diana was smiling at him and, unwillingly, he laughed.

'Anything that keeps you off the back of a good hunter is an excellent thing, Roderick. I trust you *don't* hunt, in Northumberland?' said Lord Blentham, who was an agnostic.

'I go to the meet, Father, and that's all!'

'Good.' Just then, the coachman came up to Charles, muttered something and drew him aside. 'Tell your mother I'll be in shortly!' said their father. The two men walked away together towards the opposite stable-block.

Roderick and Diana stood still and listened to the fading talk.

'I'm sure he's very sorry, my lord!' said the coachman. 'I've made sure of that.'

'It can't be helped, it can't be helped,' said Lord Blentham. 'It must be very largely Mr Roderick's fault.'

Diana stamped one frozen foot and blew on her hands. 'I don't think you realise how lucky you are, Roddy, to be a man and independent,' she said loudly. She guessed that Roderick had done something to harm one of the horses, and she said this partly to distract his angry thoughts.

'Independent? I? You try being a curate, my girl – on a tiny legacy from Aunt Emily and a stipend of two hundred a year!' He drew himself further up in his riding boots, and put one hand inside his coat. 'And my father hardly helps to make me independent, as you call it. One mustn't complain, of course,' he said: quite contentedly, for Diana nearly always had the effect of putting him in a good mood. He thought that if he had not been her brother and a clergyman, he would have wanted to marry or sleep with a girl of her type, and would have succeeded in winning one.

'Oh, I don't mean money,' said Diana, studying her brother's coarsely handsome face, and remembering the disrespectful way in which her father had spoken to him. She sighed.

'You're not back on Cambridge, are you?' he said. 'You'll be wanting a latchkey next.'

'Yes, I'd like a latchkey, but I'm not so silly as to ask Mamma!' said Diana.

'I should hope not! Poor old Didie. Cheer up. Come on, let's get out of this da – this frightful cold.' Roderick took her arm, and Diana quite enjoyed walking beside him with her head two inches above his own. Of course, she thought, no one was truly independent, not even men. Like her father, Roderick was right and annoying, and there was nothing to be looked forward to in life but reading.

Lady Blentham considered herself fairly broad-minded. She

had no prejudice against any form of intellect, or even against those who were a little Bohemian, so long as they did not offend in some way against propriety, etiquette or taste. When her husband argued that, in order to be called Bohemian, a man or woman must necessarily be lacking in a sense of propriety, she would say that absolute convention and real propriety were not quite the same thing. To prove her point, she would remind him of Edward's friend, Arthur Cornwallis, who was wholly devoted to his rather plain wife. It was not conventional to write little essays, or to wear soft collars, but it could be perfectly proper.

Arthur Cornwallis claimed to adore Lady Blentham, whom he had met several times as an undergraduate and stayed with twice since his marriage. He told Edward that his mother was a marvellous example of a dying breed or type, an Early Victorian, and that visits to Dunstanton and Queen Anne's Gate were delightful because of this. Angelina knew perfectly well that he flattered her, and must think her a foolish if charming old woman, but she liked him all the same. When they were together, they always talked about old-fashioned subjects such as Ritualism and Dickens, or about the decline in morals and good manners over the past thirty years.

Sometimes, Angelina confided in him. Cornwallis had never told Edward that Lady Blentham had once said: 'You must not think, Mr Cornwallis, that I would be opposed to Edward's – wanting to be more like *you*, to be something of an *aesthete* or a literary man, if only I could think he had talent! But he isn't up to it, as they say. Now, don't agree with me! I know you can't – you are always loyal to him, dear Edward.'

The Cornwallises came to stay at Dunstanton that year during Roderick's visit to his parents; and Arthur soothed Lady Blentham's fears that her son was not a good clergyman.

'I've made a small study of theology,' he said, 'and I couldn't fault him on doctrine when we were indulging in a little discussion after dinner last night.' Roderick had said very little over the dining-room port. 'Though I'm afraid, dear Lady Blentham, we bored your husband horribly.'

'I'm sure not,' she smiled.

Tea was over, and they were alone together at the end of the Long Gallery, protected by screens from the draughts of its dim wooden length. Mabel Cornwallis and Maud were both having a headache and lying down upstairs, while Diana was in the library and Roderick visiting a friend.

'How I enjoy a wood fire,' he said. 'Coal fires inspire a man to do nothing but wrap himself up in a dressing-gown and brood on unworthy subjects, but a *wood* fire makes one think – almost of noble deeds. Certainly of one's days of youthful activity. Medieval in the very best sense, don't you agree?'

Mr Cornwallis, thought Angelina, had the face of an eagle and the body of an owl. He was a little too dark for her taste, but that did not matter.

'I'm afraid the house *is* a little cold in winter, Mr Cornwallis. Many people say so, out of my hearing.'

'Dear lady, you're teasing me! I hadn't thought you capable of such a thing – so unkind.'

'I believe I have – some qualities I don't quite know myself,' said Lady Blentham.

'How could I doubt that? But to return to Roderick, do you know, I think that when he is – master of his own parish, with a suitable little wife, he'll settle down as a first-rate High-and-Dry man – quite of the old school, no Romish vestments, no – '

'Perhaps *too* old a school,' said Angelina, who enjoyed colourful ecclesiastical ritual, though only because she had a secret romantic nature. She was too young to remember the days of High-and-Dry theology, but she rather liked Cornwallis's pretence that she belonged to a previous age, before even surplices were commonplace. She continued: 'On the other hand, Diana is becoming quite a New Woman. Or I hope you don't think so?'

He rememberd quickly. 'Oh, Newnham and Somerville! Prunes – and pine-wood, and terrible voices! Dear Lady Blentham, it must be discouraged. Naturally you won't *allow* her to become a New Woman?' Though his choice of words tended to be flowery, Cornwallis's voice was always sober, soft, and unaffectedly kind.

'Certainly not,' said Angelina.

Cornwallis removed his spectacles, polished and replaced them. 'Diana is a most admirable girl,' he said. 'I should imagine that this wish of hers to go to Cambridge – distressin'ly vulgar, dear lady – is partly a wish for what she imagines would be more freedom of society, more intellectual companionship?'

'Yes,' said Lady Blentham.

'She must be told how wickedly *strict* these women's colleges are – far worse than school. She never went to school?'

'No. I think it can do a girl nothing but harm. I hear that nowadays there are schools where the girls actually prepare for public examinations, and play cricket.' It had not quite occurred to Angelina that women's colleges were strict: she valued Cornwallis partly because he could make this kind of revelation.

'Yes, a horrid thought. Well,' said Cornwallis, 'I wonder what is to be done?'

Maud came back into the gallery, carrying a large tapestry-frame from which dangled a piece of *gros-point* in shades of bright blue.

'Well, my dear, is your headache better?' said her mother. 'We were talking about Diana.'

'She's at the awkward age,' said Maud, sitting slowly down and arranging her embroidery.

'Very true,' said Angelina, 'but there are so many awkward ages for a woman.'

'I think you should let her go to Cambridge, Mamma.'

'My dear,' sighed Lady Blentham, and turned her head towards Cornwallis. 'Still my little rebel.'

'Oh, no,' said Maud. 'But I remember what it was to be young and I have every sympathy with Diana.'

'*You* never thought of Cambridge,' said her mother, smiling.

'No.'

'But Miss Maud, do you consider yourself middle-aged?' said Cornwallis gravely.

'I'm thirty.'

'Hush, my dear,' said Angelina, who believed that Maud was a little in love with Cornwallis. 'Never mention your age! Mr Cornwallis,' she said, 'I want your help.'

He was contemplating Maud's fleshless beauty with intellectual pleasure. In a sense, Maud's looks had improved since he first met her five years before, though she was even more thin and pale now than she had been then: for now she was a true spinster no one expected her to have the charm and colour of a nubile girl, and her features were allowed to be nearly perfect. 'With little Diana, Lady Blentham? But of course!'

'Large Diana, I'm afraid.' She saw Maud look up. 'Could you talk to her? I know how you find very young girls a nuisance! But if *you* were to tell her that Cambridge, for women, isn't what she thinks it – I'm sure she would believe you.'

Maud started sewing again.

'I'll do more, dear lady,' said Cornwallis. 'May I make a very modern and shocking suggestion?'

'Yes, Mr Cornwallis, though I doubt it will be either,' Angelina said.

'I wonder – I wonder whether you would allow Diana – and Violet and Miss Maud, too, if they would care for it! – to come unchaperoned to one of our little parties? Diana could read her poems to us.'

'Unchaperoned?' There was silence for a moment, while both rapidly considered whether Maud could be thought old enough to be a respectable chaperone. Maud considered the question too, though they did not guess it had occurred to her. 'Perhaps you think it's freedom from control Diana wants?' added Lady Blentham.

'No no *no*! But isn't my wife chaperone enough?' He had a very polite, disarming smile.

'Of course she is,' said Angelina after a moment. 'Yes, I see.

Yes. Times are changing, as we have agreed. It's extremely kind of you, Mr Cornwallis. And it might possibly answer. Maud my dear, *you* would like it, wouldn't you? You would like to go with Diana?'

'Very much, Mamma,' she said, blushing. 'Mr Cornwallis was kind enough to invite me.'

'You're old enough to have a latchkey – if you had ever asked for it I should have given you one!'

'Thank you!' Maud closed her eyes, because she felt too old and tired and stupid to be bothered with a latchkey. Last year in London, Dr Sacheverell had told her that it was not her age or even her anaemia which made her so listless, it was her fondness for laudanum. He had told her to go out, and be active.

Maud heard her mother say: 'Mr Cornwallis, will you promise me one thing?'

'Dear lady?'

'If I give Diana, the girls, a little more freedom – if we let her learn that there *are* intelligent people, moving in the first circles, who are prepared to encourage her – will you promise me never to allow her to meet Edward's wife at your house? You see, I never have allowed either her or Violet to go out with anyone but myself, or one of our kinswomen who *understands*, because of her!'

'But of *course!*' said Cornwallis, thinking that he must remind little Diana, when he introduced her to Kitty, that meeting Kitty had been forbidden by her mamma. She would like that, and so would Edward.

Both the Cornwallises were rich and well born. They lived in an odd, graceful house in Half Moon Street, with eighteenth-century furniture and tapestries, black-and-white-tiled or polished floors, and one or two modern things such as vases full of sunflowers and silver-framed photographs. Books were everywhere.

When their literary evening began with an excellent dinner, Diana and Maud were rather disappointed, thinking it little different from many formal dinner-parties in other houses.

The conversation, however, was not quite what they were used to.

Maud and Diana were impressed when, over the removes, they learnt that Arthur Wing Pinero (whose latest play had greatly shocked Lady Blentham) was to drop in for a while later in the evening. The Blentham girls had not heard that anyone else at the party was famous, but they supposed during dinner that some must be, for people were talking in a familiar way of Mr James McNeill Whistler, Mr Oscar Wilde and Mrs Humphry Ward. No one mentioned such figures to them, but Diana did manage to make intelligent, brief replies to the elderly man on her left. He wished to discuss modern novelists.

Edward and Kitty were present, and were kind to their sisters as everyone else was, but the girls had little time to talk to them either at dinner or afterwards. Both were extremely popular, and considered to be a rather good joke. When they left the dining-room and went upstairs with the other ladies, Maud and Diana were astonished to see Edward lean forward and begin to speak as the door closed behind them. His voice lacked its usual languor, and he was obviously being listened to by the other men.

Half an hour later, the gentlemen returned to them; and the Blentham girls were delighted yet embarrassed when Kitty changed the tone of the whole evening. She climbed up on one of the finest Queen Anne chairs in the drawing-room and gave a raucous imitation of May Yohé; who, she said, had no right to have taken the London stage by storm.

'No voice, no figure, and a nasty little face, gentlemen! Now, listen to this!' she said, grinning, and half the party gathered round her. She winked at her sisters-in-law, who were sitting close together by the door.

Maud and Diana, who had been allowed to see only Shakespeare at the theatre, had heard from other girls that the new American actress was able to sing only four notes. Kitty, with her hands on her hips and her butter-coloured throat raised to the gas-lights so that the good paste jewels glittered in her hair, sang a whole song on two.

'Maud, how *did* Mr Cornwallis persuade Mamma to let us come?' said Diana.

'You know how clever he is with her. It is – rather exciting, isn't it? Though I see what our mother means about Kitty.'

'Yes – just as he said – far more exciting than Cambridge,' murmured Diana, as everyone clapped and Kitty jumped down, trailing black lace which looked very well against the men's plain black and white. 'Maud, you won't tell Mamma about this?'

'I?' Maud turned to her, looking like a brilliant, beautiful girl. 'Do you really think I will?'

At that moment, Cornwallis came up and sat down beside Maud. 'I think we may enjoy a few more *civilised* recitals before the night is over,' he said. 'But I so like to entertain originals of every kind. You weren't offended, Miss Maud?'

Diana sat still, smiling at him, remembering the half-hours of his time Cornwallis had given her since January, discussing books with her instead of trying to draw morals from them as Angelina did. He was as kind as he was deceitful and mischievous.

The men round Kitty were dispersing, and she herself retired to a corner with two of them. One man, Diana saw, was making his way in her direction. He was big, blond, clean-shaven and young, a boy whose name she had forgotten, who looked more like a sailor than a literary man.

'Miss Blentham, may I join you?'

'Yes, certainly . . . ' He was rather handsome, she thought, in spite of his snub nose: firm-jawed and clear-complexioned, with light round grey eyes set beneath unusually thick and pale eyebrows.

'I think you've forgotten my name,' he said, seeing the anxious look on her face. 'We were introduced, actually. Julian Fitzclare – v-very much at your service, as they used to say!'

'Oh, you're Mrs Cornwallis's brother – she told me – Captain Fitzclare, of the Blues!' she said.

'Yes, of the Blues,' he agreed.

They were quiet for a while, looking down at their laps, and shiftily moving their feet. 'This is a good party, ain't it?' he said. 'It's unusual.'

'Yes,' said Diana, looking at the one man who was not in evening dress but in a ruby velvet coat. She was not used to feeling shy, and she had felt shy ever since the Blentham carriage dropped them at the door. 'I suppose it's Bohemia.' She smiled.

'Yes – at l-least so I'm told by – c-crusty old ladies,' he said, smiling at her dark-red eyes. 'Actually, my sister tells me you're a p-poetess – may make an awfully good poet. She admires you.'

'Oh,' said Diana. 'You do make me feel rather a fool, Captain Fitzclare.' She wondered just how old he was: twenty-five or -six.

He sat upright, and flushed. 'Why? I'm not one of those sort of idiot fellows who thinks a lady shouldn't have a brain. I don't like stupid girls,' he said.

'Don't you?'

'Most men do, you know.'

'I know.' Diana was quite unable to decide whether she liked him or not.

'I believe,' he said, 'that women are superior to men.'

Diana laughed. By the fireplace, a man was discreetly reading out a passage from a little sage-green book, which he then handed round to his small audience of ladies.

'Why do you laugh?' said the Captain. She hoped he was hurt.

'Well, I – used to want very much to go to Girton, or any women's college at either of the universities, in fact. Most people always tell me that women are so superior, and clever in their own way, they don't *need* university. But they don't deny university is for the cleverest men! The Senior Wranglers and Senior Classics – *aren't* they the cleverest of men, Captain Fitzclare?'

'Mr Pinero!' the butler announced.

There was a stir as the playwright entered; Mabel ran forward and began introductions. He was led over gradually to the other side of the room and Captain Fitzclare, who had shaken hands with Mr Pinero with stiff and deep respect, sat down again beside Diana and showed her a very serious face.

'You know,' he said, 'I knew a girl once who was very like you – talented, and pretty, and clever and all that – and she went up to Somerville and simply hated it. She was awfully cold and lonely, you see. Felt she had to stay her whole three years because she'd fought her people so hard to get there. She told me it was rather dirty, as well as cold – and everyone was dreadfully earnest, and suspicious as a governess – not a soul she knew – people rather despised her for being, well, a lady, I suppose. Wouldn't take her seriously because of it. You wouldn't like that, surely? Though I'm sure you're brave enough, and can't be a wretched snob, or anything like that. And then you see, she never did anything with all that education. Just got married, and never opened a book afterwards.'

'Goodness,' said Diana, colouring slightly because it had never occurred to her that lower-middle-class people, with accents, might go to women's colleges, although she had never supposed she would meet girls from quite her own set. 'I thought colleges were extremely luxurious – Charles the Second silver, and enormous dinners, and so on.'

'Not women's colleges. They're awfully uncomfortable, and it's difficult to work at anything if you ain't comfortable. I – wonder why you really want to go, Miss Blentham? You read on your own, I suppose?'

Obviously, thought Diana, Captain Fitzclare could not be very intelligent, let alone unconventional, because he was in the Blues: yet she felt he was unprejudiced, and capable of listening properly to a young girl whom he admired. She knew that Cornwallis had been hired by her mother to discourage her charmingly from foolish ideas. 'Yes, of course, I read a good deal,' she said.

'And when you were younger, in the schoolroom I mean – I suppose you had even more time, did very well?'

'Oh, well. I spent every minute my governesses would spare me on poetry, reading it and writing it, too. But I wasn't allowed then to read any kind of novel – I did, of course – or adult books, really, of any kind at all. Which was dull. But poetry was considered quite all right, very suitable.'

'Yes, odd that, when one thinks of some poems – mm – not that I've read much – what girls are expected – '

'I know exactly what you mean,' said Diana firmly, thinking: '*Oh my America, my Newfoundland, my kingdom safest when with one man manned.*' 'I suppose you're right – Cambridge would be very different from all I've known – in a way I hadn't quite thought of – but – ' She was still determined to go if she could: but she was beginning to enjoy this party so much she could not think about it.

'You've plenty of time to think about it,' he said. 'And I say, if you don't get married first, they'd be *honoured* to have you, Miss Blentham.'

Arthur Cornwallis came up. 'Diana my dear,' he said loudly, 'did I not make you promise to bring your poem, and read it to us? You won't be *alone* – many of us are preparing to indulge ourselves, you know – like Sir Henry here!'

The man called Sir Henry said: 'Yes, don't deny us, Miss Blentham,' just as though he were expecting her to play the piano and sing a little air. Suddenly, half the people in the room seemed to be looking at her. Kitty was beaming in Diana's direction across some tall man's protruding stomach.

'Is it in your pocket?' said Captain Fitzclare.

'Don't disappoint us, Diana!' called Edward.

She had written a poem called 'Early Winter, in Garden and Soul', and she had brought it with her, though not in her pocket as Captain Fitclare had said, because she had none. She remembered that she had tried to be exact and simple, and yet to imitate the alliterative roll of Swinburne's lines.

Diana took the hot, folded square of paper out of her corsage, and looked at it. It would be undignified to ask for time, or to be excused. She was angry with these people who encouraged her to show off: but she had come here in order to read a poem, and have it judged. Diana opened out her paper and blinked down at the words she had thought quite acceptable. The last lines of the second verse read:

THE HON. DIANA BLENTHAM 1880–1896

Cold I wait among the cherries, trained along the wall's
wire rack.
Where loose leaves of thin coral orange, hang but a few
days from branches of black.

It did not scan. She would not have thought it possible. She
must have been waiting for an imaginary lover, or inspiration,
or permission to go to Cambridge and waste her time. For
nothing. Diana crumpled the paper and put it back in her
bosom.

She said to those who were waiting and smiling: 'You
mustn't encourage me to bore you – it's bad, very bad, very
bad indeed.' Diana sat down against beside Fitzclare.

'My dear!' said Cornwallis. 'I'm very sorry you think so,
but don't let us distress you. Another time?'

'Perhaps.' She could see that people approved of her
modesty, of her throwing away her chance. Diana was angry
again.

Captain Fitzclare laid a quick hand on her fingers as soon as
attention passed over them. Someone else was reading out a
very amusing piece.

'I'm sure, you know – I've heard about all this sort of thing
from Mabel, even though I don't quite fit in this s-set either –
I'm sure that if you think it's bad, it's good, it will be good. If
you thought it was g-good, it might be absolute rubbish!'

She said: 'How kind of you, Captain Fitzclare.'

CHAPTER 6

TWO ENGAGEMENTS

In the library at Dunstanton, one wet afternoon in late July, Diana was standing on tiptoe on the rickety bookcase steps. She was looking for a copy of the *Annals* of Tacitus, for she was trying to teach herself Latin; all the unread classical authors were hidden on the very top shelf, not prominently displayed with the unreadable old sermons as they were in most private libraries.

Diana found three copies after a difficult search, took them all out, and sat down on the steps to see which had the best print and commentary. One was a brown seventeenth-century volume, another had been mauled by a schoolboy, but the third, in a fairly modern binding with firm gold print, looked an improvement on either. She opened it and read the title-page, which said:

MEMOIRS OF A WOMAN OF PLEASURE

The Celebrated History of Miss
FANNY HILL

It was an early nineteenth-century pirated edition, very ill printed and very much thumbed: yet it smelt musty, as though no one had read it since it had been disguised as the *Annals*. Before going further than the title-page, Diana knew roughly what sort of book it must be. She had had two seasons in London, and she had heard people whispering about such things. She jumped down from the steps, went to her corner armchair, and began to read, wondering if it could possibly be her father who had had the book re-bound. On the whole, now that she was learning Latin with her father's full knowledge, she thought it must have been her grandfather, or her seldom-mentioned Uncle Harold who had been killed at Tel-el-Kebir.

Diana began at the beginning, and was moved and shocked by the first twenty pages though she did not quite understand. As she read on, she remembered a well-chaperoned visit to the British Museum three years ago, and the statue of a naked man which she had come on quite by accident. Mademoiselle, who was still looking at coins when Diana slipped away, had chased through the rooms, and discovered the girl examining the man with an air of detached distaste; not with the giggling, wicked curiosity proper to seventeen. She had pulled Diana away, but had not scolded her: for fear of questions, as her charge had known at the time.

'So this is it, so this is it,' Diana murmured aloud, pulling at her hair, as, while swiftly reading, she worked out with half her mind the whole truth of the baby-mystery, exactly what must be happening in cold, very undelicious terms. Why on each do they conceal it from us, the mere facts, thought Diana; oh, well, I do see. She had guessed long ago at the reality of childbirth, and she dreaded it to the point of thinking she might never marry.

> . . . I arriv'd at excess of Pleasure, through excess of Pain; but when successive Engagements had broken and inur'd me, I began to Enter into the true unallay'd Relish of that Pleasure of Pleasures, when the warm Gush Darts through all the ravished inwards . . . the whole afternoon, till supper-time, in a continued circle of Love-delights.

Diana felt she knew exactly what Fanny Hill was talking about. She referred back to the earlier passages, where girls and their fingers figured chiefly, and men were only in the wings; then continued with the story, under the glass-strengthened heat of the Kentish sun which, outdoors, ruined by wind and damp, could help arouse no sleepy passions.

Diana found Fanny Hill's second, rather frightening lover

more coarsely fascinating than the lovely boy Charles who seemed to have as little, if good, conversation as Julian Fitzclare.

> *. . . roll'd down the Bed-Cloaths, and seem'd Transported with the view of my Person at full length . . . he drew up his shirt, and Bared all his Hairy Thighs, and stiff Staring Truncheon, red-topt, and rooted into a Thicket of curls . . . in a few minutes he was in Condition for Renewing the onset . . . and thus in repeated Engagements, kept me constantly in Exercise till Dawn of Morning, in all which time, he made me full Sensible of the Virtues of his trim Texture of limbs, his square shoulders, Broad Chest, compact Hard Muscles, in short a system of Manliness, that might pass for no bad image of our Antient Sturdy Barons . . . .*

At the thought that her father was in fact a baron, Diana giggled and looked evil, then blinked as she remembered her cool thin gentle mother.

'Oh, goodness.'

She must show this book to Violet, when she had had time to digest it. For it was distressing, with all its talk of male truncheons, engines and machines; vulgar as well as a revelation, teaching that the deepest comfort of the body was normal. The baby-making aspect of men and women's meeting had never aroused Diana's curiosity so much as the unimaginable reason for her soft, low pleasure in her own flesh.

It must be nearly nine years since she and Violet had discussed all this, though modestly, in the schoolroom the day Nurse told them she was leaving to be married. They had not mentioned the subject since then: perhaps shortly afterwards Violet, slow and dear as she was, had discovered the oozing little joy for herself. Then like Diana, she might have become only perfunctorily curious about babies and men.

Lord Blentham came in. He asked Diana whether she was enjoying herself, and whether she did not think she had done enough work. Diana did not hide the volume of Tacitus, though her hands shook; she smiled tiredly, and said perhaps she had done enough for one day. He did not ask her what she was reading, because he was busy and had come in only to fetch the *Graphic*. He made a joke about Latin and strong-minded women, a commonplace remark which was not characteristic of him. Then he left, and Diana got up quickly from her chair.

Six weeks later, Lord and Lady Blentham and their two younger daughters were staying with a friend in Argyllshire. Violet liked Scotland, but Diana did not.

'Oh, Didie, Didie! Oh, Manning, please will you go and wait in my room, I'll help Miss Diana to dress, I've got something to tell her, you see!' cried Violet, breathlessly pushing open the door to her sister's room, so hard that it rattled against the wall.

Diana had been at the dressing-table with the lady's maid behind her, looking peacefully out at the view of the moors which belonged to their host, Sir Walter Montrose. She jumped, began to smile, and opened her mouth at Violet's entrance, but Manning, seeing both girls' excitement, was the first to speak. 'Yes, Miss Violet. Do you still wish to wear the cream nun's-veiling?' she said.

'Oh, yes, anything!'

When the maid was gone, Violet threw herself on the bed and said: 'He's asked me. And he got Papa's consent before proposing, can you believe it, this is 1893? And he's never tried to kiss me. Oh, Didie *darling*. Isn't it wonderful?'

'Well, congratulations,' said Diana at last. 'I never thought he really would, I must say.'

Violet rolled over on the bed. 'Oh, just because he never – behaved like a young man. I knew – I so hoped – the way he looked at me, and the *kindness*, especially when he killed that wasp at luncheon yesterday, and I was so terrified, and Jimmy Rose thought it was funny – '

Diana began to laugh. 'Oh, Vio, you are an idiot. I do hope you'll be happy. Well, when exactly did he ask you? What did he say?'

'Oh, I was loitering in the hall, thinking I must come up and dress, you know, even though the gong hadn't gone – *why* can't one wear a tea-gown for dinner – and he came out of the gun-room passage, and started talking about the colours on the moors, you know, and how really awful it is to *pollute* them by shooting the grouse for mere sport, which I've always thought. And then there were no servants about, you see, so he opened the front door, and we went out, going towards the moors I suppose, awfully romantic, and then he proposed, and said a lot of nonsense about his being so much older than me.' Violet stopped, and patted her hair.

'Well, he is fifty-five. I don't know how – '

'Fifty-four.'

'Still, people will say it's shameful, you know they will, Vio.'

'Oh, never mind that. I'm not in the least conventional. After all, Papa gave his consent.'

'Of course he did. You're such a *big* mouth to feed, and you're old as girls go, nearly twenty-two, aren't you now?'

'Don't tease. I wish I'd heard S – Walter asking Papa,' Violet said, smiling into the distance.

Diana noticed Violet's hesitation. 'Vio, do you still call him Sir Walter? Did he say – um – "My dear Miss Blentham, my deep and sincere friendship for you and your family has grown, over these last few weeks, to –" '

'*Didie*, you *know* he's not pompous, or old-fashioned even. He said *Violet*, quite passionately.'

'I know. The whole position is just – it makes one rather nervous.'

'Yes: Mamma,' said Violet. 'She'll be so angry at not having had the least idea!'

Diana did not take this up, though she thought her mother had guessed something, and disapproved, but had refused to take the business seriously because it was unthinkable.

'Oh, Didie, I'm going to be *married*!' said Violet. She went on: 'I'll live here forever, and I'll never have to go to London again, or dance with dreary men, or try to look sweet and *jeune fille*.'

Diana turned and looked at Violet. 'Vio, have you thought about *Fanny Hill* – in connection with Sir Walter? All that?'

'Often,' said her sister, sitting upright on the bed. 'Very often. In fact, I look forward to it very much.' She said again, thumping the pillow: 'I'm going to be *married*, Didie!'

'I know!' said Diana. 'And I think you're a fool – the whole thing is ridiculous, and he's an old bore however kind he is! A widower of nearly sixty, I don't know how you can. Don't say you're going to be *married* again, I know you are!'

Violet stared at her. Until now, Diana had encouraged her confidences, grinned at her and teased her, and said that Sir Walter was just the man for her. 'Poor old Didie,' she said with ample dignity. 'I'm going to tell Mamma now.'

Before the next day's shooting began, Sir Walter Montrose hinted Lord Blentham away from the remains of his breakfast, and made the other men at table mildly curious. The two of them went out of the house, and Sir Walter proposed a stroll in the garden. As they walked, both silently examined the place which was to be Violet's home.

Auchingilloch Lodge was a convenient house, built of Scottish stone in simple, modern castle style. The gardens were poor, filled chiefly at the moment with overgrown shrubs and late, unhealthy roses; and beyond, there were the brown hills ready for shooting, lapped by streaks of morning cloud. When Sir Walter had proposed to Violet the afternoon before, the whole scene had been golden. He sighed.

'Well?' said Charles.

Sir Walter hesitated before saying: 'Violet has accepted me. I was – more delighted than I can say, of course, Blentham, and I must thank you for – '

'You don't mean to say you really hadn't even dropped her a hint about the matter before?'

'Well, a *hint*,' said Sir Walter, smiling, 'but a very discreet one.'

There was a pause, and both coughed.

'Well, she's a sweet girl and rarely any trouble, and I hope she'll make you happy. It's time she was married, I daresay her mother will accustom herself to the idea. I told you, didn't I . . . When you approached me yesterday I didn't know what to think,' said Charles. He had imagined at one moment that he could not face squashing the whole affair, which must already have been settled between the two of them; and at the next, that Violet was bound to turn the old man down and giggle about it.

He heard the other say now: 'I know I'm more than thirty years her senior. I thought – Blentham, I can only tell you that I love her deeply and asked your permission to marry her only because I couldn't stop myself – because it is my deepest wish to make her happy.'

'Yes, yes, of course, Montrose,' murmured Charles. Though he said so little, he wished briefly that more men were as articulate and unashamed as Montrose.

Sir Walter put his hands in his pockets, and Charles thought quite crossly that he was a remarkably handsome man for his age, with his tall slender figure, thick straight grey hair, fine skin; and notable grey-blue eyes surrounded by becoming, thoughtful lines. His nose was a little too large, and hooked. 'I think that Violet must have told your wife of our intentions,' he said, shyly.

'Do you mean because she hardly spoke to you at dinner?'

'Yes – I suppose so.'

'Didn't she refer to the matter?'

'No, no she didn't.'

'Oh, in that case – '

At that moment they saw Angelina, who was already dressed in tweeds. She was coming briskly round from the opposite side of the house, though she was supposed to be in bed with her breakfast tray. They said nothing till she reached them, and she spoke first.

'I happened to see you from my bedroom window,' she told the two men, and embarrassed them slightly. 'Well, Sir Walter, so you are going to be my son-in-law! I thought in that case, you couldn't object to my getting up rather early – having a little stroll in your charming garden.' She blinked up at him.

Charles pushed forward slightly. 'Angelina, did Violet tell you?'

'Yes, Charles.' Angelina had made her daughter cry.

'I mean to do all I can to make Violet happy, Lady Blentham,' said Walter.

She looked at him. 'She's of age, perhaps she knows her own mind. I mean to have a little talk with her, Sir Walter, and if what I say about – if what I say doesn't influence her as it should, then she can marry you without my – making vulgar objections. I've thought about this very carefully. I must go back into the house, I suppose, I must have interrupted a most important talk.'

'Lady Blentham, I'm glad you don't object too much.'

'Yes,' she said, and suddenly beamed, making Charles grunt and look up at the house. 'Charles and I still have our little Diana, after all – though I suppose not for *very* long.' All of them thought of Captain Fitzclare.

It was on his account that Lady Blentham had decided to accept Sir Walter's invitation: if Charles had not told her that Fitzclare would be present, she would have declined for herself and the girls.

She left the men, and they went on their way, walking rather faster than before. 'Dear Angelina,' said Lord Blentham, and added: 'Violet's the least like her mother of all the girls. Didie's really rather like her – so's Maud.'

'All women are mysterious, don't you think?' said Sir Walter.

Lady Blentham went back into the house, feeling a fool because she had just acted on impulse as she almost never did. She climbed the stairs, walked along the little passage reserved by Sir Walter for unmarried women, and stood for a moment coldly looking at the little brass-bound card on her daughter's door which said: '*The Honble. Violet Blentham.*' She went in and said: 'Violet' to the mound in the bed. 'Violet.'

'Mamma?' Violet struggled a little, then raised herself, and blinked at her mother in the half-darkness. Angelina decided not to open the curtains. 'It's awfully early, isn't it? You're dressed . . . '

'I want to talk to you, my dear.'

77

'About my marriage?' Violet said clearly, a moment later.

'About your – marriage. Because I think that like most girls – you have very little idea of what marriage implies.'

'Oh.'

'Some girls are told nothing by their mothers, Violet, and when it happens – when they marry – they get a considerable shock.'

Violet guessed what was coming, and thought of Fanny Hill, but she only stretched her toes and said: 'Yes, Mamma? What sort of considerable shock?'

Lady Blentham walked over to the window and fingered the curtain. 'Don't you think this is a very ugly, bleak sort of house, Violet?' She hated Scotland, and all unruly moors.

'Oh, I rather like it,' said Violet. 'Do go on, Mamma!'

'Well, my dear,' Angelina sighed, 'do you promise me not to repeat a word of what I'm going to say to you to Diana?'

'Yes, I promise,' said Violet, drawing up her knees under the bedclothes, and hugging them.

Angelina sat down on a hard chair, and folded her hands in her lap like a good child. 'You know, of course,' she said, 'that married people often share a bedroom? People who move in Society, even the middle classes, have separate bedrooms, of course, but usually connected?'

'Yes.'

'They have to share a bed,' she continued. 'Even if they do have separate rooms. My dear, have you read the marriage service?'

'Yes, Mamma.'

'Perhaps certain passages – certain words – have made you wonder? "Fruitful", for instance – the mention of children?'

'Actually, no, Mamma.'

'Then it's time they did!' said Angelina. There was a pause, and she looked down at her lap. 'Violet, I must explain that married men and women – come together, in bed, to make babies. Men are made very differently from women and they – they enter us.' She closed her eyes. Nearly all men repelled Angelina, but she thought Sir Walter remarkably attractive, and found it hard to imagine his taking a wife to bed. She wondered how in the world Violet had attached him, for she was so plain. Breathing deeply, she continued: 'They have an instrument attached to their – stomachs – to enter between our lower limbs. Men suffer from desire, Violet, the lust of concupiscence as they say, they *want* to do it, gain pleasure from it, constantly, that is what I mean. But it's *painful* for women – often very painful. Even with a man of whom she's fond, a woman cannot – it's only our duty, our absolute duty, to submit. That's marriage, Violet. Do you understand me?'

'Yes, Mamma,' said Violet in a very muffled voice. Even in the dim light, she could see that her mother's cheeks were bright red.

'Now, do you see why I have told you? Can you still want to marry Sir Walter – such an old man, really so plain? Isn't it vile? He *must* seem so to you!' There was no answer. Angelina's voice rose. 'Girls nowadays, one can never . . . Perhaps you know something about all this. Perhaps you thought such an old man wouldn't want it! But he will, Violet – I promise you.' She did not really think it possible that Violet could know anything, and she knew she was becoming over-excited.

'Oh,' whispered Violet.

'And childbirth – producing a baby – through a tiny hole, is quite agonisingly painful, Violet. Even chloroform helps only a little!'

'Mamma, don't you think someone might possibly hear you?' said Violet anxiously. 'The maids, I mean . . . '

Angelina swallowed. 'Do you wish to marry him? Do you? The thought of your being married to him makes me very, very angry. How dare he, at his age, even *think* of – oh, in the old days a mother would have been quite *glad* for her daughter to marry him, for mere social reasons, even though he can't have much more than five thousand a year! And would she have told you what I've just told you? But my affection for you – my caring for your happiness – matters very little, perhaps you'd *rather* . . . '

'Oh, don't be upset, *darling* Mamma, please.'

'Have you listened to what I've been saying to you?'

'Yes.' Violet sat up in bed, and pulled the pillows into shape behind her, looking at her mother meanwhile.

'Do you insist on marrying him – now that you understand?'

'Yes. I love him, you see. I shan't mind his – doing all those things to me.' At last, Violet began weakly to laugh.

Lady Blentham got up from her chair and said very clearly: 'Violet.'

'Y-yes, M-mamma?'

'Did you know before. Did you allow me to tell you, quite unnecessarily?'

Violet realised then that, for the first time in her life, she had been consciously unkind, and to her mother; but she could not stop giggling. 'I did know a – a *little*, Mamma. Other girls talk, you know – people *do* find out!'

Angelina's teeth chattered. 'Then I see that I shall have no need to say anything at all to Diana, ever. Very well, Violet. Marry Sir Walter, though I can't think you'll be happy. How you can *know* and think you *love* him? Young girls' natural feelings, towards handsome young men – when they think that marriage will be a few kisses, that they'll be treated with *respect* – that one can understand, but you are quite, quite different, I see! No, I won't say it. Marry him. I shall send the notice of your engagement to *The Times* tomorrow. Well, how little one knows one's own children. Stop it, child! *Violet!*' The girl was still laughing. Lady Blentham strode over to the bed, and slapped her daughter's face: but she could not bring herself to do it as hard as she wished, and she sobbed.

Diana walked up and down the little yew-tree avenue which was the central feature of the garden at Auchingilloch. She was smiling, occasionally laughing, over one of Shakespeare's sonnets, which Julian Fitzclare had copied out and put under her door in an envelope. He had included a note, which asked her whether she did not think it original and moving. He said he would like to have her opinion as a poet, and she meant to give it:

I have seen roses damask'd, red and white,
But no such roses see I in her cheeks;
And in some perfumes there is more delight
Than in the breath that from my mistress reeks . . .
I grant I never saw a goddess go –
My mistress, when she walks, treads on the ground.
And yet, by Heaven, I think my love as rare
As any she belied with false compare.

It was immensely kind of him to make such an effort to court
her with poetry, and to be original too. He could not have
enjoyed being so intellectual, thought Diana, even though he
worshipped her.

She sat down on a wet wooden seat, concealed from the main
path in an alcove, and thought of Violet's engagement, which
was now the main topic of conversation at Auchingilloch
Lodge. Lady Blentham let it be known that she had contrived
a wise match for an unusual daughter; and the other ladies
staying with Sir Walter were busy spreading the news round
the neighbourhood and communicating it by letter. Julian
Fitzclare very much approved of Violet's choice, and quite
believed that Lady Blentham was right to have encouraged it.
This pleased Diana, though she did not tell him of her
mother's original reaction, or of her own outburst when
Violet told her; which had surprised her at the time as much as
it had her sister.

Diana and Violet had made up their brief quarrel, as soon as
Violet had enjoyed a cuddle with Sir Walter and told him
about it, but Diana still felt guilty. As she had told Violet, she
was unhappy too, because she knew how badly she would
miss her sister; how she would hate living alone with her
parents and Maud. There would be no more smoking
cigarettes in the old schoolroom at Dunstanton, or long hair-
brushing talks about sex and other people's stupidity, about
their parents and about themselves. Her sister congratulated
her on these feelings.

Diana disliked knowing that she was jealous of Violet,
when she had never had the least cause to be so before. She did

not like discovering that Violet had a hard streak in her character, and would never in her life forgive Angelina, or be brought to think Sir Walter a rather silly man. It had been very unpleasant, Diana thought, to discover that Mamma was capable of handing out slaps.

She looked down again at the poem in her hand; and the sight of it made her feel panic. It made her think she would never really have a chance to marry and be like Violet, even though Julian's copying it out for her seemed to point to the opposite. She was not normal, and never could be.

Julian Fitzclare had been the first to make Diana see that a part of her wish to go to university had been the desire to leave Dunstanton: even though she loved her parents. Violet's engagement, and all the troubles surrounding it, simply confirmed this. So, two months ago, had *Memoirs of a Woman of Pleasure* – she could hardly think of education now.

She wanted to be a fully dignified grown-up, a clever woman with a house of her own, able to treat Angelina as an equal. Since yesterday, when Fitzclare had taken the opportunity to kiss her behind a rock on the moors, she had also felt an increased need for a man. Diana thought he had made her see that *Fanny Hill* was not just a most intriguing fantasy; that real men who danced and shot could be like the courtesan's better lovers. They did kiss with sexual passion, only slightly mixed with fear; and she would learn to enjoy the reality, not only the thought, in time.

'You know he won't propose, he's merely a little infatuated,' she said aloud, in a sensibly teasing voice, as though speaking to Violet. *Reeking breath*, she thought. Diana brushed her teeth once a day, and always gargled with eau-de-cologne after smoking a cigarette. She smiled again, and wondered whether he could be made to smile too. Diana did like Julian, but she did not think he would ever make her a serious proposal. She wished more than anything else that he would, and swore she would accept him.

Julian Fitzclare felt that he had deeply wronged Diana behind the stone on the moor. She had been shyly unresponsive as any girl ought to be, but her hot colour and the look in her eyes, and her perfect silence then and after, confirmed his view that she was unique. Only the other picknickers, wandering towards them, chattering and looking, had prevented him from proposing then. Since that day, he had not found her unchaperoned even for a moment, and he wondered how on earth he was ever to marry. He did not believe she would even consider accepting him. He was sure that she liked him, but he quite accepted that she could not love him as he loved her. He would have been rather shocked if she had, for he only wanted to serve and adore her.

On Sunday, the first of September, there was no shooting; Sir Walter's household planned to drive over to Smallburn Castle, where its owner, Mr Maclean, would give them both luncheon and tea. Several carriages were needed to transport the whole party, but it turned out on Sunday morning that the second landau had a broken shaft and was unusable. There was consternation when Sir Walter and his devouter guests returned from the local kirk.

'Well,' said Sir Walter's widowed sister, Mrs Lejeune, quickly planning excellent arrangements in her head, 'I can't think what's to be done. I simply can't imagine – it's a disaster.'

'Very unfortunate,' said Lady Blentham.

'I told Walter, of course, that hiring job-carriages for a party like this is always a risky business. They're *never* sound. A pity, I must say, he doesn't keep a proper number of his own, but I'm sure Violet will manage him better than I do. Do you think, Lady Blentham, that it would look *very* odd if he drove her in the governess-cart?' she said quickly.

'No, not odd in the least. They're engaged.'

'Violet is such a dear.' Mrs Lejeune, who had no children, looked forward to staying at Auchingilloch, making friends with her brother's little wife, and supervising her nursery. 'Mr Fitzclare – Captain Fitzclare, I always forget – might perhaps drive your younger daughter? We do have a pony-trap, and . . . so difficult!'

'I see no reason why he should not.'

'You and I can follow them, of course, in the landau.'

'Yes,' said Lady Blentham. She had been so horrified by her own folly, her emotion, and the violence she had shown to her daughter, that she was now sincerely in favour of the marriage. Her old feelings were so perfectly buried that she did not remember them, and she was being meek.

When Mrs Lejeune told him that he was to drive Diana over to Smallburn, Julian blushed.

'Shan't you be pleased?' said Mrs Lejeune.

'I'll be d-delighted,' he gulped. 'Delighted, I promise you.'

It was a warm day, and there were midges in the air. Diana and Julian drove in virtual silence for a while, commenting only on the weather and the state of yesterday's bag. About twenty minutes after leaving Auchingilloch, Diana said: 'Thank you for sending me that sonnet. I think it's one of Shakespeare's best, don't you?'

Julian flicked the horse and thought for a terrible moment that he had forgotten to say in his accompanying note that the poem was one of Shakespeare's, not his own. 'I'm glad you do – I'd give anything to be able to write like that!' She might still think he had been trying to pass it off as his, and of course she would have seen through that at once. She was a brilliant, poetical girl.

'Like Wolfe – wishing he had written Gray's *Elegy*. But that sonnet's so *sensible*,' said Diana, smiling at the roadside. 'Isn't it? The Dark Lady must have been delighted with it.'

'Just so. I say – I s-say, Miss Diana, I m-meant it, for you, even though I wrote that n-note to go with it! You *are* like a g-goddess, and snow-white skinned and all that – n-not like the lady in the poem! B-but I didn't think you'd like to hear a lot of exaggerated n-nonsense, however pretty, I thought – you're so d-different.'

'No black wires grow on my head?' said Diana quickly, without moving.

'Damn it, what a f-fool I'm making of myself! The thing is – D-diana, I love you, I think you're the most p-perfect girl, the *only* girl – I can't l-live without you. Will you m-marry me – d-do me the honour?'

84

Diana thought she liked his little stammer, before she took in his words.

Julian stopped the pony-trap, and neither noticed the Montrose landau drawing closer.

'Yes, I will, Julian,' whispered Diana. Her heart was beating very fast, just as though she were in love.

'My dear – my love – D-diana, I'll do anything for you! D-do you love me, even a little bit?'

'Yes, I love you,' said Diana.

Julian advanced an arm and gazed at her, and she wished she could be clever with him.

Behind them, Sir Walter's head-groom coughed.

'My dear Captain, you're blocking the road!' said Mrs Lejeune from the back seat of the landau.

Julian swung round so hard that he disturbed the horse.

'Frightfully s-sorry! But I've asked D-diana to marry me, and we've just got engaged – Lady Blentham!' he said in a voice brave with happiness.

Diana turned in her seat, and though with Julian's voice ringing out over the hills she could hardly see the occupants of the landau, she nodded at her mother and gave a little, wavering smile. Then Lady Blentham returned it.

'Modern children!' she said, blushing, before the laughing congratulations began. Diana wanted to say: 'Oh, Mamma! Don't you disapprove?' She could only say insipid, suitable things.

Remarks about two marriages being settled at Auchingilloch in such a particularly extraordinary way continued until the group was disturbed by a bicyling farmer, angry at the blocking of a very narrow road. It was then agreed that Julian and Diana should follow the landau to Smallburn at a distance of a hundred yards or so, and be the last to arrive.

CHAPTER 7

ONE QUIET WEDDING

The inside of Dunstanton church was light and dark in patches, full of white and yellow daffodils caught by the moving sun. As Violet came down the aisle on Lord Blentham's arm, followed by her bridesmaids, the guests turned to watch her, though not too obviously because that would be impolite. Some were smiling, and Diana believed that they were thinking of how innocent Violet must be, and what a shock she would have tonight.

She was feeling old. Julian Fitzclare, his parents and all five of his brothers and sisters were seated halfway down the aisle, watching her and not Violet. Over the past few months, Diana had frequently been told of people's saying how Julian, or Fitzclare, adored that girl, or Miss Blentham, or Diana. People said that he was an excellent catch, and this pleased her, although she despised them for not considering his personal qualities, only his eligibility. The Fitzclares were an Anglo-Irish family, who had helped keep Ireland for the English since the Pale round Dublin was first made. They were considered very respectable. Julian was the eldest son, due to inherit twelve thousand a year and a third of County Westmeath, as several people Lady Blentham thought vulgar had told her daughter at different times.

The procession halted. Violet and Sir Walter moved towards each other, and Diana thought as she knelt down and watched them that both looked like happy, handsome, rather intelligent sheep. She adjusted her bouquet, smiled, and thanked God that in four months she would be married too. Diana never forgot to be thankful.

She did not especially want to live in Ireland, but then old Mr Fitzclare was a healthy man, younger than Sir Walter Montrose; and Diana thought that probably she would not have to go to Ballynore until she herself was middle-aged and past wishing for anything else. She looked forward, in any case, to baiting her Liberal Unionist father-in-law with her strong support for Home Rule.

The congregation listened patiently to Roderick's sing-song reading of the Solemnization of Matrimony. Violet wept and smiled, which unnerved Roderick a little, and made him falter in places and turn red. Diana, kneeling behind her sister, caught the words 'honourable estate', 'Cana of Galilee', 'brute beasts', 'nurture of the Lord', 'just cause', but could not follow the whole prologue. Her lips were parted. Julian, watching her, thought he was ready to cry like a woman: it was quite extraordinary, being so much in love. Diana was an ideal combination of the original and the suitable, and he must tell her that she was as rare as a rose without a thorn.

The vows began. Lady Blentham looked down at her lap and prayed, as Sir Walter repeated his after Roderick. Half the guests in church, some of whom were watching her, thought this marriage ridiculous. She restrained her tears, of every kind of emotion, when she heard the young bride's sharp little voice saying: 'I, Violet Angelina, take thee, Walter Augustus, for my wedded husband, to have and to hold, from this day forward . . . '

He will be kind to her, thought Lady Blentham, glancing at her eldest daughter who was seated beside her, and remembering that she had once longed to hear some man say: 'I, So-and-so, take thee, Maud Victoria.' Perhaps it would still be nice for Maud to marry.

Lady Blentham was rehearsing Diana Mary's wedding in her head when Walter and Violet were pronounced man and wife. The prayers following recalled her to the present, and she looked up suddenly, with a happy expression on her face. 'Lady Montrose' did sound very well.

Angelina twisted her handkerchief into a string, then stopped because of the guests. She would at least not have to see the cold, determined Violet when she was living all year round in Argyllshire with her kind old husband, being happy.

Diana knew that the wedding breakfast would be a gloomy affair, even before it had begun. There was iced champagne, and food too cold for the bright but chilly spring day. There were not enough chairs in the hall, and under the influence of discomfort some of the guests discussed the marriage with remarkable freedom.

'Of course Angelina Blentham would have liked to have a wedding at St George's, *very* smart, with *everyone* invited, especially those who don't invite her to their smaller parties, the Duchess you know, but I ask you, how *could* it have been possible? I believe it's perfectly true that Violet simply set her heart on Sir Walter, set her cap at him in the most obvious way, poor old thing.'

'He'd no business to ask her, in my opinion. Disgusting old goat. And I don't agree that Angelina would have liked a fashionable squash in St George's, or anywhere else. Thinks that sort of thing rather vulgar. But if she didn't, I daresay little Diana would oblige her.' At that moment, Cousin Oliver noticed Diana standing beside him in her bridesmaid's dress, and grinned sadly, as though he were drunk.

'I think we're all glad that we didn't need to invite more than a very few people who would be merely acquaintances,' Diana said to him, 'and only a few relations we dislike.'

Julian, who had been trailing her, whispered: '*Bravo*, d-darling!'

Diana did not want to be praised for rudeness. 'It's hot in here,' she said, smiling at him, 'and I do feel rather unwell.'

'H-hot? Damned cold – are you hot?'

'Yes.'

'Too many people. D-darling, if you feel unwell, shall we go s-somewhere, somewhere else?'

'There's nowhere,' said Diana, looking round the hall. Violet and Walter had not separated since they joined each other in church: now they were standing together under the most valuable portrait in the room.

'H-here's my mother,' said Julian.

It seemed to Diana that it was not only his mother, but half the Fitzclares, who were pressing forwards in their direction. None of them had had a chance to speak to her all day, and they meant to speak to her now.

Mr Fitzclare was large and pasty, with Julian's thick pale eyebrows, and he looked like an old and ugly version of his son. Mrs Fitzclare was tiny, with a mole on her nose, and a perpetual worried smile on her pink face. She was quite an intelligent woman, but she was afraid of her husband.

'Diana, my dear, you looked perfectly lovely,' she said. 'So often the bridesmaids are prettier than the bride. One can't be – '

'Not so lovely as she *will* look, Frances! Don't imply that she won't be at her best on July 31st.' As he said this and laughed, he did not look at Diana: he was not paying her a compliment.

'It's July 29th, Mr Fitzclare,' said Diana.

'Yes, that's right!' said Julian's youngest sister, a pretty girl who was still in the schoolroom.

'Speak when you're spoken to, please, Adelaide,' smiled her father.

I won't be afraid of you, thought Diana, looking at Mr Fitzclare. Perhaps I'll make you hate me: she wondered what had come over her.

Mrs Fitzclare said something, and Julian replied, but Diana did not listen to what they said. She seemed to be noticing everything about her at once, Fitzclares and others and her own heat, the surrounding cold and the smell of wedding-food, Violet and Walter, her parents and the servants and the wooden-panelled walls; and yet she was thinking very intently: 'Do I love you? Do I? *Do I* love you? Julian.' But it did not matter whether she loved him deeply, romantically, improperly, or not. He would be a first-rate husband, and she had to be married. There were sexual relations to be had if she married him. Half an hour ago, she had been passionately wishing that this were her own wedding, she had not been thinking like this.

'My dear, is anything the matter?' said Frances Fitzclare. Diana jumped. 'I have a headache – just a slight one.'

'Go and take a breath of air on the terrace!' said Mr Fitzclare. Diana resented his telling her to do just what she wanted to do; it was presumptuous. 'Julian, I think you might help Diana through this crowd.' He glanced round and saw that Lady Blentham was far too busy to notice their leaving the room unaccompanied. Mr Fitzclare was in favour of his son's engagement because, though she was unusual and not very rich, Diana was better than any of the other girls Julian had seemed to like before.

Outside, Julian took Diana's hand and kissed it, then touched the chaplet of silk roses on her bright hair. They could hear the dim roar of the party, coming through closed windows, when they were standing in the drive.

'Diana, s-sit down, you'll feel better,' he said, anxiously looking at her, and pointing to a wrought-iron seat in the middle of the spring border which ran all round the house. It was not a very private place. 'D-do you know, I've been meaning to t-tell you for a long t-time, that you're as rare, as unusual, as a r-rose without a thorn? That happens to be *t-true* of you, Diana.'

'No, I'd prefer to walk.' Diana looked towards the grey portico, and said: 'Julian, I can't marry you. I don't love you enough – I'm sorry, very sorry. But I – '

'What? D-diana?'

'I can't. I can't.' She began to cry, quite quietly.

'Diana!'

The cold wind cut at her and she clutched at her dress. 'I don't love you. I don't want to marry you. I know that now.' There was quiet for a while, and Diana's tears fell.

Julian placed a fist in one palm, and said: 'You're n-not yourself, I shan't t-take this s-seriously. G-go and lie down, darling, you'll f-feel quite d-differently s-soon. It's the s-strain of all this, V-violet's wedding, I know you d-don't like . . .' His stammer disappeared for three sentences. 'You do love me. You've said so often. I shan't believe you.' He did not put his arms round her, though he wanted to, and she wanted him to, in spite of the fact that she really thought him a kindly threat, nuisance and burden.

'You must,' said Diana, and she ran into the house, forgetting to hand back her engagement ring. Lady Blentham caught her, saw that she was looking unwell, and sent her upstairs before Diana could say that she had jilted Captain Fitzclare.

Before the start of that first London Season which she was to spend alone, Diana concluded that she was very passionate by nature; but that the kindly and absolute discipline imposed on her since she was a baby had prevented her from ever showing it. Her general mood, she knew, had always been one of calm and good-natured superiority, but it was interrupted by bouts of thin depression like that from which she was suffering now. In these periods she did not rage, and rarely wept, and her campaigns for her own way were too decently conducted ever to be effective. It was horrible that there was so little in the world to be passionate about: she could not claim to have one justified and real resentment, or one overpowering, positive desire.

Julian Fitzclare would not release her from her engagement. He thought Diana did not know her own mind, and sometimes she agreed with him. Thus she could not be too angry with him, and she knew she ought to be grateful for his patience and fidelity. His soft, brave stammer quite prevented her from thinking he was arrogant: no one who spoke in that way could be other than well-intentioned. She was telling the truth when she said that she was not in love with anyone else, for there was no other man in London whom she could like half as much. This made Julian very happy.

Diana did not raise the subject of not wanting to marry him every time they met, and several times she agreed that they would be happy together. She began to hate herself, and Lady Blentham, who had become oddly unobservant since Violet's marriage, called in Dr Sacheverell and advised him to prescribe a tonic for her.

Dr Sacheverell, who had attended the Blenthams in London

for years, prescribed nothing. He told Diana that she reminded him of his wife who, when she was a girl, had been quite a *malade imaginaire*. She had been bored and unsuccessfully in love, and had only needed the right man to look after her.

'I've told Captain Fitzclare he is not the right man,' muttered Diana, suddenly, looking at her hair stretched out on the pillow.

The doctor snapped his bag shut. 'You have? And you're still engaged to be married?'

'He won't let me go,' said Diana, and thought this too romantic an expression.

'Well. That's hardly the way to keep you! Goodbye, Miss Diana. I think,' he added, 'that I won't tell Lady Blentham there's nothing the matter with you. I shall advise a glass of port after dinner every evening.'

Diana stared after him as he closed the door.

Julian came to call at Queen Anne's Gate at half-past five that afternoon, as he often did. On these occasions, Lady Blentham would go upstairs for a little while and leave them in the drawing-room. Diana was not supposed to be alone in a room with Julian at any other time.

'What did the d-doctor s-say this morning, D-diana?' said Julian.

'Nothing very much,' said Diana. She hesitated. 'No. In fact, he told me a good deal – about myself – by implication. You know I've been – worried about our marriage, Julian, well, now I know I can't marry you. And I want you to believe me this time.'

She was not looking at him, and her tone was disinterested and firm. Julian, horrified by the thought that Dr Sacheverell might have fully explained the physical side of marriage to her, put down his tea-cup with a shaking hand. Then he pulled himself together.

'Darling,' he said, 'I w-want you to know one thing. When we're m-married I shall b-be *gentle* with you, k-kind to you, in every way. Every s-single way. I'll n-never hurt you, and you m-mustn't be afraid!'

'Oh, don't talk like that!' She got up from her chair. 'I'm not afraid! I'm angry. Extremely angry!' That sounded false, she thought, but she did not start crying.

'W-with me?' He was not upset or cross, only surprised. 'Darling what have I d-done?'

'Why didn't you, don't you, *believe me* when I say I don't want to marry you? How dare you not believe me and say I don't know my own mind. It's insulting, Julian! Look – look –' Diana, white-faced, tugged at the ruby ring on her finger and pushed it at him. 'There, I've given it back, and I'll never take it back from you. Why didn't I do it before? I will not marry you, Julian. Do you understand now?'

Thickly he said 'Yes', and Diana trembled. His eyebrows were lowered, his mouth was down at the corners, and his colour was high.

'You look remarkably like your father at the moment!' Diana said. She thought: but I've *never* found him appealing, attractive. He's quite plain – plain and heavy. A blond stupid weight, a mere Army officer, admirable only when viewed far off in his uniform.

'If you'd only *believed me*, at Violet's wedding. I wouldn't have disliked you – I wouldn't have learnt positively to hate you – I might have *wanted* to marry you. Oh, *damn* you.'

'Diana!'

'I won't be trapped. I won't have it implied that I am a fool. I will not be patronised, in fact I don't know how I've endured it all this time.' She paused. 'How can you be so – so confident? You don't believe anyone *could* jilt you, do you, Captain Fitzclare! In spite of your forever saying how *inferior* you are to me?' Her voice was very loud, but the anger in it was unmixed with fear or misery. She looked womanly, not like a girl.

'V-very well,' said Julian, getting up. 'Very well. I d-do understand you, and believe you. And I sh-shan't ask you again.'

'Good! Good!'

Lady Blentham flung open the door and saw Diana in a tantrum.

'*Diana.*'

There was two seconds' immobile silence.

'I've broken it off,' she said. 'I won't marry him, Mamma. I told him so weeks ago, but he would not listen!'

'Do you realise that I could hear you from outside my room? You were shouting.'

'No, I didn't, and I'm afraid I don't very much care.'

Angelina's voice grew even quieter than before. She had taken in Diana's first words, about the engagement, and she was afraid of fainting. 'I don't think, Diana, that I have ever heard you shout before.'

Julian went over to the window and stood there unsteadily, cursing under his breath because he had knocked over a chair on his way.

'I shall shout, Mamma,' said Diana.

'I trust not!' said Lady Blentham.

'D-diana has absolutely p-put an end to our engagement, L-lady Blentham,' said Fitzclare, turning. 'I h-hope she c-comes to regret her d-decision!'

'I hope she does *not*.'

Angelina's attitude filled them both with shame. Although the breaking of the engagement was none of her doing and the last thing she wanted, she felt very powerful for a moment, when she saw the pair not knowing where to look. As Julian, mumbling, tried to express himself in a more proper spirit, Diana thought rather wildly: we're like Adam and Eve, being cast out of the Garden of Eden.

94

Part Two

MRS MICHAEL MOLLOY
1896–1901

CHAPTER 8

IN BATTERSEA PARK

Diana turned twenty-two in January, 1896. She ceased to be a very young girl, and became more independent; though, since her jilting of Fitzclare, people had tended to treat her as a wayward and troublesome child who might have yet more dangerous qualities growing inside her. Some mothers of fresh debutantes went so far as to advise their daughters not to make friends with Diana Blentham.

When Lady Blentham heard of this she told Diana that, if her father had not been so conscientious about attending the House of Lords, and if she, Angelina, had not felt it her duty to go with him, there would have been no more London Seasons for any of the family. Diana would have had to make do with the local society, and occasional visits to relations, none of whom except Violet was likely to find a husband for her.

It was Angelina who implied this, but it was Lord Blentham who thought Diana a pure idiot for throwing over Julian Fitzclare. He had said so, quite calmly, when she was still in a very bad state of mind over her broken engagement. No one seemed to believe that it had been a hard thing to do. Though their own lives were absolutely guided by convention, most people whom Diana knew paradoxically supposed that it was both easy and a great entertainment to behave unsuitably in Society's eyes. But as time went on, Diana did begin to find it easier than before, and quite amusing too. She learnt to say shocking things in a very deadpan, even impatient way, without sidling or smiling; she had a latchkey made with Angelina's cold permission, and she went alone to the theatre to see Ibsen's *Ghosts*.

She bought a bicyle in 1895. Though her parents disapproved in principle of women riding machines, they could not seriously object to her bicycling, because it was the Season's craze and every girl was doing it. Diana often enjoyed herself when she was twenty-one and twenty-two, but she was not happy, and believed she never would be.

One Sunday afternoon in her fifth London Season, Diana went to bicycle in Battersea Park with two other girls in their twenties, but she left them with a wave of her hand after a short while, and turned down a narrow path alone.

Diana was not a good bicyclist, but she was determined, and quite capable of keeping steady on a straight, flat road. One could have, as everyone said, a great sense of freedom on a well-managed bicycle. Diana did not feel it unless she was by herself, unafraid of falling off, and able to go fast and ring her bell unnecessarily. Now, as she rode under a line of budding plane trees, a remarkably handsome man on an old-fashioned penny-farthing raised his hat to her; and Diana dared to remove her attention from the road and bow, just as though she were in a carriage.

She did not notice the coming slope until her bicycle wobbled at the change of gradient. She found herself going faster and faster, then she veered round to the side, crashed into a pedestrian and fell.

The man was knocked to the ground and, as the machine went spinning from Diana's grip, he broke her fall with his hard stomach, and his arms.

'Well,' he said, 'you've a fine pair of legs to show, I will say, if you must be knocking me over on a Sunday afternoon!' He did not smile as he said this, and released her.

In the struggle, Diana's skirt had been pushed up to her waist to reveal blue serge bicycling knickers.

'Thank you – I'm sorry!' Diana gasped. Then she realised what he had said and added steadily, 'I hope I didn't hurt you?', pulling down her skirt. She did not blush.

'To be sure you hurt me, Miss – ?' The man frowned, and rubbed his shoulder.

'Blentham.' Diana wondered why she had given him her name, instead of saying it was quite unimportant. He was a dark and ugly man, with a long, intense face, a broken nose, extragavant clothes, and a faint Irish accent.

'Miss who Blentham?'

'My name happens to be Diana.' She immediately felt she had been pompous.

'Well, you have hurt me, Miss Diana Blentham. But have I hurt you, is more to the point? You've not damaged yourself, apart from showing your legs?'

'Don't mention my legs!' she said, quite angrily, and stopped.

'*My* name is Michael Molloy, and I happen to be a painter. Do you know, you're one of the most handsome women I've ever seen? You'd make a fine model. And you seem to have plenty of spirit. On the whole, I think I'd like to marry someone very like you.'

'Oh, don't talk rubbish, just in an attempt to embarrass me further!' cried Diana, staring.

'Well, I shan't say it again. There, you can't be offended, can you, Miss Blentham? Here's your hat, my dear, put it on, there's an old lady looking at us as though she'd heard the Last Trump sounding. You must never be hatless out of doors, didn't you know?' he told her.

'Or unchaperoned!' said Diana, taking her hat. She realised that she was still sitting on the grass, practically leaning against Michael Molloy. He had not troubled to get up and was lying flat on the ground.

'As you say, ma'am. Now, do you have a chaperone near? Or elsewhere?'

Diana straightened her shoulders. 'I came with some other girls.'

'And you've left them?' He had narrow but very bright dark grey eyes, set under black eyebrows which grew together in the middle and were even thicker than Julian Fitzclare's. They were commanding eyes, Diana thought, and though of course his words were amusing, his voice was grim and his eyes looked sad. They were also full of sex, she was sure of that, quite quite unlike Julian Fitzclare's. She had had other suitors, too. Diana looked away from him, and said: 'Yes.'

Michael Molloy raised his torso from the grass. 'Perhaps I'd better not ask you to have tea with me, all the same. You'd best pick up that machine of yours, and be rejoining them. By the by, where do you live?'

'Queen Anne's Gate – and in Kent!'

He stood up, and did not ask for the number of the house in London.

'Goodbye, Miss Blentham,' he said, nodded, and turned.

Her lips moved quietly as she watched him lope swiftly away: she had been perfectly sure he was going to flirt with her. Diana picked up her bicycle and, with quivering legs, pushed it back up the little slope which now seemed a full-sized hill.

One week later, a large parcel came to Queen Anne's Gate by the afternoon post. It was addressed in a pointed, sloping hand to '*Hon. Diana Blentham.*' The Blenthams were alone together in the morning-room when it arrived.

'Not from Cerisette's, surely, Diana?' said Angelina.

'No, it can't be.'

'But it can only be clothes,' said Maud; 'a box of that size.'

'From one of your admirers, Didie?' said Lord Blentham. 'Well, open it!'

Diana, sighing at them, was already doing so. She took the parcel over to the table when she had removed the wrapping paper, and lifted off the lid. Inside, covered with tissue-paper, was a tweed coat very like a man's Norfolk jacket. She did not show it to the family, but took out the envelope which lay beneath, and opened it. The letter said:

> *My dear Miss Blentham,*
> *I discovered that you and I have a mutual friend as they say in Arthur Cornwallis.*
> *The enclosed will better show off your limbs than a skirt and knickers, should you choose to go out bicycling again, after our encounter in Battersea. I hope you will wear it, but in any case, I remain,*
> *Yours very sincerely, Michael Molloy.*

Diana put it in her pocket and, trying desperately not to smile, laid the jacket over the back of an armchair. Next she pulled out an Eton collar and a belt.

'But I thought it was not from Cerisette's, Diana?'

'No, Mamma, someone else sent it. Look! Shan't I look ravishing in it?' She held up the knickerbockers which completed the suit, and started to laugh, clutching them. 'Oh, dear. Oh, Lord.'

'Bloomers!' said Lord Blentham.

His wife blushed and said: 'Rational Dress. Diana, no.'

'You won't wear it?' said Maud.

'Of course I shall wear it, it's a present,' laughed Diana.

'Oh, no, you won't, my girl,' said her father.

Diana turned. 'Maud, you should have a set made for yourself, then we can go out together.'

Angelina got up. 'If this – monstrosity is a present, it is a present from whom, Diana?'

'Oh, a very nice person,' she said, calming down.

'Let me see that letter you were reading.'

'No, Mamma.'

'No daughter of mine is going to wear bloomers in public!' said Charles, and then was a little ashamed of having been pompous. Diana saw this.

'They're not bloomers, Papa. As Mamma said, they're called Rational Dress nowadays. And it *is* rational. So sensible, don't you think? Practical,' she said.

'I ask you not to wear it,' said Angelina, raising her face. Maud followed the others' exchange with her eyes, but did not speak.

'You're a disgrace, Didie,' said Charles.

'We shall see, Mamma,' said Diana, after a pause. 'I'll take it upstairs for the present.' Gentle, happy tears began to fall from her eyes, and she gathered up the jacket and breeches and crushed them to her as she left the room.

'Better burn them, Angelina,' said Charles when Diana closed the door. He opened the newspaper to show that he took no further responsibility.

'Yes,' said Lady Blentham. 'Yes.'

'Why should you?' said Maud. 'What right have you to do so?'

Her parents stared at her: it was so long since she had been even theoretically rebellious, and she had not been rude since she was a child. 'You have no right to burn Diana's clothes,' she said. 'No right at all!'

'I think you are not yourself,' said Angelina.

'Maudie, help yourself to more tea!' said her father.

'No, thank you. Do you know, I think I *might* learn to bicycle!'

'Charles,' said Angelina, deciding not to encourage Maud by listening to her, 'do you realise that those clothes may – just possibly – have been sent Diana by a man?'

Lord Blentham jumped, and let out a crack of laughter. 'What? You don't say so! I say, what a – how monstrous! I must say, that is absolutely disgraceful. It can't be true,' he scowled foolishly.

Upstairs, Diana laid her Rational Dress on the bed and continued to cry over it, because she was in love. She had known for days that, in three minutes in Battersea Park, Michael Molloy had succeeded in making her feel alive, and she must love him for it. Ludicrous as it was, she had become extraordinarily aware of everything about her, and had been given telescopic eyes for seeing trees and flowers in the outside world, foolishness and intrigue and comedy in her own. She had tried to put him out of her mind, because it had been a hateful encounter for all its delicious unconventionality; and yet because she had met him it seemed wonderful merely to be in England doing the London Season.

Now it turned out that he knew the precious Cornwallises, who had provided Julian Fitzclare years ago. Diana laughed and hugged herself and called herself a fool.

She put on her suit and examined herself in the mirror, planning and wondering at how Michael Molloy had guessed her size. At last, still wearing it, she sat down at her little writing table and began to scribble a letter to Violet. It was not written in her ususal discreet, elegant, faintly amusing style: she should hardly be expected to write like that.

Dearest Vio, In your last letter, you said that you and Walter might perhaps be hiring someone or other's house in Green St for a few weeks in June/July, and that you were trying to dissuade him because you do hate London so. But you must come, and help me, because I need you to provide a meeting-place for me! I'm in love, and Mamma and Papa are not, I think, going to approve, so do please agree to play gooseberry (blind and deaf gooseberry) now that you are a married lady as Nurse would say.

Only consider, dearest. When I was out, bicycling in Battersea, I knocked over a very rude and ugly but quite remarkably fascinating man, a painter! called Michael Molloy who in fact knows the Cornwallises. Well, I thought very little of it until today, when he sent me a parcel containing – do guess – the most charming suit of Rational Dress. Imagines-tu, ma chérie. I opened it in front of Mamma and Papa! And I'm wearing it at this moment, and it's extremely becoming – he did say I have awfully good legs.

Vio, you must see I need you. One look at him is enough to tell one that, even though Mr Molloy may be one of Arthur's junior lions, whom he doesn't invite to his best parties, I shan't be able to meet him in the ordinary way elsewhere, unless you're game. And you must know how it is here, even though I do now have a latchkey, my comings and goings are continually noticed.

If I do meet Mr Molloy chez Arthur and Mabel, I shall tell him about you, and I expect – I hope so much – that he will leave his card with you. No, nothing so ordinary, of course! He will probably ignore your butler's saying you're not at home, walk in, discover you in bed with a headache, explain the situation, compliment you on the state of your décolletage, and ask you whether you can please arrange a large party for your sister's benefit and invite him as guest of honour. Chérie, do you see how intriguing?

When this letter had been finished, addressed and posted, Diana was miserable for hours, because she had imagined and said that Michael Molloy was serious in his intentions towards her. It occurred to her that he might want simply to seduce and not to marry her, but it was not this thought which made her ashamed, only her presumption in writing confidential nonsense to Violet about his being a magnificent man. She had worked a spell against his ever wanting to see her again. This, thought Diana, is love.

Arthur Cornwallis was amused by Michael Molloy's version of the bicycle accident, and because he supposed that Diana was too strongminded a girl to be seriously embarrassed at seeing Molloy again, he agreed to invite both her and Maud to a soirée one evening when Molloy intended to come. Michael Molloy knew very well that Cornwallis would be as shocked as Lady Blentham at the idea of his marrying Diana, and he said only that he meant to persuade her to model for him, clothed.

At their second meeting, Diana was the first to see Molloy across the Cornwallises' familiar drawing-room, but he turned round within a moment of her sighting him, and pushed through the crowd towards her. She waited, and did not let her eyes leave him.

'Well, a fine evening, is it not, Miss Blentham? And dear Mabel does give such very good parties!'

'As you say, Mr Molloy. Let me introduce you to my sister. Maud, this is Mr Molloy, whom I've met – '

'At some ball or other, was it not?' said Michael, without a trace of his Irish accent. His attitude this evening startled Diana, but his appearance did not. He wore a very old dinner-jacket, braided dark green trousers, and a soft collar. 'How do you do, Miss Blentham?'

'How do you do?'

Two minutes later, Michael had presented Maud to another man who looked as patently Bohemian as he did himself, and taken Diana into a corner. 'Diana,' he said, 'I want you to marry me. I came here tonight because I knew you'd be here and I wanted to ask you.'

There was a space of two seconds, then Diana said in a low steady voice: 'Ask me again in six months' time.'

'Six months! I can't be waiting that long.'

'I can't be waiting less.'

'Don't you know your own mind?'

'No.'

'You do.'

'Please don't bully me, Mr Molloy.'

'Michael.'

'Michael.'

He looked at her and watched her bosom heave. A lock of his thin brown hair was stuck to his forehead with sweat.

'You said,' she told him, 'that you wouldn't – talk like this again. Do you remember?'

'I do. I didn't mean it. I merely thought I was being too precipitate. The first meeting is not the time to be making a regular proposal to a girl.'

Diana laughed.

'But I knew my own mind, even then,' he said. 'And I'll make you know yours.'

'Tell me about yourself, Michael,' she said.

He crossed his arms over his chest. 'I'm a painter as I told you, and I'm thirty-seven years old. I'm an Irishman, my father's a builder with a firm of his own in Dublin, and I haven't a penny in the world beyond what I earn.'

'Dear me,' said Diana.

'I'm not eligible, am I?'

'No, indeed.'

'Well, Miss Prim!'

'You're ridiculous. Don't look so angry.'

'I'm offering you love. Don't think I don't feel my ineligibility – even though I may try to make a joke of it! I've no sense of humour.'

'It wouldn't work, Michael – I mean, if we were in fact to marry!' said Diana, looking into the crowd with red cheeks and ears.

'And why would it not?'

'We should quarrel.'

'No, we shouldn't, if you loved me. I'm not quarrelsome, and I should protect you from all that makes life hell, Diana – even though I've no money.'

'Do let's change the subject for a while, Mabel's staring at us!'

'Very well,' he said, 'we'll discuss the Royal Academy private view.'

They did discuss it, although he had not gone there, and then Michael began in earnest to talk about painting, just as though she were not the woman he loved.

He was sharing his passion with her, and she was learning, and she loved him. It occurred to Diana that no other man had ever talked to her seriously, and she believed that Michael would like it if she talked at length on serious subjects, too. She felt tipsy: not with juvenile adoration or the longing to be married, but with powerful excitement; and she knew she wanted to be in bed with him. He was so very determined. She remembered that Julian Fitzclare, for all his love of her, had not proposed instantly because he did not know his own mind. She had had to take charge, and use silent pressure to make him stop worshipping and ask her to marry him. And then, drowned in responsibility, she had realised her mistake and taken all the blame. If Michael Molloy ran off with her, nearly everyone would blame him, not her, and he would think them right to do so. She, Diana, would be able to relax in his arms on crumpled sheets, to ignore other people's prejudices and do exactly as she pleased.

'When shall I see you again? Can I call on you?'

'No.'

'Parents, is it?'

'Yes.'

'Is there nowhere – '

'My married sister's coming to London next week. I'll tell her to ask you to something.'

'Is she eccentric, your sister?'

Diana started at this idea of Violet, but said: 'Yes, I suppose so, in a sense. She fell in love with a man old enough to be her grandfather.'

'Very well done of her, to be sure. Is he rich?'

'Tolerably so.'

'And what's her name, so that I'll know her invitation when I see it?'

'Violet – Lady Montrose.'

'You don't mean to say she's already widowed!'

'No, of course not. I didn't – mean to put a comma between Violet and Lady.'

'See how well I know what's what in English Society,' he said, opening his eyes wide.

'I'm impressed,' said Diana.

'My father was a Land League man in his youth – and so was I – but a great, great snob, Diana. Knew all these things by heart, so he did, and could have told me that your Papa's peerage is not old by any means. A fourth baron, is he not?'

'Far better than a Dublin builder, at all events!'

'Oh, Diana, Diana. How was your Rational Dress?'

Then she realised that she had not even thanked him, and it seemed positively cruel of her not to have done so, when he had no money.

Michael and Diana courted each other in peace in Violet's Green Street house, once Sir Walter had said that Michael seemed a good, intelligent man, and the whole affair was no concern of his. At other times over the following few weeks, Diana behaved with more propriety than usual. Lady Blentham noticed how amicable she was, but said nothing, only worried. She had made a private vow to speak to Diana only if she tried to wear the Rational Dress, but Diana did not wear it.

When she told her husband that she was puzzled by Diana's behaviour, Charles told her that, odd as it might seem, very likely Hugh Parnell was about to make her happy. 'Rather too young for marriage, of course, I gather he's only just down from Oxford, but I don't think that's a very serious objection. James Parnell was at my tutor's, must be young Parnell's uncle, no, cousin perhaps. Really, my dear, he's a nice young chap, and she could do far worse than marry into that family.

The Parnells of Combe Chalcot, you know, are nearly as good as the Venables.'

'Please don't try to tease me, Charles. Diana would never fall in love with a young man so – commonplace as Hugh Parnell, and I don't believe for a moment he is serious in his intentions, as they used to say when I was a girl!'

Diana overheard this conversation when she passed the drawing-room door. She opened it, and said: 'Maud and I are going, Mamma – Buxton says the carriage is ready.'

'Very demure you look, Didie,' said Charles. She was wearing white, with lilies of the valley in her hair, and huge puffed elbow-sleeves which were suitable for an afternoon dress, and original in a ballgown. Her cheeks and lips were slightly rouged, but her mother did not notice.

'Then I hope you enjoy yourselves, my dear,' said Angelina. 'Give my love to Violet, of course. I wonder if it will be a good party? Giving one's first London dance is always rather difficult, and her drawing-room really isn't quite large enough.'

Lady Blentham, who was going to dine alone with her husband and then go to bed, suddenly felt both old and wretched when she parted the drawing-room curtains and watched her daughters climb into the waiting brougham. Even Maud looked young at this distance. Dear God – whatever Diana does, she thought, I shall be too tired to take an interest. My favourite child – but *nothing* seems to rouse me to feeling. She told herself not to exaggerate, and turned resentful eyes on Charles, who was to attend a late-night session at the House while her own visit to the opera with her brother and sister-in-law had had to be cancelled because Mrs Venables was ill.

At one o'clock, Violet sat down for the first time since her party began. From her seat behind a bowl of roses, she watched her guests trying to dance in the inadequate space, and imagined Diana's future life in which nothing like this would ever be seen. She envied her extremely.

Violet was pregnant, footsore and looking unusually plain, and she had given this party only because she knew Lady

Blentham would have been triumphant in displeasure, had her daughter done no more than invite close friends to dine with her, and wholly neglected her supposed society duty. Walter and Violet both said that they despised social fetishes, and loved unconventionality, and they were pleased that Diana seemed to share their views. Violet supposed that when her sister married Molloy, she would lead a life much the same as her own, though London-based and of course, rather more eccentric.

She did not think Michael's lack of money a real objection, because she and her husband regarded money only as the means to buy worldly things which were quite unnecessary, and in any case, however angry the Blenthams were, they would not cast Diana out completely. Her parents would be very, very angry, that was true. Violet resolved to stand by Diana whatever happened, and she guessed that Edward and Kitty, Maud and even Roderick would support her too, if Angelina were over-ferocious. She smiled, and at that moment, Edward came up and asked her to dance.

'You've invited quite a few oddities, haven't you, Violet?' he said as the little band struck up the tune for a valse.

'Oh, I suppose you mean the Sacheverells. You are such a snob, Teddy. Why shouldn't one invite a doctor to a dance? Anyway, Mrs Sacheverell was presented the same year as poor old Maud.'

'Why not, indeed?'

'Or an *actress*, or an *artist*, or a person in *trade*!' said Violet, stamping her feet to the music.

'You're the worst dancer in London,' said Edward.

'You've aged terribly since I saw you last. Your face is so red, Teddy, I suppose it's because it's so very hot in here – I must tell Angus to open another window, oh, how I do hate being a hostess – tell me, are you happy with Kitty?'

'Never regretted it for a moment,' said Edward, refusing to look surprised.

Kitty, who never regretted having left the stage to marry Edward, saw him dancing with his sister and decided to go upstairs for a short rest. Edward's only fault, she thought, was

109

a tendency to admire other women; but she knew he did not have a full-fledged mistress, and so she refused to criticise him. He would be safe with Violet for the moment.

Edward was her dearest possession, but though he was attentive, and handsome, and charming, he had never made her well-imagined bodily passion for him magnificently real. As she edged and smiled her way through the noisy press of idlers on Violet's staircase, Kitty reflected that, in fact, the mysterious satisfaction about which even the immoral did not talk directly had never been so very important to her. What with Teddy and the kids, she thought, I'm happy, and loving's pleasant enough, I'm sure. A nice little thing.

On the second-floor half-landing, Kitty raised her head; and up above her at the very top of the stairs, she saw the grey-lit figures of Diana and Michael Molloy. As she focused her eyes, Kitty took in her breath, for she recognised true, troublesome passion now that she saw it. 'Well!' she muttered.

Diana was moaning, and her hair was in a terrible state. Michael's hands were on her waist, pulling her lower half towards him, and his face was pushing her head back as he kissed her over and over again. When he began to raise Diana's skirt from the back, Kitty swung round, opened the bathroom door, and deliberately slammed it behind her as loudly as she could.

CHAPTER 9

PUSHED TO THE LIMIT

Kitty soon decided that violent lust and emotional intensity were more immoral in a girl born with Diana's advantages than they would be in anyone else. Diana had enough good things in life as it was; the folly and ingratitude of loving a man like Molloy made her sister-in-law truly angry.

Kitty knew that Lady Blentham would be furious too: and she told Edward that she meant to write to her, because Diana must not be allowed to wreck her life. Edward was shocked by his wife's description of what she had seen, but he refused to do anything, and said that would be the wiser course for her to take as well.

Perhaps he was right, Kitty thought, when the letter to Angelina had been taken away. Perhaps her mother-in-law would not be in the least impressed by her writing, would even refuse to believe what she said. Lady Blentham had not once received her in the six years of her marriage, and Kitty hated her, though she understood. She wished that she were Angelina, able to be cruel sometimes and save Diana from ruin. Diana was a good, innocent girl, and worth saving.

Dear Lady Blentham,
You will, I am sure, be very surprised to receive a letter from me.

Angelina looked at the signature, and moved her lips silently, then returned avidly to the beginning.

I do not doubt you will be displeased, even insulted, but I feel obliged to write to you, because there is something you ought to know, concerning Diana. I do not imagine you can be aware of what I have to tell you, because you would have done something long ago, if you knew.

Angelina looked across the breakfast table at Diana, who was dressed in her riding habit and had opened *The Times*. Probably she was reading the Divorce Court proceedings. 'How dare – *can* you read the newspaper in front of me,' said Lady Blentham in a low steady voice, and pulled it away from her daughter. 'You know what my feelings are.'

'Mamma!'

'Be quiet, if you please.' Lady Blentham was truly thankful that they were alone together. Charles was out, and Maud was in bed.

Diana watched the London dust floating in the sunlight before her mother's pallid face, and with her eyes narrowed and blinking rapidly she thought of how she would marry Michael and live in Camden Town.

I am afraid Diana has formed a very unsuitable connection, – Angelina supposed that Kitty had searched a long time for that phrase – *with an Irish painter, called Michael Molloy. I have met him at Arthur Cornwallis's, and I suppose Diana met him there too, though exactly when I do not know. Whether he intends marriage or not, I also do not know. However, I do think that Violet* – not even 'Lady Montrose' thought Angelina! – *is in favour of the idea of them marrying. I hate to say anything so vulgar, but I saw Diana kissing Mr Molloy, at Violet's little dance on Thursday.*

'Oh – '

'Yes, Mamma?'

Angelina read on without replying.

I inquired from Arthur Cornwallis more about Mr Molloy, though I hope I do not need to tell you that I did not drop even a hint, about him and Diana. It seems that he is not only quite penniless, and the son of someone in trade, as you would say, but that he was actually concerned in the activities of the Land League, or some other violent, Irish Fenian organisation. Whether the police have their eye on him now, Arthur does not know, but I hope I am not exaggerating, when I tell you there is a danger of this.

He is considerably older than Diana, of course. I hope that you will consider I have done right, in writing to you about this subject – I know that I have. I do not doubt, in any case, that you will quite agree with me, that it is of very great importance that Diana should not be allowed to throw herself away, and make a scandal. She would, I am sure, be very unhappy with Mr Molloy, for many reasons. Among others, she does not know what it is to live without elegance and comfort, on very little money.

You will be pleased to hear, I know, that Edward, Frankie, Charlie and Little Angel are all very well indeed.

Little Angel, an ugly baby, had been christened Angela after Lady Blentham, who considered the name a very inferior form of her own.

> *Trusting that you will receive this letter in the spirit in which it was intended,*
> *Yours sincerely, Kitty Blentham.*

When Angelina laid down the letter, Diana said: 'Mamma, I'm no longer so young that I cannot be allowed to read the newspaper for fear of knowing about things I should not.'

Angelina scarcely heard her. Her chief thought, for several moments, was of the woman's insolence in doing right. Then, silently, she made herself concentrate on the sense of the ill-expressed letter.

'Is that letter to do with me?'

'Yes,' said Lady Blentham at last.

Diana bent stiffly over her toast, and looked at it. 'I should think it's an impertinence.'

Angelina got up. 'It is intolerably impertinent. From your sister-in-law.'

'*Kitty*?'

'Is it true, Diana, what it says?'

'What does it say? I haven't seen it.' She guessed, although she did not know, and had never confided in Kitty.

'You may read it,' said Angelina in a voice of contempt. Diana took it. No doubt, she thought when she finished reading, Kitty considered her letter a model of efficient dignity.

'Well?' said Lady Blentham.

Diana put down the letter and her napkin and went to the door. 'I can't talk about it now, Mamma. I'm going to see Kitty and ask her what she means.'

Angelina ran to her. 'Then what she says is a falsehood? It's slanderous, Diana?'

'No, it's not altogether a falsehood.'

'Diana!'

'No, Mamma!' She left, and Angelina heard the front door slam.

Diana walked to the nearest cab rank, and told the driver to take her to Cadogan Square. Though in the past year she had had so much more freedom than before, she had been alone in a hansom cab only four times in her life. 'I thought you were a friend,' she said aloud to an imaginary Kitty, then realised she must not say anything so commonplace. She was as puzzled as she was bitter, and she was still trembling a little from her rejection of Angelina.

The hansom drew up before the young Blenthams' house. Diana paid the cabman, rapped on the door, and was admitted by the butler, whose shocked and curious glance made her remember that she was still in riding-dress, and that it was far too early to be paying calls. She intended that, very soon, such things would no longer concern her.

'Is Mrs Blentham at home?'

'Yes, miss, that is – '

'It's important. Please ask her to see me – no, I'll go up! Where is she?' Kitty and Diana had had several friendly talks at odd moments in public, but no one could think them intimate. Diana had rarely been to their house even since her coming of age, and the butler had taken a moment to recognise her. 'Come, tell me!' she said to him.

'I believe in the boudoir, miss,' said the man coldly. 'But I fancy . . . '

Diana went upstairs and found the room. 'Hello, Kitty!' she said. Kitty, who was reading a novel on the sofa in her dressing-gown, looked up.

'Well! You're up early – you don't want me to come riding with you, do you, because I'm afraid I can't. Do sit down, Diana!'

'Thank you. I've come about the letter you wrote to my mother,' said Diana, sitting down and thinking that the pink-and-gold boudoir full of huge photographs and too-expensive flowers was just the thing for an actress. She assumed that Edward and Kitty were heavily in debt: an inexcusable, foolish thing to be. 'She had it this morning.'

'Oh, you're cross, are you?'

'Yes.'

'Well, I meant it for the best, Diana.'

'Nonsense.'

'Why *do* you think I wrote, then?' said Kitty, slowly closing her novel.

'Some kind of spite – or jealousy. I can't think what I've done to make you feel like that, to do what you have.'

'Spite and *jealousy*?' said Kitty.

'Am I putting it too strongly?' said Diana, consciously raising her eyebrows.

Kitty imitated her. 'Rather, Diana. Of course I didn't do it for *spite*, I did it for the very reasons I said. Because Lady Blentham will be able to stop you ruining your life, at least I'm pretty sure she will, which is what you'll be doing, if you marry him – never mind if he seduces you. I'm sorry to speak so crudely, I'm sure, but you're old enough to know what I mean!'

'He wants to marry me. There's no question of seduction.'

'So much the worse!' said Kitty. 'In a sense.'

'My mother won't be able to prevent my marriage, neither will my father. I'm of age, though everyone seems to forget it.'

'They'll be able to – well, put pressure on you, and I just hope you'll listen,' said Kitty.

'My mind is made up,' said Diana.

'So you'll marry him, will you? And what will you live on, an allowance from Papa?'

'Michael earns something and yes, I expect that once my parents have – recovered, they'll give us something too,' said Diana. She never took her eyes off Kitty, and her toes wriggled angrily inside her boots.

'And supposing that's so, how much do you suppose you'll have?'

'Four or five hundred a year? Many people live on less, though I don't see quite why you . . .'

'They do indeed, Diana. They live on much less, and do you know what it's like! Now do stop looking as though you'd swallowed the poker, I thought I was a friend of yours.'

'Diana, you don't know what you're doing, you're just a girl in love, and you think you don't care if you upset your family. D'you realise that if Michael Molloy marries you, you won't be in Society?'

'Realise it?' said Diana. 'Do you think I want to be "in Society" as you call it, any longer? When I could be . . .' She did not say 'just with him', but she smiled. Until she met Michael, Diana had despised people who believed in what her father called love in a cottage on nothing a year. She felt much older now than she had felt a month ago, and not only older, but braver, wittier, stronger, more beautiful and wise.

'I suppose he makes poverty look positively heavenly!' snapped Kitty. 'Well, I wash my hands of you.'

'I'm so glad. Do you apologise for writing to my mother?'

'No, I do not,' said Kitty, sitting upright, with her hands crushed beneath her thighs. 'Oh, I'm sorry if my doing that has only made you more headstrong about it all, and it looks as if it has! But I did the best I could and I can't be sorry.'

'If you wanted to save me from ruining my life,' said Diana, 'why didn't you write to *me*, and give me your advice? Why did you write to my mother, Kitty? Why couldn't you say all that – all this to me?'

Looking at Diana, Kitty herself wondered why for a moment.

'Was it an attempt to please her, make her pleased with you?'

'I daresay, but what nonsense you do talk.'

'It didn't please her.'

'I should imagine not.'

'Well,' said Diana, 'I don't want to have an irreparable quarrel with you. I'm going – let's forget it. Will you cut me, Kitty, when I'm married?' She got up and arranged her skirts.

'I just might.'

'Oh.'

'Diana, do you remember coming to call on me when you were a flapper, and we were just married? You managed to come alone in a hansom, and, oh, you were so excited and pleased with yourself. No harm in that at that age. But you haven't changed a bit.'

'You're so jealous, Kitty,' said Diana. 'Do cut me in future, it should be quite amusing in the circumstances.'

'Diana Blentham, you're a bloody idiot!'

Diana smiled, because the Cockney swear-word shocked her, and of course it ought not to, things being as they were. She left the house feeling quite calm, and on the whole decidedly the winner: though at the back of her mind there was a new picture of Kitty as a powerful, well-intentioned yet unpleasant woman. Diana did not think she would see her again. Once Kitty had represented a wild and intoxicating, quite improper world; but it was hard to remember that now.

Within a day, Diana's family seemed to her to become caricatures of their old selves, dancing foolishly around her in bewilderment and rage. She remained quiet and determined, observing their vagaries; and the thought of Michael entirely prevented her being made unhappy by them. They were almost strangers, and Diana felt free, because she no longer belonged to them.

Five days after Violet's dance, Diana met Michael down by
the trees north of the Serpentine, a part of Hyde Park visited
by few of her friends. She could have met him in her sister's
house, as she had already done twice that week: but she
wanted nothing to do even with Violet, who had been so
sensible and kind.

'Well, darling? Why's the need to be so clandestine?' said
Michael, folding up his Irish newspaper as soon as she came
up looking anxiously for him. 'Lady Montrose hasn't turned
nasty?'

Diana jumped. 'Oh, dear one! No, she hasn't, but I don't
want to use her.' She blinked at him and took in her breath.
'Michael, tell me, are you perfectly *sure* – '

'Do you want us to be married soon? Is that it? Why,
Diana? Don't you remember saying six months?' he told her,
smiling suspiciously, and putting one thin, heavy arm round
her waist.

'My love.' She squeezed his hand because he understood
everything at once, more quickly than she did herself. 'It's so
difficult, you'll be horribly insulted and I can't blame you.'

'Ah?' Michael reached up and picked a sticky leaf from one
of the lime trees. There were a few late boats on the
Serpentine, and its water was soft steel blue: dark green in the
shade.

'Papa had the – impertinence, when he'd read Kitty's
wretched letter, which I told you about as you know, to get
one of his friends at the Home Office to make enquiries about
you at Scotland Yard. Words dropped in the right ear at
Brooks's, all so very discreet, don't you know?' She longed
for him to kiss her.

'Did he now?'

'Well, of course, there's been such a dust kicked up at home
that Kitty's letter was *nothing* to it. Of course I wasn't *shown*
anything yesterday, because I know there could be nothing to
show, no *papers* but oh, you can imagine. Papa insists you're
the very worst kind of Fenian, and of course, he says he'll cut
me off without a penny if I marry you. Truly. So old-
fashioned – so humourless – he was shouting so that people

must have heard it across the street. I never guessed he could behave like that.' She sucked in her lips as she thought of it.

'So what precisely did he say, about my being a wicked *Fenian*, Diana? Which to be sure, I am.'

'My dear,' said Diana, turning her umbrella in her hands and looking at him with eyes as determined as his own, 'he actually said the police suspect you of having been – mixed up in a minor way with that group of Fenians – is that quite the word – who murdered Lord Frederick Cavendish in Phoenix Park. Years ago. Apparently, there wasn't enough *evidence*.'

'Ah,' said Michael. Suddenly he gripped her elbow. 'And do you believe them, Diana? Would you believe me a murderer?'

'Don't be so melodramatic!' said Diana, thinking irrelevantly of all he had said to her so fiercely on the subject of free Ireland and the treachery of Parnell.

'You don't? Say you don't.'

'Michael, I do not believe that, whatever you had to do with the Land League when you were young, you had anything to do with that kind of violence.'

'I did not.'

Her head jerked. 'Stop looking at me so coldly. *Damn* you.'

'Diana! Ah, darling, don't cry then – don't cry – hey. But I have to be sure of you, don't I?'

They cuddled, softly and warmly, and a nurse with a perambulator clucked at them. Michael took his head from out of her hair.

'Well, shall I be making the arrangements for us to be married as soon as possible, at the registry office?'

'Yes, Michael.' How marvellous to submit.

He took hold of her chin, and studied her face, which was on the same level as his own. He had often wanted to be taller and to look down on more people. 'Diana, this isn't rebellion against your family? You want *me*, myself, all I can truly give you – not just to escape from home and shock the lot of them? It's for love you're doing this?'

'Yes, I want you . . . dear one, you do understand? It's got *nothing* to do with rebellion, as you say. That would imply that I almost enjoyed their – hatred of you, wouldn't it? And I hope to God they'll come round one day.' To look at him make Diana feel charitably towards all the world.

'Well, so they may, but I doubt it.' He did not sound very displeased about this. 'We'll be poor, you realise that? I'm not deceiving you.'

'Yes, of course I realise.'

'You won't have more than one maid, for everything. No *servants*, Diana. No pretty dresses.'

'I can do very well without.'

'Yes, you'll look your best without. And when you're my wife, you won't be able to see your friends, only mine,' Michael said, putting another arm round her.

'*Some* of my friends may not cut me.' Diana smiled.

'Perhaps they won't, then. So we'll be married in a day or two.'

'Yes.' He was reality, she thought, the only reality.

'I'd have you down on the grass now, if it weren't so damned public,' Michael said. He looked with a gleam in his eye at her dark grey dress, which had obviously been chosen because it was sober, suitable for Bayswater and almost middle-class. 'But of course I can't disturb your costume. My dear, your discretion is *admirable*,' he said.

'Kiss me,' said Diana.

'We've years to do that, and more,' said Michael. 'I said I wouldn't disarrange your clothes, but I love you.'

When Diana returned to Queen Anne's Gate it was twilight, and her parents guessed what she had been doing. She had meant them to guess. They hustled her into the morning-room at once, though it was time to dress for dinner at Lady de Grey's.

Diana wondered why she had never before seen how stupid they were, and how idiotic was their way of life. She remembered her nursery and schoolroom and debutante days, Julian Fitzclare and the battle of the latchkey fought a year ago, and it seemed to her that never before had she questioned anything, or seen any truth at all. Now that she was perfectly certain in her own mind, nothing they said could affect her even for a moment. Yesterday, she had been affected for moments together: thrown back for whole minutes into their world by the mad revelation that Michael was a murderer.

The cynics about love are wrong, she thought: 'a cynic is he who knows the price of everything and the value of nothing.'

'For the last time, Diana, *have you been to meet Molloy?*'

'No, Papa, I have not.' How glorious to lie, and how curious it was that she had never told a direct lie to either of her parents before.

'Diana, it is – very difficult to believe you are not telling an untruth,' said Angelina. 'You hardly seem to want us to believe you. It's your manner.'

'Unconvincing!' said Charles. 'I am going to repeat myself, Diana. If you do marry this man – and I'll never give you my consent, blessing, whatever arguments you use, I wouldn't even if I were satisfied that the police's suspicions are unjust – I'll give you absolutely nothing to live on.'

'No, Papa.'

He glared at her under his eyebrows, and she thought what a fine picture he made. 'What a pity we don't live a hundred years ago. I'd have no hesitation in locking you up in your bedroom – absolutely none. I'd do it now, if you were a couple of years younger. Oh, I give you credit for not being fool enough to try to elope, but I'm warning you,' he added.

Diana imagined climbing down a rope-ladder. 'Why are you so angry with me?' she said. 'You've never been angry before. You didn't shout at me even when I gave up Julian – although you disapproved so much.'

'Isn't it clear!' muttered Lady Blentham.

'You weren't proposing then to marry a man who's very possibly the worst kind of anarchist!' said Charles.

'He is not an anarchist, and he's never plotted to kill anyone.'

'Whether he is or not,' said Angelina with an effort, 'he is a – a freethinker, Diana, and though I suppose you don't object to that he . . . He would be an impossible match on every count. My dear, I know you are in love, but you *can't* marry him. You know that. It won't last.'

'Mamma . . .' said Diana, turning. Her father stared at Angelina too.

'In love!' said Charles, interrupting. 'Don't be ridiculous.'

'I am in love, Papa. Even though you may hate the expression – do you think it vulgar?'

'I tell you you're not going to marry him. You can't possibly do so if you have no money and *I-will-give-you-nothing*, do you hear me, girl?'

'Please don't speak to me like that, Papa.'

'Don't you – '

'Diana, neither of us will be able to see you, if you do this,' said Angelina, though she did not mean this quite literally. 'You must not do it. Oh God, if I only had not consented to your having a latchkey, a bicycle! If only I hadn't tried – so hard – to accept that these are modern times – none of this would have happened. I wanted you to be happy. I blame myself, entirely.' She was not going to horrify herself by treating Diana as she had treated Violet three years ago.

'Angelina, don't be so emotional. Really, my dear!'

'Mamma, very likely something worse would have happened if I'd been – more innocent, ignorant. Isn't that what you're implying? Ignorance isn't always a protection.' The full truth of this struck her for the first time.

'Oh, heaven help us.'

'I won't have any child of mine create a scandal. God, how does one cope in these cases – like a damned bad novel!'

Diana stood still, looking straight ahead of her at the undrawn curtains, still faintly smiling, because nothing could touch her save Michael's hand. She was amused because her parents had at last surprised her, by acting just a little out of character. She had not thought Lord Blentham would be deeply distressed, as Angelina was, but she had expected him to persuade and to try to understand. She had supposed Lady Blentham would threaten and be unrelenting, in her own cold, disgusted style. It was her father, who made a show of his indulgent fondness for her, who was doing that now.

'Love is not what you think it, Diana,' said Angelina.

'It's silly to talk like this,' said Diana, looking from one old person to the other, and thinking how odd and impotent both looked. They had been tyrants, but she forgave them. 'If you don't want anything to do with me – if I marry him – ' she said 'if' as a precaution against being locked in her room like a heroine, but she did not really feel vulnerable – 'then just cut me, I shan't mind – really, I don't think I shall. I know what I want, what's best, and if it happens, after a few months no one will remember – it won't matter – it'll be all right. Life is like that!'

This was the longest speech she had made to her parents on the subject of her love. Obviously, they hated her. Diana thought how frail a thing was family love, dependent always on good behaviour. It was that, of all things, which they expected her to try and preserve as the most precious thing in life. She did feel badly when she said: 'Of course you're quite right, I shan't do anything very stupid, like eloping. I do hope you'll consent.'

'Don't talk rubbish!' said Lord Blentham.

CHAPTER 10

MICHAEL

Diana stood outside the registry office and wondered already what on earth she had done. She looked about her, blinking as though it were a brilliant morning, though in fact it was a damp summer day: 15 June, 1896.

She noticed everything, above all the hand on her arm: it was as though she now had to look at the most commonplace things from a wholly different angle. In the street there was a grey horse, a dirty boy, a sweet-shop and a gutter running with a plait of fresh rain. She was glad, she thought, that they had gone to be married in Holborn. Glad that Michael had not chosen territory she knew, which she now imagined she would not try to see again.

'Frightened?' he said, leading her down the steps and on to the pavement.

'Oh, well, the die is cast!' she replied without hesitation.

'Love can be a killer,' said Michael, patting her arm as she smiled. 'Come, we're going home! I'll teach you not to regret marrying me, Diana Molloy.'

'Home,' said Diana, crying with happiness at last. 'It's *most* efficient of you – to have made a home for me, just like . . . Dear one.'

For the time being, they were to live in Michael's studio near Charing Cross. He had persuaded his landlady to let two extra rooms by telling her that his future wife was an Honourable, and that he would soon be able to pay.

'Shall we take an omnibus? Have you ever been inside one, Diana?'

'No,' said Diana. 'Let's take one!'

She felt properly transformed by the ride in the smelly, crowded omnibus, and when they alighted two streets from the house she had never seen, it seemed to her that she had always been Mrs Michael Molloy, wife of a poor artist. And yet the most extraordinary moment, at which Michael might prove that the descriptions given in *Fanny Hill* were based on fact, was still to come. She was as nervous as an unkissed virgin was expected to be.

Michael looked down at his wife's hot face, and took a strand of hair off her forehead. She had taken kindly to the delightful pain which was his gift to her, every bit as kindly as he had supposed. He had been very careful with her, pressing but gentle, as he had been ever since their first meeting – six weeks ago. He meant never to change, because he loved her so much and, against heavy odds, had succeeded in gaining her. He reflected in his present triumph that despair was ridiculous, that all his life he had been able to gain anything, so long as he desired it with all his mind and made full use of his talents for insolence and obstinacy. Michael smiled. Whatever it cost him, he would not let Diana suffer too much from the change in her circumstances, which he understood so much better than she did. She had cost him quite a lot already.

'Alanna,' he said, a word Diana knew from novels set in Ireland. 'Sleepy?'

She stirred in the curtained daylight, and a chink of sun picked out the freckles on her pink nose. 'Michael?' she whispered.

Diana looked up at him. His odd face was now mauve and blue, shadowed like a face in one of his paintings. Love strangled her and she began to cry: but these were not the quiet tears of bewildered joy which she had shed several times before. Her sobbing was tumultuous, and loud.

'Diana! Are you regretting this – are you? D'you want a divorce then, d'you want to go back to Papa?'

'No! No! Never – how *could* you think so!'

'Why are you crying like this?'

'I don't know – I just don't know. M-michael, you must never be angry, never – you're all I have now, all I could ever want, just you, just you truly, I'll die without you, I'll die if you're angry! Oh, try to understand.'

'Ah, it's the power of sex,' he said. 'I won't be angry then – and I'll look after you as well as well can be. So long as you never regret it.'

'How could I do that? Oh, you must understand!'

'I do.' Michael held her closely in the hot and crumpled bed. He had already had the sense, in view of her virginity, not to undress her completely or to take off his shirt. 'We shan't do this again for two days – not till you're stronger, and wanting it. What's more, I shan't die in the meantime.'

Diana giggled, but did not stop weeping. 'So much more than I imagined – love – my first time, doing this, and it wasn't painful, not terrible – not in the way they say, but quite differently! I ought to have felt – oh, it's more than any human being can stand, it's not safe, such *intensity*.'

'Write a poem about it,' said Michael, stroking her neck.

She calmed down for a moment. 'Perhaps I will. And will you paint me?'

'I'll paint you. Did I really not tell you I would before?'

'So odd,' Diana said quietly, 'what we *did* tell each other – and what we haven't yet.'

In August 1896, the Molloys bought a house in Mornington Terrace, Camden Town. Diana was pleased that her house overlooked the lines running north from Euston, King's Cross and St Pancras: Michael's old studio had been next to a railway station, and she found the noise of trains erotic. The house was hers, bought with some of the £500 left to her by her godfather more than a year ago. Michael said it was better to rent, but Diana had an idea that any house was a good, solid possession. She was glad that the Married Women's Property Act enabled her to use her money as she liked and that Michael, who was willing to give her anything, did not seriously object.

She stood now in Michael's airy new studio, and thought about servant problems. She had engaged a girl who called herself a cook-general, who cost twenty-five pounds a year but was a good-natured slut and would have to go. Diana believed that now she had learned to cook eggs and sausages and stew, she could manage the house tolerably with a charwoman alone. Michael, though he had once told her she would have no servants, was now encouraging her to engage two. He wanted a cook and a house-parlourmaid, and he swore they could afford it.

Diana had learnt early that he expected a girl of her class to be thoughtlessly extravagant, and her instinct for economy both impressed, amused and annoyed him. She had explained that, by the standards of their own set, the Blenthams were not rich, and that she had been used to dressing herself on fifty pounds a year. Michael teased her, saying she had a genius for exaggeration, and told her he insisted on employing two servants for her comfort.

Lady Blentham never had any difficulties with her servants, even though she was not able to pay the highest wages. She considered it vulgar to discuss servants' failings. She had told Violet, though not Diana, that they would work well and stay if given good living quarters and treated with considerate but firm authority. That, she said, was all that mattered. Diana assumed she was perfectly right, but the system did not work with her cook-general. She felt rather a fool when giving instructions about how to buy food economically, because it was an art which she had so recently learnt herself from Michael's kind, snobbish, former landlady.

Life in the old lodgings had not been serious, it had consisted only of learning and playing and love. Michael had barely worked at all. Things were to be different in Mornington Terrace, where Diana was drifting down into peaceful sediment, having been shaken up and down in a champagne bottle ever since the spring.

On the day after her marriage, Diana had written to tell her parents that she was safe, happy and married, and that she would soon send her address so that they could write to her. This she had now done, and she knew that they would have to look Mornington Terrace up on the map. She had had no letter from them in a fortnight, but one had come today, and it was from Arthur Cornwallis.

My dear Diana, he had written,

I was nearly as distressed as your dear mamma when I learnt of your marriage, and naturally, I blame myself in part. I have, I think, succeeded in persuading her that not in a hundred years would I have encouraged you to become so wretchedly entangled, as Violet seems to have done. My fatal, wicked desire for entertainment!

Enough of this. I have been speaking hitherto from my worldly standpoint, but I most sincerely pray for your happiness, my dear, and in fact, there are moments when I think the social milieu you have chosen may suit you very well – so long as you are not too distressingly poor. I know that you will never pine and complain, and make life very much worse for yourself in so doing. Love does not invariably lead to personal disaster – only to social setbacks, shall we say?

Perhaps you will think me too horribly condescending, if I say that I shall do all I can to advance Michael's career, now that he has so wickedly caught you, my dear. As you know, his earnings are very irregular, and the money he occasionally receives from devoted maternal relations cannot amount to much. Money he must have, and there is but one way for an artist to gain it – not by way of the Turf.

He must prostitute himself, alas. He must do his best to become a fashionable painter, that is, one who paints portraits of vain women in just the style they like. À la Sargent, need I say. A faint suggestion of flow, but no hint of impressionism – a glorying in rich silks – a hint of mystery, and not mere beauty, in the faces of his more intelligent subjects. Of course there can be no mystery about such subjects' faces for the most part.

Diana laid down the letter and looked at the half-finished pictures lining the walls. She had made a discovery since her move, and Michael, before she spoke, had accused her of making it and confessed that she was right.

He would never make a great, innovative painter. The work he liked to produce was in a very advanced style, in which splotches of strange colour were used to enhance the immediacy of an evening, morning or lamplit interior. Painted with his hand, these bright shadows did not produce the impression that the subjects were living persons with hidden depths.

Michael was humble about the artists who succeeded in doing what he longed to do, but he was often angry too. He said that there was only one English artist worthy of consideration: Joseph Mallord William Turner. Some French moderns approached his genius. He, Michael, was at the bottom of the heap. When depressed, he would drink whisky by the half-pint, and invite his least reputable Irish friends to insult his paintings and himself. Then Diana, thinking that it was easy enough to be Patient Grizelda, would comfort him.

Cornwallis's letter continued:

One never knows, my dear, what will take in this world of ours. Of course a great many people don't wish for portraits, not even the most sugary nonsense, they only wish to be painted and have it known they were painted by the most presentable and expensive Academician to be had. Michael's talent however is real, though not what he likes to think it in his moments of high optimism. In short, he may turn out a more than competent portraitist, admired and commissioned though never, I think, highly fashionable with the great and the good.

Very few people besides myself will like to entertain him, but my dear, one never knows. In time your marriage may prove a distinct advantage to him, and your romance, skilfully presented, may help him to gain and you to regain just as large a footing in 'Society' as you desire – no more, no less. Your birth and his talent together may produce all manner of marvels. If only it were not for his Fenian connections! But as dear Lady

Blentham says, Society is declining at such a rate that it may soon enough be considered that it is delightfully amusing to be a suspected – how shall I put it?

I think I may be able to persuade the correct authorities to hang Michael's portrait of Mrs Baring-Wilder's charming children (that is the style I mean. He knows full well he is a master of it, though he insults it – so rightly! But he was glad enough to be commissioned) in next year's Academy exhibition. Do not, I beg of you, permit Michael to inveigh against the wickedness of further corrupting his art.

Our unfortunate friend may have said of Mr Frith's great memorial, was it really all done by hand – but there is not the least likelihood of your Michael's ending either as a latter-day Frith, or as poor dear Oscar did, to be sure. I have the oddest feeling that hard work at hack portraits will paradoxically improve Michael's real work.

I have the highest regard for you and for Michael, and believe me when I say that, though I was perfectly horrified by the story of your elopement, I shall never have the impertinence to 'cut' either of you as I believe your unamiable sister-in-law was ill-bred enough to do in Regent St. She shall receive no more invitations from Mabel.

Both of us, my dear, send our love. Mabel adds, I may say, that there is no use crying over spilt milk. An expression of wisdom none the worse for being used by servants.

Yours in the best of good faith, Arthur Cornwallis.

The letter's tone angered Diana, but there were parts of it which softened her.

She knew that Michael must do more or less what Cornwallis said, and she meant to talk to him about it. She had no intention of going into places where it would occur to people to cut her: the memory of that world sickened her, and she wanted only to live on it, never inside it. Occasionally, it seemed to her remarkable that this view of hers had not been modified in the course of three whole months of marriage and Bohemia.

Diana sat down, opposite Michael's charcoal sketch of herself in the nude, and thought about her meeting with Kitty in Regent's Street two weeks ago.

She, Diana, had been wearing her new style of clothes: fashionable enough in cut, but without whalebone or padding, or hot bands encircling her neck and wrists. Now she wore only one petticoat, and when she went out, low shoes and an old boater hat. A combination, she supposed, looking back, of the Aesthetic Lady of the previous decade and the New Woman of today. To Kitty, dressed with absolute propriety in clothes buttoned tightly over every curve, Diana had looked like one trying to ape a street-urchin from her native Commercial Road.

Diana, walking along and carrying a parcel, had called up to Kitty sitting in her borrowed landau with a hat-box at her feet. Kity had looked at her, turned aside, and spoken to her son, Diana's eldest nephew. He had been sitting in the corner with his back to the horses, complaining loudly about the treat of being taken out in Mamma's carriage.

Diana had laughed. 'Do call on us in Mornington Terrace, Kitty – we shall be moving there pretty shortly, you know. Come and see your Aunt Diana, Frankie!'

She had attracted attention, one man had recognised her, and it had been one of the finest moments of her life. Diana closed her eyes now, and remembered swaggering down to Piccadilly Circus with her brown-paper parcel in her arms. It had been delightful to be young and notorious, yet protected, full of virtue unrecognised by the world.

Looking once more at the charcoal portrait, Diana let a few angry tears fall out of her eyes. Soon, she hoped, she would have a baby. She wanted a girl, and she would call her Alice, after Alice in Wonderland and Alice Bateman, her nurse: who now no longer remembered her birthdays.

That evening, Michael returned from some race Diana had

never heard of, and threw a wallet of gold sovereigns into her lap. He also presented her with a necklace made of delicate links, from which hung silver-framed moonstones the colour of unthreatening summer cloud.

'Michael!'

'I backed the first outsider whose name I liked and it won by a head. Fifty to one, Diana!' Michael looked like a boy reciting poems as he said this.

'How much did you stake? What was the horse's name?' she said, handling the necklace, which could not be worth more than thirty shillings, but which she thought the prettiest she had ever seen.

'Wearer of the Green, is the answer to your last question.'

'Of course!' She laughed, and after a pause said: 'Goodness, what a lot of money. Darling, how much *did* you stake?'

'Ten quid merely, my dear Diana.'

'Michael, promise me . . .'

His sudden frown came down on his face. 'Never to gamble and game again, is it? My lady Blentham's warnings and the Reverend Roderick's sermons again, is it?'

'Oh, don't be so unfair. I just want you to promise never to bet more than ten pounds – if we can afford it.'

'I'll promise,' he said, picking up his wallet and throwing the coins at her one by one, glowering all the while. 'Now, have I been extravagant, Diana? Have I wasted the ready? Are we going to end in the workhouse, then?'

'Just when I was a trifle worried about the bill for bedroom china,' said Diana, fending them off. 'Do you know, a man, a dun, came round the other day and was quite rude to me?'

'Was he, by God!' said Michael, looking rather like Lord Blentham.

'I saw him off, Michael, but it was rather unpleasant,' she told him.

'There's my brave girl,' he said, squeezing her shoulder. 'But it won't happen again, that I promise.'

'Oh well, it happens a good deal, to people like us, doesn't it?'

'I won't have tradesmen importuning you with their rubbish,' said Michael with his hands in his pockets. Diana smiled, but he ignored it. 'They're to come straight to me – when they've anything to complain of, which won't be often. I'll tell the girl. Or whoever we have in her place. Yes, I don't want a char,' said Michael.

Quite suddenly Diana suffered one of her rare panics, which would spin her for a few unreal moments round the pivot called *but this is for life*.

Michael saw her dead expression, and took her in his arms. 'Come, I want to take you to bed – don't take off that necklace. Ah, I knew how well it would suit you.' He kissed her until lust overcame her, and then said: 'Ah, passion's the thing, damn you.'

When they had made love, and eaten the cook-general's liver and bacon, Diana drew the curtains in the sitting-room, and showed her husband Cornwallis's letter. Michael tore it up after one reading, then pieced it together like a jig-saw on the table. He examined it, while Diana stroked the cat and looked at the crowded bookshelves in the space between the windows. Next week they were to give their first party, to several of Michael's friends whom she did not know very well, and she wondered whether to ask Cornwallis.

He would find this house amusing, for Diana thought most of its interior falsely artistic, rather old-fashioned, and even faintly vulgar. The previous owner had put up a dado of tulips, and wallpaper designed by Morris, and the fireplace was made of black iron and lined with china tiles. The Molloys had bought little furniture so far, and in this sitting-room their few pieces looked over-important, set against the dark patches on the blue carpet and the wallpaper where once there had been low bamboo stands, pictures and Japanese fans. The chairs, table and tallboy they had bought were all Queen Anne, like the Cornwallises', but they were scuffed, country-made pieces of furniture, not good of their kind. Diana was determined to imitate nobody, though she knew that conscious originality was to be despised. She had put some large cushions down on the floor for comfort and economy's sake, and this was an arrangement she had never seen before.

She sighed, then suddenly remembered that Michael had been angry enough with Cornwallis to tear the letter up. Yet she had quite forgotten him. She felt frivolous, and too young.

'Intolerable,' said Michael.

Diana got up from her cushion. 'I know,' she said, fingering her new necklace. 'But do you think – possibly – there's another side to the case?' She put her arm round him, and waited.

'Oh, I know he means well! But he knows nothing – nothing about us, you may be sure – it's clear he didn't even expect you to show this to me.'

'No, I don't think he did.'

'Expected you to be a cunning little wife and use your wiles to get your own way, damn him. And I'm painting no more flash portraits of anyone, not now I've got you. I'm obliged to him for all he's done for me, putting me in Mrs Wilder's way, and others', but from now on I'm not footling around, Diana. Oh, I'll support you, and I won't quarrel with Cornwallis because I can't damn well afford to, but I'll ask him please to recommend me as a drawing-master to young ladies of his acquaintance. That's how I'll earn enough.'

'But dear one – Fierce Fenian Seducer –' Diana said, 'just think. Your marriage to me has put that quite out of the question, beyond the pale. Do remember!'

'Under a false name, I mean,' said Michael, who failed to laugh at the oddest moments. He was scowling now.

'Oh, darling! Yes, Arthur might be amused – why not? Oh, it *would* be amusing. And you'd be so good.' She watched him.

'Would it, indeed? I suppose so. Oh, you have a sense of humour, Diana, a neat little English girl's sense of *the amusing*.' He looked at her with his mouth twisted, making Diana love him as though he were a child. He was remembering the suit of Rational Dress which he had once sent her. 'Raphael Macallan from Glasgow, that's who I'll be – Digby will be able to recommend a Scottish school for me to have gone to – no, no, it will be better to stick to Paris and M. Clement's atelier, won't it? That should impress the ladies, indeed. A grain of truth strengthens any lie you please, as my uncle who was hanged was used to say to me. Ah, Diana.'

Diana's slight anxiety vanished. Michael took hold of her shoulders, and she noticed for the hundredth time how unusually pale he was and how, when he flushed, the colour took only on his jawbone and round his eyes. 'Diana, I'm going to be a great painter, if it's at all within my power. I'm not wasting any energy on rubbish fools will think grand.' He paused. 'I believe you have the power to make me one – to save me from bloody mediocrity. Look at that picture of you, upstairs!'

'It's good, Michael.' She looked down at his waistcoat.

At that moment, the maid came in, snuffling and holding a letter on a tray. 'This came for yer by the afternoon post, mum – I forgot it.'

'Thank you, Eliza!' said Diana crossly. The handwriting was Lady Blentham's: Diana put it in her pocket before Michael could say anything. With her heart beating fast, she told him: 'We'll be happy – so much happier than others – even when we cease to be passionate as all married people do – because we have no *illusions*, even though we're in love.'

He said: 'My noble wife,' and he vowed not to bet, drink, or run up debts, and never to hit Diana in one of the hot little quarrels which they so much enjoyed. She was so very beautiful, and cleverer than he was, and the most truly sexual woman he had ever known. 'I'm not good enough for you but I'll make you good enough for *me*.'

He compared Diana daily with his dead mother who had adored him, with his loud father, and with his skinny sister, Eileen: but he did not talk to his wife about his family, it was as though that would be to contaminate her when she loved him for himself alone.

Eileen had regarded him as an immoral person and one to be despised ever since their father, whose favourite she was, had been able to send her as a day-girl to the local convent school of the Sacred Heart. His father, who had taught him to read, write and keep double-entry books, had considered Michael too sinful and shrewd to benefit from a religious education. Michael thought himself sinful, but in the grand manner.

CHAPTER 11

ONE YEAR LATER

The Blenthams and Montroses gradually mended their quarrel over Diana's marriage, and who was responsible for what, in a series of letters and meetings in London. For a long time they did not go to each others' houses except for parties, but met privately at Gunters' and the Ritz, in Brooks's and at the House of Lords.

It was not until November 1897 that all except Kitty gathered together at Dunstanton. They meant to assure themselves and each other that the matter was closed, and also to reassign small portions of blame. Then they would be a good family once more: for the public scandal had long since faded, and Diana was forgotten.

On the day the Montroses were coming down to Kent, Maud found an announcement on the front page of *The Times*, and read it out to her parents after breakfast. Diana had had a daughter without any of them knowing.

Late that afternoon, when Violet and Walter were newly arrived, and were seated with the others at the end of the Long Gallery, Maud came in with the paper in her hand. She held it up to her spectacles, as Violet continued to chat about London and the trains from Scotland.

'I just went out to fetch this . . . please listen.' They were all silent, and her parents and her brothers stirred their tea. ' "To Diana, wife of Michael Molloy, a daughter, Alice Maria." Isn't it most interesting news? I had an idea that it was rather vulgar to put one's child's name in the announcement,' she said, which showed she was not as dull as her family thought her. 'At least, at one time I thought it was rather democratic.'

'Very well, Maud, you've read it out once, twice is quite

beyond the call of duty,' said Lord Blentham, getting up. 'I imagine Violet and Walter have already seen it.'

'I'm sorry, Papa. But we knew, of course, didn't we, Mamma?' said Maud. 'Diana did drop us a line about it, before.'

Violet looked about her, and stroked her sables. Her husband was now gently snoring in the armchair nearest the fire. 'Really? How awfully odd. She wrote to me – quite a long letter – and said she was hoping for a girl, so I'm awfully pleased, because actually we didn't see the notice – but I thought she told me she wanted it to be a surprise for the rest of you. Sorry!'

'What a deuced bad moment,' mumbled Sir Walter.

'Maud is telling an untruth,' said Angelina. 'We've had no communication from Diana. Naturally I intend to go up to London to see her, now, in view of this.' She did not say when.

Roderick swallowed some tea. 'You would do well to take plenty of cash, Mater. I fancy that Irish bounder of hers is pretty deeply in debt. You know, I went to call on her as soon as I had her address – I was very glad to be able to lend her a few guineas.'

'Thank you, Roderick,' said his mother.

'You'll give her very little besides advice, if you take my advice, Angelina,' said Lord Blentham. 'I told her we would do nothing for her, and . . . I'll take care of matters as they ought to be taken care of.'

'There is the child now, Charles,' said his wife.

'Yes, there's the child, Angelina, I know,' he said. 'Alice, indeed! I had a pointer bitch called Alice once – but it's rather an unsuitable name for a child, in my opinion, though I did once hear some old lady or other say it was a very good sort of name for a maid. Together with Ellen, and Jane, and Dolly, and Cora,' he said, and smiled. He looked very old and ill, though he had made a marvellous recovery from a stroke the previous winter; and he very seldom smiled. 'I have no intention of visiting Diana yet – I see she means to have us all under her thumb pretty soon.'

✻   ✻   ✻

Alice Molloy was a seven-pound baby, whose aged face looked just like her father's an hour after birth, and like a black-haired Diana two weeks later.

'I'm going to get myself knighted before it's time for her to be presented at Court,' Michael said.

'Oh, Fierce Fenian,' said Diana.

He lowered his eyebrows. 'That'll be no bar by the time she's eighteen or so. The world will have changed a great deal by then, you wait and see.'

'Oh, I wonder,' said Diana. 'Anyway, I have no intention of presenting her, and dragging her through all those terrible parties one has to endure when one's young. And besides, why on earth do you want *your* daughter to be presented to the English sovereign, Michael?'

'Oh, I'd like her to catch a glimpse of Ireland's oppressors at home.'

'You are ridiculous. And you've been drinking,' said Diana, sitting up in bed.

'And so why not? I've something to celebrate.' He took hold of Alice, who was sleeping on Diana's lap, and cooed at her. She woke, screamed, and was quietened by his putting his finger in her mouth. 'I've found a nurse for her, Diana.'

'A nurse?'

'Didn't I tell you I'd keep you properly? I made up my mind long ago that a nurse you should have for her.'

'But how can we afford one? And do you think any self-respecting nanny would work in this house? We don't even employ a cook, let alone – oh, heavens. And I won't have Alice shut in a cupboard, or forbidden to suck her thumb, or spanked, or – '

'You're still weak from the birth,' Michael said, looking down at her. 'And this isn't a self-respecting nanny, not in the sense you mean! She's a good girl from Kerry who's lost her place, because she was pregnant, poor child, and then she lost the baby. I found her drowning her sorrows, that's how I know. She's not trained, but she was eldest of her family, so she told me in the Crown, and she's looked after infants since she herself was weaned. Oh, and you needn't be thinking she's a drunkard, she was drinking her port as though it were nasty as medicine. And not to be wondered at, given the port at the Crown.'

Diana stared at him. 'But Michael – '

'I've got her downstairs. You'll see if you like her. She'll do any work which will keep her off the streets, she said – I said ten pounds a year and her keep for looking after Alice and having an eye to the housework, and she said, Done!'

Diana revived a little. 'Didn't you tell me once that the stupidity of the Kerrymen is a standing joke in Ireland?'

'It is so. I prefer to make jokes about English stupidity.'

'Michael, does this girl speak English? Isn't County Kerry part of the Gaeltacht?'

'Of course she speaks English! How do you suppose I managed to talk to her! And do you think an Irish girl would get a place as a skivvy in England if she spoke only Gaelic?'

'Very well. I'd like to see her, at least. What is her name, Michael?'

'Bridget O'Shea. You may have some trouble at first in understanding her, her accent's very strong.'

Michael went out to fetch the girl, and he stayed away for a long time. Diana began to cry for no reason. Then she imagined, and next convinced herself, that Bridget O'Shea was or would be Michael's mistress. Physical passion held their marriage together, and made all their differences negligible: now this would not be so. Michael would keep Bridget O'Shea on the collapsed bed in the studio.

Diana was just beginning to remember the full ferocity and tenderness and loose ache of making love, and to want her husband inside her again after eight weeks' abstinence. She let out a sob, and Alice too began to howl. At that sound, Diana thought of her own incompetence in changing her baby's napkins, winding her and even feeding her. She was prepared hopelessly to welcome her husband's pert Irish mistress. Afterwards, she thought, she would go back to her family and mourn these eighteen happy months of her life forever.

When the door opened again, Diana's self-control snapped back into place.

'This is Bridget, my dear,' said Michael.

'Ah, the poor little mite!' cried Bridget, looking at the roaring, tousled baby at the foot of the bed. Then she blushed.

Michael smiled, and Diana sat up straight. 'I – understand you wish to apply – to be Alice's nurse?' said Diana above the noise. She blew her nose and wiped her eyes.

'Yes,' said Bridget wonderingly. 'Mr Molloy did say – '

'Yes, I know. Oh, how ridiculous this is! My husband said you had had experience in looking after your brothers and sisters – if you can only make the child quiet, you can be her nurse for as long as you like!' Diana fell back on the pillows, feeling like a caricatured tyrant. She loved Alice dearly.

Bridget O'Shea picked up the baby and hushed her for a moment. Diana saw that she might have been pretty, but was not because she was so thin. The shape of her face was round as a muffin, but her cheeks were hollow, and there were grey shadows of hunger about her snub nose. She had expected a black-haired and blue-eyed colleen, but Bridget had frizzy golden hair, and light freckled eyes.

Alice began to grumble again. 'She's wet, mam – where do you keep her little napkins, then?' Bridget said.

'Over there.' Diana pointed to a chest of drawers.

Bridget proceeded to change the baby on top of the chest, watched by the Molloys. Her hands shook a little, but that did not seem to disturb Alice. 'Do you feed her at the breast, mam?' said Bridget, when she had finished. She spoke quite naturally, because she was so bewildered at this sudden change in her life. She had eaten well for the first time in two weeks, and hope and curiosity had temporarily blown away her private unhappiness.

'Oh, yes. So much less trouble than one of those dreadful bottles!'

'And so much better for the little one, mam!'

Bridget then said something to Alice in Gaelic and Diana guessed that, even before her pregnancy and miscarriage, she would not have made a good under-servant in a conventional household. She was a spirited girl and seemed to be only feebly aware of class distinctions, and the necessity of treating

140

body functions as taboo. Diana herself was now a socialist as well as a bohemian, and believed all people of spirit and intelligence to be equal, all stupid people to be objects of compassion.

She had a vision of making Bridget a companion, of merely having a woman she liked in the house. She realised then how long she had been cut off by Michael from her own sex. Michael was standing there now, smiling away. He must have thought of all this too.

Lady Blentham and Violet called at Mornington Terrace the day after Bridget O'Shea's arrival. Angelina had not seen Diana since her marriage, but she had written several letters and received teasing, evasive replies. As she stood on the doorstep, she felt tears in her eyes, and she told herself she would not be angry. Camden Town upset her very much.

Violet, who was dressed for the grouse-moors, said: 'Isn't this a rather charming part of London? Variety, you know. Awful pity about the railway line, imagine poor old Didie's bed rattling every single night with the trains going past. I believe there are quite a lot of artists living in this district, or somewhere else, I can't remember. Walter was being rather a bore about it the other day. Isn't there quite a famous music-hall very near here?'

'I've no idea, Violet.'

'She *is* taking a long time to answer the bell. She wasn't looking very well, physically, when I saw her last – rather overworked with only a charwoman, and her writing to do. She takes it awfully seriously now, Mamma. But so happy!'

'Happiness is indeed a blessing,' said Lady Blentham.

Bridget pulled open the door, with Alice on her arm, and said: 'Good morning, your Ladyships, Mrs Molloy's been expecting you! Will your Ladyships please to mind the step and follow me – this is Alice, Miss Alice, and I'll be taking her in to Mrs Molloy directly!' She held the door wide open, and ran upstairs.

Lady Blentham, who had understood only the gist of Bridget's rapid speech, was very shocked, yet inclined to smile. Violet laughed.

'Oh, Didie is *extraordinary*!'

They followed Bridget upstairs, to the double-windowed sitting-room from which all the Aesthetic decorations of the early eighties had now been removed. There were paintings by Michael on the walls, and Persian rugs as frayed and faded, but not originally as good, as those at Dunstanton lay on the bare floor. The room was extremely untidy. They saw Bridget give Alice to Diana, who was seated in a cane armchair, and then run out past them on to the landing.

Diana raised her head, and Lady Blentham tried to decide whether she was plainer or prettier than before. Her own hands were shaking on top of her cane.

'Vio,' said Diana, 'I didn't expect you to come with Mamma.'

'Oh, I decided to. I haven't seen Alice, after all. Darling, let me hold her!' Violet ran forward and picked up the child with expert hands. 'Oh, she's so like you. Look, Mamma!'

Diana wished passionately that Violet had not come. She thought her mother had aged terribly in the past year. She was not yet sixty, but her hair was nearly white.

'She used to have quantities of black hair but it fell out quite suddenly a couple of days ago,' said Diana.

'Oh, she'll be blonde,' said Violet. 'Look at that.' She pushed at a cobweb-thin line of hairs at the nape of Alice's neck.

'Mamma, do sit down,' said Diana. 'Why are you using a stick?'

'I sprained my ankle a month ago. At my age, these things do not mend quite so easily as they did when one was young. Violet, I wonder – do you think you could leave us for a little while?'

Violet stared and wrinkled her nose. 'Didie?'

'Do you mind dreadfully being sent out, Vio? Mamma has something to say to me, I can tell,' said Diana, looking out of the window.

142

Violet put her head on one side. 'Tell me Didie, is that very odd girl your *maid*?'

'She only came yesterday. She will be Alice's nurse – she's not a trained palourmaid, as you will have noticed.'

Violet looked from Diana to her mother, returned Alice, picked up her skirt and left, smiling crossly.

'My dear,' said Angelina, 'my dear.' She paused, and said in an unstately way: 'Violet was trying to make this easier for us both, but – '

'Yes, I know,' said Diana. 'I hope she isn't too much offended.'

'No.'

Diana adjusted her child's dress and shawl. 'I presume you came on Alice's account?'

'Yes, yes.' Lady Blentham looked at the baby. 'It's been too long, in any case. Diana, where is your husband?'

'In Bloomsbury.'

'This room is most – artistic. Are you comfortable here, Diana?'

'Oh, yes. It's extraordinary how quickly one grows used to having very few luxuries – to lacking what one used to consider not so much as essentials but as part of nature's order.'

'I daresay. Could your maid bring us some tea, do you suppose?'

Diana smiled. 'I'll ring the bell. This is not her first place, she does know the sound of a bell.'

'I imagine you found her in a somewhat unorthodox way?'

Diana began to enjoy herself, and to feel a little ashamed of it as she rang the bell. 'Oh, yes. Michael discovered her in the pub – the public house round the corner, weeping because she'd lost her place, poor child.'

Angelina studied her gloved fingers and, to her own horror, quiet tears began to glide down her cheeks. 'This is the way you prefer to live, Diana?'

'Yes, Mamma. I should hate to be very poor, but we're not. Don't cry!' she said lightly. After a moment's thought, she presented her mother with Alice. 'Do you know, I've earned a

143

little money myself – I published two short poems in a small journal the other day? Publishing is not easy.'

'A charming child,' said Lady Blentham. 'Yes. I came chiefly to talk to you about Alice, my dear. You understand that your father will not – can never – forgive this marriage of yours? I forgave you long ago, as you know, Diana.' She stopped. 'I had no right – cowardice has kept me from visiting you before.'

'Don't let it distress you too much, Mamma.'

'I wish I could invite you, and Alice, down to Dunstanton, but your father makes that impossible. Did you expect him – ever – to be so cruel?'

'No. Only bombastic.'

'He is not bombastic. He is a highly determined and *intelligent* man, whose mind I have – whose mind it is impossible to change. He holds to his original intention of cutting you out of the family, his will, but he says – he is just beginning to consider . . . You see, I have explained to him that there can be no reason for Alice's suffering from your – I ought perhaps to quote him exactly . . . from your disgusting folly and ingratitude.'

Lady Blentham hesitated, and Bridget came into the room, carrying a tray on which there stood two chipped cups, a silver teapot and a Toby jug. Although she had not yet been asked to bring it, she was beaming.

'I thought as you might like a drop of tea, mam.'

'Thank you, Bridget, I was about to ring a second time.'

'Glad I am then that I saved you the trouble, mam.' She nodded, smiled, and went, banging the door. The theatrical noise made Diana want to laugh, and made Angelina close her eyes.

'Diana, I suggested to him that he leave three thousand pounds in trust for Alice. It would have gone to you, of course. The others are all well enough provided for, even Maud – your father agreed with me that it might be possible to do this. He has even been thinking of possible trustees, if he should decide to set it up.'

'Three thousand. Who is he considering as a possible

trustee?' said Diana a moment later, setting down the teapot.

'Her father – and your brother, Roderick.'

'Her father? Michael?'

'He – would think it proper. His views on a father's duties, whoever he may be, whatever . . . Of course, because he insists on your husband's being a trustee, he may never make the trust at all.'

'So he can forgive my poor old Fenian seducer, but not me,' said Diana very quietly.

'I consider it abominable.' Angelina did not use such words easily, Diana remembered.

'If it happens, of course I shall be very glad for Alice's sake. I shan't be especially grateful, I'm afraid, Mamma.'

'No, you won't be.' Lady Blentham's tears had stopped.

'Michael too would be delighted.'

Angelina got up and changed her chair. She gave Alice back to Diana, then said after a little while, watching the baby: 'Diana, tell me, did you marry that – did you marry him for love?'

'Mamma.' Diana stared at her. 'Did you think it was for his social position – I'm not being sarcastic?'

'Yes – no. But love, Diana. Did you not find married love, after all my warnings . . . has nothing been a disappointment to you?'

'Almost nothing. Certainly not love.'

'You are too thin for a woman in your condition,' said Lady Blentham, though her daughter's bosoms were the normal size of any nursing mother's. She felt it impossible to discuss Diana's confinement in detail. 'Far too thin, but I must admit that you are still a beauty!' There was a glow in Diana's face, which might be mischief, not motherhood's fulfilment. 'How did you bruise yourself? You have a bruise on your wrist.'

'Michael hit me with a paint-brush. I do bruise very easily,' said Diana after a little hesitation. She smiled.

Angelina raised her face. 'He does not – oh, my God.'

'Oh, *Mamma*, he isn't what one might call a – a police-court wife-beater! I oughtn't to have have told you, but the fact is, we rather like a little mild fighting, in an odd sort of way. *I* hit *him* a great deal harder than he hit me on that occasion. I can promise you I did.' For the first time, she looked a little embarrassed. 'It's quite a little bruise, look. His is much larger.' She laughed, and fiddled with Alice.

And then they went to bed, thought Lady Blentham.

'Your Irish girl's tea is so stewed – it makes me feel quite unwell,' she said.

Angelina would have liked to hit Charles in the past, to beat him for assaulting her in the name of love, with what he called when speaking to her 'the instrument of love, you know'. And for refusing to become a Tory and a Cabinet Minister, and refusing to forgive Diana; and even for liking Walter Montrose, whose self-centred vagueness and feeble, poetic affection was now making Violet unhappy.

'Don't drink it,' said Diana. 'Next time you come, I shall make it myself. Formosa Oolong is the kind you like, isn't it? Can I offer you a little brandy – a restorative?' She was not being too ironical.

'I understand, Diana,' said Lady Blentham, thinking only of her own desire to inflict pain to induce understanding.

Of course, Diana could not really enjoy married love. She felt it her perverse duty to claim that she did, because she was now living a world of forbidden novels, in low, eccentric company. Angelina longed to protect and embrace her small daughter more than she had ever done, even when Diana was a faultless child of three.

When Violet came back, she was very cheerful, and told her mother and sister that she had had a most instructive gossip with Bridget. She folded Diana in her arms, and made her promise to bring Michael, Alice and Bridget up to Auchingilloch in the summer. Diana agreed, and after that there did not seem to be much to say except about Alice's beauty and goodness. Very shortly, the Blentham ladies took their leave. Diana remained in her sitting-room trying to re-read *Leaves of Grass* as she waited for her husband to come back and embrace her.

CHAPTER 12

MATURE PERSONALITIES

The dining-room at Auchingilloch was big enough for twenty, but Sir Walter liked to use it even when he and Violet were alone. It was not a particularly pompous room despite its size, for Violet had had it painted green, taken up the florid carpet and replaced the Landseers with family portraits of children. She had even had these cleaned. Diana, looking across the silver and fruit and flowers, objected only to the overmantel loaded with Benares brass.

Sir Walter had aged in appearance since his marriage, and his hair was entirely white. He was now talking in a rather ignorant way about the pleasures of Bohemia. His wife and her sister had returned from a long walk too late to change for dinner; Diana was wearing her old suit of Rational Dress, and seemed perfectly at ease.

'How one longs to be freed from convention,' Sir Walter said. 'But it is rather difficult for some of us.'

'To be sure,' said Michael.

'I think my father rather longed to be freed from convention, sometimes,' said Diana, who had never thought of this before.

Lord Blentham had died six months ago, in January, before he had quite made up his mind about Alice's prospective trust. All the Blenthams but Diana were still in full mourning; and yet it seemed to them that he had died a long time ago. It was as though they had not fully realised until his death that Charles had been the head of their house, the person who bound them together as children.

Kitty and Edward were already at Dunstanton, and Lady

Blentham, in deepest mourning of all, had gone to live permanently in London which she hated. Maud had amazed the whole family by taking rooms of her own in a mansion block in Wigmore Street, instead of going with her mother. The Blenthams had always supposed that it was Angelina who had perfect authority over her middle-aged daughter, not Charles at all.

Everyone in the family was richer than before, but only Roderick was glad that Charles was dead. Lord Blentham had told his second son that he disliked him only a few weeks before his stroke; but on the other hand, he had relented towards Diana. He had added a codicil to his will, leaving her three bits of good jewellery and £200.

Walter said: 'It's rather a strange thing, to find oneself deprived of a parent in adult life, though of course it ought not to be, when one considers the matter rationally. To find oneself the oldest generation – really and truly grown-up, as the children say!'

Violet laughed, and remembered why she had married him. She reached for a nectarine, though she was in the middle of eating a lark, and said: 'Well, Didie, Walter's awfully keen on talking about *Bohemianism*, but what *is* it, precisely? In essence, as Walter likes to say?'

'Oh – well, it's not dressing unsuitably, or painting or writing, or caring very little for – formal meals and the rules of mourning shall we say – or making friends of one's servants, or visiting Scotland in June,' said Diana, gazing at the door. 'No – in essence – I suppose the difference is that in polite society, at least when women are present, one never, ever contradicts or argues. And also, it's not done in the best circles to supply information – not even when one is asked, do you know, in so many words. One must pretend courteous ignorance, unless one's talking scandal, of course.'

Sir Walter laughed flirtatiously. Violet assumed her struck expression: the same she had used since schoolroom days.

'Ah,' said Michael, smoothing his dinner-jacket. 'Now I understand. Well do I remember, Violet, talking with some man or other at Arthur Cornwallis's.'

'Arthur's?' said Violet, surprised.

' "In that part of southern Poland – what used to be Poland – what is its name?" he said. "Galicia," I said, and he couldn't have looked more offended if I'd said Saskatchewan.'

'No, you don't understand,' laughed Diana, 'when you say he couldn't have looked *more* offended! He'd have been rather pleased if you'd said Saskatchewan, and the subject would have been changed, gracefully.' She paused, smiling. 'No. Anyone who says directly, in mixed company, "No, *that's not true, this is*" is essentially a bohemian and not someone who belongs in polite society, however literary and artistic!' As she said this, she felt satisfied, and quite at home.

'My Diana,' said Michael, before Walter could pay her a compliment.

Diana sat down on a stone in the middle of the moor, and Violet flopped down beside her with an exaggerated sigh. They had brought a picnic basket, which they meant to share with Michael, but it was early yet and there was time to be filled in with conversation.

There was no animosity between them, and little irritation, and yet it was hard to remember that once they had been very much in harmony. People who met them casually had been surprised to learn they were sisters. They felt now like women who kept up a schoolgirl acquaintance only from habit. It chilled Diana to think that such a strong emotion need not die or even change its nature, but could simply become less of the same old thing. She believed she could only understand and cope with disastrous or glorious, enormous change.

Diana squinted down the slope of the valley to the white-lit stream where Michael was now fishing for anything that would take his bait. His tweed figure was just perceptible. The truth, thought Diana, was of course that nothing mattered to her now but him, and his world, which no one else could understand.

She turned her thoughts towards her sister's husband, and tried not to compare him with her own. So long as he was not challenged or criticised in earnest, Sir Walter remained a fond, indulgent but indifferent husband, and a very great bore. But Diana knew that he could be very frightening, and that Violet, who had married him because he seemed the least frightening of men, did not dare oppose him seriously even over little things. Though Walter often said lightly that he was in the wrong, he never believed it. Diana could see that in his eyes when he took off his spectacles.

She wished she could feel more for Violet, and asked now: 'Dearest, tell me – when you row with Walter, is he ever – *violently* disagreeable?'

Violet was startled. '*Violently*? Didie, gracious. He couldn't swat a fly, let alone his wife. Besides, we don't *row*. We're not like you and Michael, my dear Diana!'

Diana saw that she was telling the truth. 'It's a good thing, to be able to fight openly,' she said, and kicked the grass.

'To be able to say clearly, "You're wrong, I'm right," like a child?' said Violet. 'I don't in fact see – oh, never mind! Dearest, must you really go on Wednesday? I thought you would be able to stop with us for three weeks at least.'

Diana repeated her explanation of the previous day. 'It's partly Michael's work, and partly Bridget. She says the air up here is bad for Alice.'

'What nonsense! *Bad* for her? How the child can be *healthy*, growing up in the *fumes* of King's Cross and Euston – '

'But she thrives on it.'

'Oh, Didie. I know.'

'Sometimes I wonder whether Michael does. He's far too thin, and his cough worries me – the London fogs, I'm sure, make it far worse in the winter than it would otherwise be.'

Violet opened her eyes wide. 'Didie, he's not consumptive? People do say it's the Celtic scourge, you know.' She rubbed her knees with her palms, then rubbed her hands together.

'No, I don't think so. Occasionally he claims to be so, which is what makes me think it rather unlikely.' They smiled at husbands.

At that moment they heard a faint splash. Then a curse was caught up by the little valley's echo, and its hollow roar made them laugh with comprehension.

'Hoy!' called Violet, and her voice came pounding back – O-yy. 'Hoy!' Oy – oy.

'Michael!' cried Diana, standing up and facing the right direction.

'Uhl-l-l,' said the echo.

The noon sun was high over the far hill, and it turned the moors pale. Diana turned round, away from the view, and glanced behind her.

'Botheration,' she said, pushing back a strand of hair. 'Look at that cloud coming up, it's going to rain soon. I – ' she stopped.

Violet said in a lower voice than her sister's: 'Ought we to go and see what's happened to Michael?'

'Of course!' whispered Diana, quite angrily. They left their small picnic-basket on the rock, and tripped down towards the stream.

'If either of you giggles, I'll hit her!' said Michael when they came upon him five minutes later. He was drenched, and puffing far more loudly than they were.

'Wind up your tackle and don't talk nonsense,' said Diana. 'Dearest, did you lean too far forward? Did you fall? My poor one.' His appearance, though she had expected it, shocked her into making foolish remarks.

'No, Diana, a great brute of a killer-whale pulled me in and tried to swallow me.'

'Rubbish,' said Diana, recovering. 'Just take off your wet clothes behind that gorsebush over there, you can very well wear my knickerbockers, and Violet's coat – Vio, I'll borrow your petticoat, please.'

'Women!'

'Thank goodness you did give me a bicycling-suit, all those years ago,' said Diana. 'Go on, Michael!' She was enjoying herself. Self-confidence was the next best thing in the world to love.

Grey-lipped and shivering, Michael retired. Diana stripped off her breeches, took Violet's coat, and went in her stockings to join him in the gorse. Violet, holding out her petticoat, heard their argument. When they came back, Michael looked ridiculous, but no warmer.

151

'We must go straight back to the house,' said Diana.

'But he ought to be fed before attempting such a horrid walk, surely?' said Violet, as her sister took the petticoat from her. 'There's our little picnic waiting for us, and the sun will *soon* dry you, Michael.'

'I want to go back,' said Michael. 'Will you look at those storm-clouds, sister-in-law!'

Diana looked at Violet. 'Very well,' Violet said. 'Just leave those wet clothes here, one of the servants will come down and fetch them.'

'Oh, one of the servants will, will he!' said Michael.

They had a difficult walk, back up the hill and on to the stony moorland path. There were two miles more to go when they reached it, and the heather-coloured clouds were advancing from the north. They did not drop so much rain as they might have done, but they cut out all warmth, brought midges swarming from the damp ground, and drew behind them an ugly cold wind. The moor was utterly empty.

'Oh, Mother of God, I'll die,' said Michael, now in tears.

Diana slapped his face, and he lunged at her. She laughed, tired out. 'I'm sorry, darling,' he said when he was warmer. Diana did not stop laughing. Violet, twenty paces behind them, could not speak.

'Leddy Montrose!' called a horrified voice.

'Oh!' she said. Rushing round on the spot, she saw a man with a beard, driving a gig, and recognised him within a moment. 'Oh, you deliverer, Dr Graham! You don't know what straits we're in. I – '

'What's this, you've noo coat on – and who are they?' The doctor gestured with his whip.

Violet ran towards him. 'My brother and sister-in-law – I mean sister and brother-in-law – Mr and Mrs Molloy. Mr Molloy fell into the water and he's so dreadfully cold. *Please*, could you drive us back to the Lodge?' She was now quite composed.

Diana and Michael hurried towards the gig.

'You're a doctor?' said Michael.

'Well, ye're properly soaked, sir. Climb up, man, and

cover yourself with this! The doctor looked at Michael's bare calves and pulled up a horse-blanket from the floor of the gig. Diana and Violet crawled up unaided, shaking the carriage. 'A brisk drive, a tot of whisky, and to bed with a hot brick,' said Dr Graham, whipping the horse and facing Violet, 'and a good thing I happened to be driving to Mollie Campbell's – she's expecting her fifth, and if it's not a breech-birth I'm a Dutchman – else you'd be in trouble by the looks of you, Mr Molloy.' He turned back to Violet. 'I can't be staying a moment at the Lodge, Leddy Montrose, not with a difficult confinement on my hands.'

As soon as Michael's chill turned to pneumonia, and the others became seriously worried, he himself began to maintain he was perfectly well.

Diana did not leave his room except for meals, and Violet cried over the whole inconvenient, frightening, embarrassing affair. Walter told her kindly not to do so, and that every man must die at some time.

A week after Michael's fall into the stream, Dr Graham said to Diana: 'You're a faithful wee nurse, Mrs Molloy, but as things have turned out, I'd rather have had a professional – I thought at first, I admit, 'twould not be necessary.' He folded up his stethoscope and put it in his bag. 'It happens there's no trained nurse in the district just now, but if you've a mind to send now to Glasgow, Oban even, mebbe – '

'Dr Graham, how seriously is he in danger?'

The doctor paused. 'He's no reached the crisis yet, ma'am. When it's upon him, we can say just how seriously.'

Diana clenched her fists. Until now, the doctor had agreed with Michael that his illness was trifling. 'He has weak lungs,' she said.

'So you told me before, ma'am.' He returned to his old, severely jocular manner. 'But I dinna think ye'll be a widow yet a while. He's wiry, and he's fighting.' Michael, asleep and exhausted, did not look like a fighter at the moment.

'His mother died of consumption – tuberculosis.' Her voice rose.

'Consumption, as you call it, is by no means the same things as pneumonia.'

'I know!'

'Had I only been able to see him into bed that day I found ye – I didna think it would be so serious, a ducking in the burn.'

'Your instructions were followed.'

'Ay.'

'We put him to bed, we gave him hot bricks, and a hot toddy,' said Diana, looking very self-controlled. 'Are you going to stay now?'

'Give him another poultice, ma'am, and bind it tightly mind, about the chest. You can do that as well as I.'

'Yes,' said Diana, 'I've done it before.'

Dr Graham picked up his bag and said at the door: 'I shall back in the morning, early, Mrs Molloy.'

When he was gone, Diana knelt down by her husband's bed and prayed. She knew no Catholic prayers but the first few words of the 'Ave Maria', in English, and she muttered these now although Michael claimed to be an atheist and was certainly anti-clerical: 'Hail Mary full of grace, blessed art thou among women and blessed is the fruit of thy womb . . .' Even in her worst moments Diana believed that the superstitious rituals of his childhood could prevent Michael from reaching the crisis of his illness, and make him recover as though it had never been.

This was a very bad moment, worse than any before. Before, her most dreadful hours had been flavoured with a romantic terror which Diana now thought wicked. She had had a tiny bit of confidence in Michael and the doctor then, it had been hard really to imagine that he would die and leave her empty. 'Hail Mary – ' Diana stopped, and got to her feet, crying with shame.

It was dark in the room; outside it was raining and the sky was solid grey. Diana did not light a lamp, but she looked down at her husband. Michael's skin was so pale it looked like candle-grease, though his nose was swollen and flushed. Thin locks of unwashed hair lay like flatworms on his forehead, and his open mouth was lifted in a sneer. Michael was very worried about life. He had told Diana yesterday what she had never known before: that they had debts amounting to nearly two thousand pounds.

The crisis of pneumonia came upon Michael sometime before midnight, and progress after that was swift. He said 'Sorry,' several times, probably referring to his debts, thought Diana, and often added, 'I'm not dying.' Dr Graham came at nine in the morning, gave Diana a mild sedative, and stayed on through the hours till late afternoon. But for one brief period during which Alice was screaming, there was silence in the house.

Michael's last words were: 'My wife' – addressed to Diana whose hand he was clutching; then he died, at seven o'clock. Five minutes afterwards, a triangle of sunlight cut through the rainclouds for the first time in days. Diana thought of what she would do, tomorrow, outside in the warm.

'But he's *dead*,' she whispered, making the doctor say: 'Hush!' 'Oh no no no, he can't just – be dead.'

In spite of being sixty years old, Sir Walter could not remember how one dealt with a death, with undertakers and funerals: Violet, who had never seen a dead person, had no idea at all but knew she must do something. Walter's steward, Brown, advised her.

'If you could ask Mrs Molloy where she wishes her husband to be buried, I would be more than happy to undertake arrangements, Lady Montrose.'

'She's already told me he wished to be *cremated*, can you believe it? She won't hear of burial.'

'What a monstrous, irreligious practice – cremation!' he observed. 'To be burned – I'd be afraid – wouldn't you, Lady Montrose?'

'Yes, I know, he even refused a priest and he was a Catholic, you know. We might easily have fetched old Father Mayhew for him. But what is to be *done*, Brown?' said Violet.

The steward got up and rubbed his hands together. Violet noticed how chapped they were, and how pale he looked, though he was a large handsome man. 'So far as I know there's no crematorium in all of Scotland. The coffin will have to be sent down south with Mrs Molloy.'

'Oh, poor Didie!'

Brown said, after a little hesitation: 'I wonder why *you* should be forced to be so anxious, Lady Montrose? Sir Walter and Mrs Molloy ought between them to see that you're not distressed – troubled in any way.'

'They don't, and I don't see why my sister should,' said Violet, looking dignified.

'I beg your pardon. Leave everything to me, Lady Montrose.'

'*Thank* you, Brown.' She smiled, then rose from her chair and looked woeful again. 'But my sister's mourning! I don't think she *owns* a black dress, in spite of Papa – oh, well. I can at least deal with that.'

'I'm sure you will deal with it admirably, Lady Montrose,' said Brown, holding the door open for her and bending over her very slightly. Violet blushed.

That night, Walter ate alone in the big dining room, while Violet and Diana dined together, upstairs. Diana, looking very plain and tired, listened to Violet's description of Brown's arrangements and agreed suitably with all that was so tactfully said.

'Thank you, Violet.'

Diana was dressed in a loose blue gown, while Violet wore a black day-dress, her mourning for Lord Blentham.

'It must be so hard for you to realise – always – that he's gone.'

'Yes, it is hard. Don't talk about it, please.' Diana had not yet even been angry with fate. Since Michael's death twenty-six hours ago, she had felt only anaesthesia, interrupted by moments of panic. Now, lax and miserable tears came. They were, she thought, so very unexpected.

'Michael,' she said. 'Oh, Michael, darling.' Hours ago, Dr Graham had given her laudanum to stop her thinking about him. But it had not worked.

'Darling – dearest, oh, Didie, don't!' said Violet, pushing

her sister's plate of chicken away and pressing her hand down on the table. 'I wish I'd never said anything. But cry, darling.'

'Michael. What'll become of Alice? What shall I do?'

'Didie, let him be buried up here. Stay with us for as long as you like.'

'No. No.'

'Oh, dear! Darling, remember – *try* to remember you still have Alice.'

'What does she matter?'

'Didie! Dearest, you are shocking. You *must* stay here for a while.'

Diana sobbed harshly for a few minutes more, then said: 'Ring the bell for Bridget, Vio, I want Alice – I – '

'Yes, yes of course,' said Violet, getting up.

Walter, who had finished eating, opened the door. They were all still for a few seconds before he came in and closed it, making the two women shift in their places.

'My dear Diana, I felt I had to come up,' he said.

'Yes?' She was polite.

Violet walked away from the bell-pull, and sat down.

'I feel I haven't done all I ought – haven't even expressed my sympathy for you. I'm so very sorry,' said Walter with tears in his eyes.

'Thank you,' said Diana, remembering drearily that a minute ago she had been crying as though she was being torn apart and flung into airless black space.

'Didie,' said Violet, interrupting her husband who had opened his mouth again, 'before I ring for Bridget, I must just tell you – don't worry about your mourning, I've had Mrs Bell dye that green dress you told me you didn't like. It'll be quite dry by tomorrow. And I sent off an order to Glasgow for more things, so – '

Diana looked up, and her face was strange. 'You dyed my dress black? You've decided I must put on weeds – you've even ordered clothes from Glasgow, without asking me?'

'Yes, dearest, I thought you wouldn't want to be troubled with things like that.'

Diana left her chair, trembling. She spoke in a low voice,

157

but gave the impression of shouting. 'No, I'm not *troubled*, Vio! How dare you try to dye my clothes, try to drag me down, to make me – you of all people. How dare you think I'd bother with such an idiotic superstition – it's what women who hate their husbands do, wear mourning!'

She stood by the door. The Montroses gaped at her in horrified pity.

'But *Didie* – '

'My dear Diana, Violet meant only – '

She raised her hand and brought it slapping down again on the air. 'I do not care if she meant it for the best. I'm going, by the first train tomorrow. Michael happens to be dead and it was only – because of him – I could stand you. All of you, my *family*, this – oh, God. You can burn the dress, Violet, and your dear handsome Mr Brown can see to it that Michael's coffin is sent on the same train. I'm going home. I won't wear black. I shall be alone – alone.' She stopped and choked.

'I shall send Brown with you, Didie,' said Violet, who was very pale. 'You will need him, to organise things, the cremation you want, when you're in this state! Oh, darling!'

Diana said nothing. She ran out of the room, down the corridor, up the stairs and round the corner to Bridget and Alice's little brown room.

'Thank God you didn't have to share the nursery,' she said unsteadily as she looked at the child. 'I couldn't bear you to be in Violet's nursery. Nurse Tomkins would have made your life wretched – because you are not what you are not!'

'Mam, what on earth!' Bridget pressed her hands to her chest.

'Nothing, nothing, nonsense. We're going home first thing tomorrow, Bridget,' said Diana, turning towards her. Alice was asleep, and she looked perfectly happy in the clean womb of her wicker cradle.

'I'm glad, mam,' said Bridget then. ''Tis best to be over with things, and at home it'll seem like . . . Oh, poor Mr Molloy!' They were quiet for a moment, looking at each other. They had never been so intimate as this.

'I loved him so very, very much. So much.'

158

Diana lay face down on Bridget's bed and cried into the night. Bridget stroked her hair like a mother, and several times she prevented Diana from getting up and smothering Alice in wayward grief-sick embraces.

'She's only seven months, mam – only seven months.'

CHAPTER 13

POVERTY

In November 1898 Diana, Bridget and Alice were living in three small rooms above a greengrocer's in Museum Street, WC. From the attic bedroom, there was a view of the Museum. The other rooms were too low down to have a view of anything but brown walls, pipes, and dusty windows.

The sitting-room was roughly partitioned off from the kitchen, where there was a tiny stove and one cold-water tap. The only lavatory was an earth-closet in the back yard, which was used as a dumping ground for torn soggy paper and battered wooden crates. Diana took some of these, covered them and used them as makeshift stools and bookcases. She even made a bed for Alice, but then the greengrocer found her out, and obliquely accused her of theft until she paid him two shillings.

'Two shillings!' she said when she had recovered from her anger. 'Remarkable! To think that even when I was in Mornington Crescent – let alone before – I could have had as many orange boxes as I liked from him or any other tradesman for nothing. Ironic, is it not, Bridget?'

Bridget, who was trying half-heartedly to scrub away the flaring smoke-stains on the wall, said: 'You were not in arrears with anybody's rent then, mam. Lucky you are not to be turned out to eat grass like the cattle, like we were in the Great Famine, before I was born to be sure.'

'Oh, Bridget, I heard enough about the Great Famine from Michael! Of course I'm lucky – lucky – lucky – even though no one will employ me even as a shop-girl and all my possessions are in pawn or sold.'

Bridget sighed, and picked up Alice, who was grizzling with

a desire to be included in the conversation. 'There, there, my darling. The trouble is, mam dear, you look too much like a lady still, and sure 'tis that makes all suspicious, but 'twill be to your advantage to one day, mark my words, will it not just!'

'And can I find employment as a *lady* typewriter?' said Diana, looking into the saucepan, where the evening's mutton stew had burnt. She imitated the senior clerk who had interviewed her that afternoon. "I regret, Mrs – er – but, despite our recent advertisement, Mr Blenkinsop has changed his mind about the desirability of employing ladies in this office." Damn Michael for dying – I said damn him, Bridget, and don't correct me!'

'Wonderful you were with the bailiffs,' said Bridget, ignoring this. "Can I help you?" says madam, and makes them slink about the house, lifting their hats every two minutes.' She looked up, and saw that she had not cheered Diana.

'How dared he spend so much money, without even *telling* me?' said Diana. 'I'd like to spit on his grave, if he had one, I'd like to – '

'Holy Mary Mother of God, mam!' cried Bridget, crossing herself. 'Do you want to bring the Evil Eye upon us, talking like that about the poor misguided gentleman, and him your husband too?'

'The Evil Eye is already upon us,' said Diana. She banged the saucepanful of stew down on the table, and sat down before it. 'Why, should I not be angry, Bridget?'

'Yes,' said Bridget slowly, 'you didn't know men, and you didn't expect to be deceived. 'Tis an innocent you are.'

'An innocent? Now? Good God!'

''Tis no insult.'

Diana waved a hand, and they ate their stew. Between them they fed Alice, and when they had finished, Diana said calmly: 'Bridget, I know, of course, how very fortunate I am in having you. It's most good of you to have been such a friend, to have stayed with me all this time, and I promise you that I shall be able to pay you very soon. When you want to go, I'll give you a very good reference, and – '

161

Bridget stood up and narrowed her eyes. 'What's that you say? Are you trying to turn me off then, mam? After all I've done for you, may the Blessed Virgin forgive me for mentioning it?'

'You can't want to stay!' cried Diana.

'Sure and I want to stay! For one thing I'd never get a place, not if a lady took it into her head to check you and your reference, Mrs Molloy!' She said nothing just now about her affection for anyone.

A moment later Diana laughed, and Bridget relaxed a little, though she was offended. 'You said you would not desert me, when I was afraid,' she said.

'It's hardly a question of my deserting you! You could find a very much better place than this. We could still see each other.'

'Place, indeed! Oh, it's noble you are. It's of no use talking,' said Bridget. 'But I'll tell you this, mam, of the kindness of my heart indeed: it's a plain fool you're being when you'll take no money from your family, nor go to live with her ladyship. You took your twenty pounds from Mr Roderick, but now you say you'll have nothing more to do with any of them, and poor Lady Montrose in her grave and all!'

'Be quiet, Bridget!' Diana got up and left the room, knocking over an orange box as she went.

'You're cracked, mam! Oh, forgive me, then!'

Diana came back. 'If it weren't for Violet's dying, and if we were only not quite so poor, Bridget, I'd – I'd be as nearly happy now as I could ever be with Michael dead. If I could only earn a little more money, but I shall, one day.' Diana hurried on, pushing a straggling curl out of her face. 'Don't you see, Bridget? My family are not really trying to help me. If Edward offered me an allowance – as he ought to do, but won't, because of my dear sister-in-law – I'd take it.' She paused. 'They want to see me the repentant Magdalen, in attendance on Mamma. And I'm not a repentant Magdalen – if it's necessary to point that out.'

'No, mam, but for all that her ladyship would be a very good source of income.'

'Oh, you're impossible!'

Diana went into her own room, which measured ten feet by ten, and which she knew in greater detail than she had known any room she had lived in since childhood. She could have drawn the chips in the paintwork round the window from memory. Now she sat down before the typing machine, which a friend of Michael's had lent to her in a moment of careless kindness, and closed her eyes.

She meant to practise, so that one day someone would employ her in a dusty office as a lady typewriter. No one wanted her. Michael's Irish and artistic friends, who had liked her well enough, had proved to be as unforgiving of mistakes and misfortunes as people in the fashionable world. One man, a journalist, had enabled her to do a little penny-a-lining on women's subjects for the newspaper he worked for, but he had not come to see her since she had been forced to sell Mornington Terrace. Neither had anyone else she knew.

Diana sometimes thought it was all her own fault. As Michael's wife, she had felt no need of real friends, and had thought of those outside her house as amusing, living scenery. Her husband's cronies had not liked her being well born and very beautiful and careless, and they thought, like Bridget, that now of course she would return to the place she came from.

Diana put a sheet of paper in the machine:

> She tried to wipe out the past
> as they told her to do
> but she could not
> for the past is an ogre
> and sometimes a Prince
> like Beauty's Beast.
>> Pluck the rose and pay for it.
> Kiss the Beast, but in this life
> He does not change.

Try to make something tolerable of this. Try Faraday at the Nineteenth Century?

*   *   *

163

She tore up the nonsense.

Perhaps she would go back, and take over the place of Maud, who was now such an active member of the Fabian Society, and was not addicted to laudanum any more. Diana no longer cared for political ideas of any kind, and though she often re-read *News from Nowhere* because she liked it, she held socialist beliefs as thoughtlessly as she had once held Anglican ones. Her indifference was odd, she thought, because now she knew what poverty truly was, and surely that ought to make her more ardent. She ought even to be a syndicalist, like a working person, or an anarchist or a communist, but she had not the energy and was, after all, naïve. She had no place in the world from which to fight, or to make friends, and she never would have.

There was only Bridget, and Alice, and herself, and none of them belonged anywhere. Violet had died of a miscarriage which she had suffered in August; Diana sometimes imagined now that, had she lived, she would have left Sir Walter and joined them all in some better lodging in, say, Bloomsbury Square. Diana's grief for Michael was seldom tearful now, though it was ghastly; but she cried whenever she thought of her sister's dying at twenty-seven because her old husband had no self-control. She sometimes thought the loss of Violet even more shocking than widowed disgrace.

Some months ago, Diana had asked Bridget to call her by her name, because they were not only friends but equals now. It horrified her to think that Bridget could be seen as an ever-faithful abigail – a literary creature who could not exist and was most unsocialist. The thought would have amused her in happy times. Bridget had taken time to consider her mistress' request. After two days, she had concluded that the use of her name would highlight the differences between them, not rub them out; and had told Diana so.

'And 'twill be difficult, mam, when our luck turns.'

Diana knew that Bridget was wise, but she felt rejected: the girl could not really love her.

'Help me,' she muttered to the typing-machine.

✳   ✳   ✳

And my greatest desire now is to help her, thought Lady Blentham as she folded up Diana's letter. Although I am so poor. She thought resentfully of the coarse Sir William Harcourt's budget of 1894. Had it not been for the heavy death-duties introduced by him, she would have been able to live on in the Queen Anne's Gate house she had inherited from her father and dutifully made over to Charles. As things were, it had had to be sold, and Angelina had been forced to spend part of her jointure on the lease of a little house in Sumner Place, South Kensington. She lived there now in an obscurity she thought excessive even for the widow of a man who had not succeeded in his world; on an income of a thousand a year with one manservant, two maids and no carriage.

Angelina could not understand how any woman so warm-hearted as she was could have five children who had all deserted her in their separate ways. Edward was intolerable, Maud unbelievable, Roderick both puzzling and dull. School-girlish to the end, Violet had died without even telling her mother she was pregnant; and Diana was possibly the worst of all.

Angelina would always love her the most, for she considered that of all her children Diana was most like her. Charles's seeming to love Diana best had been pure self-deception: Maud, thought Angelina, had been his real favourite, though he had never indulged her and had used her as an unpaid secretary. Diana *must*, surely, be as lonely as I am, she thought, turning swiftly with a rustle of weeds. Why won't she come?

Lady Blentham sat down, and reread the letter, which had no date and no address. Diana had asked her to write care of the post office.

My dear Mamma,
   You seem to have a pretty good idea of my situation and, indeed, I am still in debt, and therefore poor. The interest on the money Michael borrowed is still outstanding, although I have paid most of the principal. Do not judge him too harshly now he is dead

165

(what a pious remark) for the fault was partly mine. I don't doubt you would tell me so.

He was determined to take care of me, to see that I had no worries, and so he took it upon himself to pay all the bills. I let him do so, I never inquired, I was relieved not to have the burden of housekeeping on a small income after the first heady days, as they say. I trusted him too much – perhaps you know that men should never be trusted?

He went to a moneylender because he was quite convinced that, soon, he would be earning a good deal. (In your letter you inquired pretty closely into all this, and so I hope you will believe what I tell you.) Once, he was entirely opposed to the idea of painting Academy portraits – but in the last few months of his life he changed his mind, realising our necessity, I suppose. Two commissions made him think that, very soon, he would be putting Mr Sargent's nose out of joint. And so, before he earned any money, he borrowed, convinced he would be able to repay. Very little of the money was in fact spent on backing horses – your accusations were unjust. If he had not died so suddenly, everything would have been well.

The rooms I have taken are extremely squalid, and so I cannot wish you to visit me. I hope soon to be able to find somewhere better.

Bridget is a tower of strength, and Alice seems to be thriving in spite of all these trials.

You say, Mamma, that it would be natural and right for us to live together, as we are both widows and have lost Violet – "who was such a comfort to us" – as well as our husbands. That is an argument I would have accepted without question five years ago, but not now. I must learn to be independent (New Woman) and I shall do so. Please, do not criticise me for this.

Perhaps, if you could accept that I shall never be a "lady" again, that Bridget is more my friend than my

*servant and that I intend to bring Alice up to be
something very different from the "innocent" young
girl of our times – perhaps then we could make a home
together, even make new and mutual friends. But I
don't think you could ever do any of these things, and
perhaps I could not either.*

*When I am better settled, I shall come and see you.
But until then I don't intend to see any of the family,
not even you – I don't want to explain all my reasons,
I cannot do so.*

*Well, on to horrid business. Violet sent me her
quarter's allowance before she died, and poor old
Roderick found me out at Mornington Terrace and
kindly forced me to accept twenty pounds from him.
But I still need money. I was of course very sorry to
hear that owing to the last Liberal budget you are in
straitened circumstances, but I would be extremely
grateful for anything you could send me, including old
clothes. But I cannot pay you back yet, in kind, by
coming to see you and, if you'll forgive me for saying
so, allowing you to examine me. I don't belong to you
or to anyone, any longer – neither, I suppose, do you.*

*This has been an extremely difficult letter to write –
rather a melodramatic essay, is it not? I wonder
whether its frankness will turn your thoughts away
from charity towards me. But I still remain your
loving daughter,*
Diana Molloy.

Lady Blentham did have a pretty good idea of the
conditions in which Diana must be living, though she thrust
the thought of rats and leaking roofs out of her mind. Her
mental picture alternated between a vision of some bank-
clerk's dark cottage with a cornice and rosette in a twelve-
foot-square ceiling, and the famous painting of Chatterton on
his garret windowsill. Curiously, the poet's garret was less
repulsive to her than the bank-clerk's house: even though she
had disliked the few poems of Diana's she had read. She

considered that no woman could ever be the equal of Tennyson, Arnold or Wordsworth. Angelina did admire the works of Christina Rosetti, and nearly all poetry, except Diana's, was a comfort to her now. She filled in two hours of her day by reading it, the two hours she would have spent in driving out if she had kept a carriage.

I never realised that I had so few friends, thought Lady Blentham. And yet I am not a cold, unpleasant woman – I am not. I was merely ambitious, but always for others, not for myself! Do I deserve this, do I?

She decided to send Diana seventy guineas, enough to be a sacrifice.

On a cold day in January, Diana returned from visiting half the fashionable milliners in the West End. She had asked for a job in each one. Every modiste had seen firstly that to be served by a woman of her class would embarrass the customers, and secondly that she was too poor to buy a straight-fronted corset and a black stuff dress for working in.

In one establishment, a lady in furs had suddenly cried out: 'Diana! My dear – where *have* you been?'

'Hello, Millicent,' said Diana.

The modiste's mouth was pruriently open.

'Doesn't it seem an age since we came out?' said Countess Vladiska, staring. She had been a pudgy freckled heiress in 1892, and was now a less rich *jolie-laide*, notorious in her circle since her first divorce.

'Yes,' said Diana. 'Could you use your influence with Madama Lis to get me a job here?'

'A job? My influence? But my dear, why?'

'Come, come, Millicent,' said Diana clearly. At that, she looked at both women's faces, and left the shop.

Millicent Vladiska told a garbled version of Diana's story to another customer, who had not recognised the underfed beauty in a worn-out ulster and pork-pie hat.

When she arrived back at Museum Street, Diana curled up on her bed. It was exceedingly cold, and grey snow was falling, and the cheerful noise being made by Bridget and

Alice beyond the wall did not help to warm her. She shut her eyes and stopped her ears, as she thought that she had no right to inflict unnecessary suffering either on herself or on Alice. If she could not make a hundred pounds honestly within a month, she would go to Lady Blentham. One day soon, Millicent Vladiska's story of how she had tried to find work in a fashionable milliner's would reach her mother's ears. Unless she acted quickly, the embarrassment caused to the Blentham family would never be forgiven her. She realised now that she cared very much for being a Blentham, and for their forgiveness.

Diana had tried to be independent for eight months, partly out of love for Michael's memory, and partly out of hatred for him. She did hate him, for sheltering her from the reality of their position and then abandoning her to discover the worst of it for herself. He had left her to choose between life as a poor relation and earning her own living. He would have liked her to earn her own living when he was not by, that she knew. She must carry on trying. Diana cried a little, than got up and went down to the kitchen to join Bridget and Alice. The place smelt of mice and burnt onions.

She told the dull story of her day, and was halfway through it when there was a knock on the battered street-door.

'It's a dun,' she said, and then after a second's quiet screamed out loud: 'Oh, my God, no, not tonight! Not tonight!' It was weeks since she had lost control of herself. 'There's no coal – and practically nothing to eat – oh, God, have mercy – '

'I'll be seeing just who it is, mam, and I'll see him off,' said Bridget. 'Do you calm yourself!' She went clattering down the stairs.

Diana tried to comfort Alice, who had toddled over towards her mother and was roaring with sympathy into her lap. Diana prayed in Alice's ear, softly and repetitively, that Bridget would be successful in turning away the dun. The sound of her voice quieted the child.

At length, Bridget came back, with a strange look on her face.

'So?' said Diana. 'You were a very long time.'

''Tis not dun, mam,' she said, taking out a card from her pocket. ''Tis a gentleman, calls himself Major Julian Fitzclare. Gave me his visiting-card he did, and said he wanted to see you for old times' sake, for I'm afraid – '

'*Julian Fitzclare?* Are you sure?'

'Well, I'm afraid I said you was at home to visitors.' She wiped the card on her apron, and gave it to Diana, who read the words. Bridget was illiterate.

Alice took the card from her mother's slackened grip and put it in her mouth. 'So who is he, mam?' said Bridget at the door. 'He's downstairs still, but I'll be seeing him off if that's what you wish.'

'I was engaged to him once,' said Diana slowly. 'Show him up. I'll touch him for a loan – he's rather rich, you know. Even though I did – did *jilt* him, and it will look rather bad. But why has he found me out? Oh, dear, don't look so astonished, it was years ago, and he married some Scotch girl or other only two months afterwards, so we weren't precisely deeply in love. I don't have any scruples left.' Diana did not mean any of this, but she was nervous. 'Alice, darling, that paper will be bad for your digestion. Give it to Mamma.'

They went to dine, through Julian's horrified kindness, at a steamy old-fashioned chop-house in High Holborn. He would have taken Diana to Romano's but that, as she told him, she had nothing to wear. Her frowsty rooms had seemed an extraordinary setting even to Diana, at the moment he came through the door; and because of this, their first conversation in five years had been extremely uninhibited. Julian had exclaimed with rough shock and pity, Diana had said all was just as he saw it, and he had insisted on taking her out after being introduced to Bridget and Alice.

Now, in the chop-house, formalities began. They remembered properly that they had once been engaged, and that Diana had behaved badly. As they exchanged questions, Julian noticed that Diana drank a good deal of the burgundy. He had had a bottle before going to Museum Street.

170

'How is your wife?' said Diana.

'C-Catriona is well, thank you.'' He had not lost his stammer, though Diana had expected him to do so with age.

'Is your father still alive?'

'Yes, c-certainly. And M-mother.'

'I always liked your mother.'

'Did you?'

'Where are you living now?'

'W-we've got a little p-place in Shropshire, I bought it myself, it's not a f-family place. I thought p-perhaps you knew.'

'No, I left the world some time ago . . . oh, dear, that sounds rather bitter, and I'm not.' Only in debt and hungry, thought Diana. 'Congratulations on your becoming a Major,' she smiled.

'N-not necessary to c-congratulate me, I've r-resigned my commission. Of c-course if there were to be a war, I'd g-go back if I c-could. We've also g-got a house in London – Chester Square,' he told her.

'How delightful. How many children do you have, Julian?'

'Three s-so far.'

'I see. What are their names?'

'M-mabel, C-charlotte and Agatha, Diana.'

Diana thought what ugly names they were. 'I'm sure they're all very pretty. No heir yet? Catriona was charming, as I remember.'

'Y-yes, she is.'

'Julian, why did you want to see me? How did you find me, in any case?'

'H-heard you were in difficulties – London version of the b-bush telegraph, you know. And actually – I g-got an inquiry agent to discover where you w-were l-living.'

'What? The sort of Private Inquiry man who provides evidence for the Divorce Courts?'

'He d-doesn't do divorce w-work,' said Julian, looking very military. 'It's against his p-principles.' He smiled. 'All q-quite above board!'

Diana laughed. 'But why?'

171

'L-lady Blentham wouldn't g-give me your direction. In f-fact, she thought it w-wasn't a good idea for m-me to see you. Nor would Edward. H-however, I wanted very much to s-see you – and s-see if there w-was anything I c-could do for you.'

'They don't know my direction. I didn't give it to them, on purpose. I wonder why they did not confide in you?' Diana paused, and they looked at each other. 'Julian, the thing is, I'm in the devil of a hole. Could you lend me a thousand pounds or so, do you think?' She felt very bold and bad saying this, though she knew it sounded most unpractised.

Diana looked down at the table, and Julian shouted: 'Waiter!' She thought of the face at which she was not looking, and drank up her burgundy, which was not so good as Michael's. She was reminded of Michael's wine-merchant, one of her most unpleasant creditors.

Julian still looked a subaltern, though he must be over thirty. His whitey-blond eyebrows and his hair were both as thick as ever, and the only change in him was a redder complexion and a harder look in his eyes. Once or twice he had gazed at her sentimentally, and so Diana put the slight hardness of his expression down to the influence of his wife: Catriona Graham had been her name, Graham like the doctor who had attended Michael.

Diana had aged greatly, thought Julian, but he knew that was the effect of insufficient food, worry, and the lack of a protector. Her eyes, hair, mouth and nose were as striking as ever. Her complexion had barely suffered, but he guessed that a few more years' poverty would produce red veins and crow's feet, and stiff lines running from her nostrils to her mouth. The thought produced first nasty satisfaction, then pity and almost love. He was unhappy with his wife, but was far too polite and intelligent to say so.

'I hope,' he said, 'I hope you were h-happy with your h-husband.'

'My Fierce Fenian,' said Diana with her elbows on the table. She dropped her eyes then.

Julian paused. 'To h-how much do your d-debts amount?' he said, in a voice suitable for addressing a junior officer.

'Roughly – five hundred in all. I asked you for a thousand because – well, in short, I'm desperate for a tiny bit of temporary capital. And you are very rich.'

'I'll lend you a thousand. No interest, of course.'

'That is – impossibly kind of you, Julian. Thank you.' Diana had never expected him to lend her so much: she remembered her bravado in asking for it with amused shame.

'N-nonsense! W-we must forget that b-boy and girl nonsense – at l-least, it ought to be a b-bond of some kind between us. D-don't you rather agree, D-diana?'

'Oh, I do,' said Diana. 'I do. And don't distress yourself – I *shall* be able to repay you one day.'

Julian unbuttoned his top-coat, which he was obliged to wear because the chop-house was so draughty, and pulled out his wallet. Diana watched the snowflakes melt on the mirror-like dark window-panes to her right. He handed her five Treasury notes and said: 'Now l-look, that's b-beside the thousand. I want you to b-buy just one pretty dress.'

Diana looked up. 'So that you can take me to Romano's?'

'Exactly.'

'Julian, I won't be *seduced* by you.' She blushed, and tried to stop a smile.

'*What!* Good G-god, Diana, l-life with that man has – you're my oldest friend – my very oldest woman friend! Although you've changed, you're b-bound to have ch-changed . . . Of c-course, you always were u-unusual, that was w-why – '

'How odd it seems. Just imagine,' she said, sitting well back with her glass of burgundy, as she had often done when dining with Michael. 'I could have married you, and then we two, just we two, would have been living in your little place in Shropshire. You have riches and security and position, have you not, Julian?' He did not look too embarrassed, he knew her. Diana continued: 'Paying long visits to Ballynore, perhaps that would not have been so agreeable. And in the – in due season, perhaps we'd have gone to – oh, Trouville and Deauville, Baden-Baden, Monte Carlo. No, I was right to say no. I was right.'

Diana's eye prickled with a tear. The reckless but unhappy bravado she had shown tonight frightened her more than it did Julian. She knew where all this must lead, and of course it was very wrong: but she was too proud to leave a course once chosen, and Diana felt now that she had tacitly chosen to be Julian's mistress when she had made her disgraceful, wonderful marriage.

CHAPTER 14

JULIAN

'No w-woman *like* you,' said Julian, as he patted Diana's shoulder and tried to disarrange her shift. 'We ought to have married.'

Diana was shocked by what she had done – and had enjoyed, even though her new lover was not Michael. I've taken a lover, she thought.

It was not that Diana, after three years of life among people who cared little for propriety, believed it sinful for two people to make love if they were not married. But she thought adultery wrong, the use of prostitutes unforgiveable, and careless lovemaking a sordid business. She wondered whether things would have been better or worse if the man had been someone other than Julian. She could not decide. He was a good man.

'Yes, it's a g-great p-pity you threw m-me over,' said Julian.

She leant back into the pillow. 'Do you really think we should have been happy?' As he advanced, Diana pushed him gently away, because she was really very comfortable as she was.

'We *are* g-going to be happy.'

'This is nothing,' said Diana, listening to her words, and watching him. 'It won't be repeated.'

Julian, who had been pressing against her, withdrew to the far side of the bed. 'S-suppose you – er – have a b-baby, D-diana, as a r-result of our b-bit of – of this?' He saw her eyes open like a child's. 'You're not to worry! I m-meant only that I will t-take care of you.'

'Oh!' said Diana. She did not move towards him for protection as he had hoped.

'H-human beings have s-such a n-need for each other,' said Julian a moment later, and Diana watched the pair of brown moles below his left nipple move nervously up and down. When he saw her looking, he covered them up with his shirt. '*I* d-don't regret this. I'll m-make sure you d-don't either. I'll l-look after you – you r-really must let me l-look after you.' His face was grim.

'No,' said Diana. 'I want a little time to think, before . . . You're doing quite enough for me in lending me a thousand pounds – and though of course it was rather a shock, this, now, was very *much* what I needed!' she continued rather breathlessly: 'One does so miss – a mere *man*. Do I shock you rather?' Diana adjusted the pillows.

Julian said calmly: 'I k-knew you were p-passionate, Diana, as w-well as c-clever – and I l-liked you for it, I l-loved it in you. I d-didn't think it what some – elderly l-ladies would c-call immodest, or s-something.'

'Oh, Julian, I'm not a *lady*,' said Diana.

'I shall s-see to it that you are – and that you l-live l-like one.'

He closed his eyes. His sudden thrust of good fortune in capturing Diana without even fully intending to do so had given Julian a headache. The noble beauty who had rejected him, he thought, would be his kept mistress, but he would be very kind to her, and there was, he believed, no malice in him. He did love her. The keeping of her would be so very discreet that he hoped Diana herself would not put the unkindest interpretation on their love-affair until it was absolutely necessary.

'Well, this will have to be love free from ties,' said Diana, making him jump. 'You could not marry me, could you, even if Catriona didn't exist. Just think of the talk there would be in the Cavalry Club!' She looked out of the bed at the typing machine, at the orange-boxes, the deal wardrobe and the chamber pot. She was trying to concentrate on reality, but she was unable to see the nasty objects properly.

Julian smiled. 'One doesn't t-talk m-much, you know, in the C-cavalry Club.'

Diana was thankful to see that he had a little sense of humour, and a certain adroit intelligence which enabled him to avoid painful subjects. Before they made love again, she told him calmly to withdraw from her person at the suitable moment. Diana would have liked one more baby if Michael had lived.

'Too s-sudden!' Julian whispered. 'Isn't it?'

'Yes.'

Diana had imagined that Julian, who could not be expected to bear the squalor of Museum Street, would give her odd presents of money. These, she had supposed, would be enough to allow her to rent a reasonably comfortable lodging and employ a maid-of-all-work while she looked about for a job. She had not expected Julian himself to pay the rent of a charming house in Hampstead, and the wages of two servants, or to make her an allowance of forty pounds a month. But she understood, and acquiesced in his arrangements, and tried not to feel she was robbing him, for debt and poverty had been very terrible. It was illogical, thought Diana, but the less likely the prospect of more poverty became, the more frightful it appeared to her. And yet she still had doubts about her present life, though it was so agreeable, and moderately moral.

Julian said one day after luncheon: 'Dearest, if w-we were m-married, you w-would hardly object to m-my s-supporting you. Where is the d-difference?'

'Well, we are not married. And although we are very fond of each other – I don't like being a kept woman. Even by you, even – temporarily. But unfortunately I have little choice.'

'That's a v-very v-vulgar expression, and I d-don't like you to use it.'

'I am glad we are not married,' said Diana. 'We shouldn't have suited, Julian.' She meant: if you love me, why don't you leave your wife? Diana did not seriously want him to do this, but she wished him to make the suggestion.

177

'As you l-like,' he said, and looked at his watch and told her he must be going.

'So I've hurt your feelings,' said Diana.

He kissed her lightly, and said goodbye. At the doorway, he turned back and looked at her, sighed and wished that this could last. Diana looked very lovely now that she was at ease, well fed and well, if unusually, dressed. She wore her hair down like a girl's, tied in the nape of her neck with a large black bow, and her crimson dress was plain, but not severe. The cream walls and bright window behind her made a flattering background.

'Diana,' he said, 'I rather w-wish you l-loved me as I l-love you, b-because I do s-still love you. Do you r-remember the p-poems I used to c-copy for you, w-when we were young?' His tone of voice was most unsentimental as he put his hand on the door.

Diana looked away and said: 'Julian, wait one moment!'

He turned back a second time.

'Tell me,' said Diana, 'how secret are you keeping me? Have you told anyone about our arrangement? Anyone at all?' She lifted her eyebrows.

There was a slight pause. 'G-good God! I've only t-told old M-monty, and he won't g-gossip, Diana. Why are you s-so – suspicious, dash it? B-besides . . .' said Julian.

'Besides what?'

'I'm not ashamed of y-you.'

Diana laughed. 'Oh, go away, darling!' It occurred to her that women in the best circles had been forgiven before now for having financially advantageous love-affairs, and she tried to comfort herself.

Soon after Julian was gone, Alice came staggering into the room. She was now a square-faced, black-browed child of eighteen months, with thick dust-coloured hair and pretty hands. Diana dressed her in simple loose frocks, and did not make her wear complicated underclothes, or unnecessary boots and hats and gloves.

'Unca Julia bring present?' she asked, planting her feet well apart on the carpet.

'A present for Mamma, but not for you, I fear,' said Diana.
'Not for Alick? Mamma?'

'I need presents,' said Diana. 'In fact, I almost live on presents, Alice. He brought me a little ruby ring. Look.'

'Roobyring.'

'Look.' Diana pointed, and the child came forward.

'Sparka,' said Alice, putting her dirty fingers on the little table where a cheap but well-set ruby lay, uncovered, beside its box. 'Not much use, ask me.'

Her mother put an arm round her. 'Oh, darling, darling, where did you learn that!' She sent Alice back to Bridget.

Diana put the ring on to go for a walk on Hampstead Heath. When she found a quiet bench, she took off her glove, looked at it, and wished she truly loved Julian. She had an idea that if she were only able to love him, her life both now and in the future would be enormously changed. Julian very much wanted to be loved: in that one way he was like Michael, and unlike other men. Diana dreaded the future.

He was not a bore, he was generous, he had a fine body, and he did not dismiss her writing as rubbish. But I can't love him, thought Diana. After all, he does not love me. She could not even respond fully when he touched her, though she liked having him in bed with her, and tried hard to please him by making the noises she had made with her husband.

She looked down at the celandines near her feet, and up at the promising March sun, and thought how pleasant life could be. It was only when she thought of how many years and years of life she no doubt had ahead of her, that Diana became depressed.

Secrecy, she thought, and wondered whether she wanted it. Diana was lonely, but she refused to go with Julian to fashionable places where he said she might meet people. The idea of meeting a well-dressed crowd of people of all kinds, which might even include her relations, frightened her and she did not know why. She supposed she wanted others to come to her, and yet she did not like the idea of Julian bringing his friends. The only man who did come to visit her in Flask Walk was Julian's brother-in-law, Arthur Cornwallis.

Diana was angry with Julian for pretending that Arthur did not know they were lovers, for saying that 'only Monty' had been told. Cornwallis was far more charming to her now than he had been when she was a girl, or a wife. He was, she thought, probably the only more or less charming person amongst Julian's friends. Diana imagined these friends to be a set of hard-drinking, hard-whoring cavalry officers, though Julian was so kind and polite and knew many people who were not in the army. Her lover said he knew no women to whom he could introduce her, and he added that it was an awful pity Diana had not kept up with friends of her girlhood. He had admitted, without her prompting, that that was a foolish and hurtful remark.

But he has made me an inferior, thought Diana, getting up from her bench and walking slowly down the path. She twiddled her thumbs inside her fur muff. 'It can't be helped,' she whispered to a clump of dead willowherb. Perhaps other people will not quite see the truth, and I'm happy enough, after all.

In the fullness of spring, Diana began to feel strongly that she wanted her mother. For the past few months she had written cautious and short, though very affectionate, letters to Angelina, but these were now not enough.

Lady Blentham was so pleased to see Diana that she cried a little and spoke sternly as soon as her maid was out of earshot.

'You should not have stayed away so long, my dear. I was very much hurt by your thinking that I should – despise you for your poverty. Was that it?'

'I'm sorry, Mamma.' Diana sat down.

She looked about her at the little drawing-room, full of those solid pieces of Adelaide furniture which she remembered in their old setting at Queen Anne's Gate. Lady Blentham was seated in a black papier-mâché armchair inlaid with mother-of-pearl, which Diana had once called 'fit for a queen'. She looked old, sweet-natured, tough. The skin above her lips had tightened across her teeth while that beneath her chin had gently collapsed. Her clothes had barely changed since the early eighties, and her back was as erect as ever. She considered modern fashions unbecoming to most women, and rather vulgar: the straight-fronted corset Diana was wearing so thrust out her bosom and behind. The silver top of Angelina's stick emphasised the beauty of her heavy-veined but pale and slender hand.

While thinking to herself, 'how very extraordinary, painful life is – I don't know that I can bear this,' Angelina said: 'My dear, I wasn't able to write to you, although I've been about to do so now that I have your own address in – in Hampstead, is it? But did you see the notice of Roderick's engagement in *The Times* yesterday?'

'Roderick's engaged?' said Diana. 'Heavens, I thought he was a confirmed bachelor!'

'A Miss Cicely Vane, her father is in the Indian Army,' said Lady Blentham carefully. 'A Major, I think, or a Lieutenant-Colonel. Not related to any of the Vanes we know. I've met her only once, when Roderick brought her here.'

'Is she pretty?'

'She's timid, and very fair,' said Angelina. 'She should do very well as a clergyman's wife.'

'Has Roderick succeeded in becoming a Canon yet?'

'No,' sighed Lady Blentham. 'But he was appointed Rural Dean the other day. I don't think, myself, he will advance much further in the Church. It was so different when I was young: corrupt, of course, though very much better than in my grandfather's day!' Lady Blentham's grandfather had been the Bishop of Launceston.

They smiled sadly at each other, agreeing silently about Roderick's irritable temper, love of comfort, occasional bursts of charity, and the horrible time his wife would have.

'Poor Roddy,' said Diana, breaking the quiet. 'I suppose he grew quite tired of being pursued by all the widows and spinsters of Melton Balbridge.'

'I daresay,' said Angelina.

'Tell me about Edward and Kitty,' prompted Diana.

'Oh, Kitty – ' Lady Blentham pronounced the word carefully – 'Kitty has become quite a *grande dame*. The

181

moment your father died, Diana, she decided to hide every last trace of Whitechapel and the stage. You remember she used to speak in a decidedly vulgar way? Well, it seems that that was all *side*. Remarkable, isn't it? Edward is entirely under her influence, of course. That's quite unchanged.'

'Does she carry a lorgnette?' said Diana. She was not surprised to learn that Kitty had made a thorough job of copying Angelina. She had five children now, just like her mother-in-law.

'Yes, she does. She carries it a good deal more than is necessary.'

'And I suppose she no longer gives her – ridiculous imitations at dinner-parties? Of course, May Yohé's passée now, but I do so well remember Kitty getting up on a chair at the Cornwallises', and howling out something from – from "Little Christopher Columbus"!'

'Diana, you horrify me,' said Lady Blentham, and smiled, making her daughter's heart squeeze with eagerness. 'What I exposed you to as a girl, all through my desire to be modern!'

'Mamma.'

'It was so difficult to keep you entirely out of her way!' said Angelina, looking aside. 'Oh, how long ago it is – what were you then, nineteen, twenty? Now my dear, tell me. Is your new house perfectly comfortable? And how have you – well, you're very well-dressed, although I can't say I care for the ridiculous hats one is supposed to wear nowadays, or for – but you are not *too* fashionable! You always had taste. Perhaps now that your husband's debts are paid your income has increased? Has your stockbroker been able to make some good investments for you? You know, I myself have been fortunate, I'm able at last to keep a carriage – just a second-hand brougham, but I did so miss not having any carriage of my own.' She began again. 'Or perhaps – perhaps you have borrowed money from a bank, and set up a little business of some kind? You always were independent, and nowadays trade, even for a woman of – ' Lady Blentham lost herself. She did not want to think.

'I borrowed money from Julian Fitzclare, Mamma.'

Angelina's nose twitched. It had never twitched in that way before she was a widow. 'Did you seek him out?'

'He sought me out.' Her stomach was now churning inside her. She wanted to confess, and could not quite believe that her mother would entirely condemn her once the first shock was over, and she knew the whole.

'Well,' said Lady Blentham, 'when none of us succeeded in discovering you . . . I wonder how he did so. Diana?'

You did not try, thought Diana; you didn't send for a detective. Her mother looked away from Diana's face, down at the handle of her walking stick.

'My dear. You've been so much out of the world that it's necessary for me to tell you certain things. You see, although Fitzclare was a very charming young man once, since his marriage his character has not improved. Of course he married Catriona Graham from pique, but we needn't go into that. He neglects her, I'm afraid and – oh, you can very well guess the rest. I heard from his mother that he's very fond of gambling, as your husband was, of course.'

Diana, blushing, looked just like a debutante. 'I'm afraid – I ought to tell you – he neglects her for me. I wanted to tell you myself because one day I suppose you'd hear an exaggerated rumour . . . perhaps it's rather a pity I jilted him all those years ago but I can't say I regret it myself! I prefer this, now. I don't want any man to live with me constantly, after Michael. I'm sure you'll understand!' She stopped herself at last, and gradually raised herself in her chair, in an effort to regain the years from twelve to thirty.

'Of course,' said Lady Blentham in the end. 'Of course, Diana. You're what the young men when I was a girl used to call a pretty horsebreaker. Fitzclare provides you with your clothes and your house? And servants?'

'Yes,' said Diana, wide-eyed. This understanding was not what she had expected from her mother. She had never heard the euphemism 'pretty horsebreaker' before.

'So,' said Angelina. 'No, don't speak!' Quietly she held up her hand as Diana opened her mouth. 'For the time being, Julian Fitzclare is keeping you. Why?'

'We are in love, and I was very poor. I fell, as they used to say in those awful novels Violet was so fond of!'

'Don't tell me lies, they're insolent,' said Lady Blentham. The mention of Violet made her stand up, as Diana had been expecting her to do for the past five minutes. 'You were *in love*, once, I suppose, with that repulsive husband of yours. You never were in love with Fitzclare, and you certainly are not now. I can see it in your face.' Angelina turned, and Diana turned away. 'You could have provided amply for yourself and Alice by coming to me. You could even have gone to Edward and his wife, if that is what you would have preferred! But no, no,' her mother went on. 'How many people know of this, Diana? Gossip, of course, takes a long time to reach me nowadays. Do you suppose Fitzclare is discreet, that he doesn't want to set men laughing in the clubs over how he – he robbed you of all your *dignity*, after you made him ridiculous? Think about it, Diana.' Lady Blentham swallowed.

Diana said nothing. Angelina pressed her hands to her cheeks. 'Within marriage, of course, it is unavoidable,' she said, half to herself. 'And poor wretched girls, who are seduced in all *innocence*, cannot be blamed. Oh, some of them are knowing, but no servant of mine ever was. I got two maids married suitably, Diana, when they were *ruined* by men, and I sent Templeton home to her mother to have the child, and I gave her an excellent reference – wilful unchastity is the most unnatural sin in the world in a woman, but I never, never turned off an innocent servant who was in that condition, and left her to fend for herself and become a – a *soiled dove*, as they like to call it!'

Diana, who was very pale, gathered up her gloves and reticule and placed them on her lap. 'Mamma – are you objecting, chiefly, to the thought that I might – enjoy the act of love?'

'No woman *can*!' Lady Blentham almost shouted. She lowered her voice at once. 'Do you realise, Diana, that it is almost treachery of a kind, to our sex, to encourage a man to think his attentions are anything but disgusting? Oh, God, I remember having almost this conversation with Violet, when she was a girl.' She closed her eyes because she was shaking, though her voice was so quiet. 'You're not in love, you're merely a mercenary, common little whore!'

Angelina sat down again, and vowed privately never, ever to express herself again. To express oneself was to be wicked.

'Very well,' said Diana, before her mother could speak, 'I am being kept by Julian Fitzclare because I need a comfortable income.' She swung one foot determinedly back and forth. 'I don't drive in the park in a ridiculously trigged-out victoria with – with half a pound of paint on my face.' Tears were spoiling the little bit of rouge she had put on that morning.

'No, no, that will come later, will it not? And when it does, I beg you to disgrace us in Paris and not in London. And I'd be grateful if you did not become the Prince of Wales's mistress, I gather that's not so well-rewarded a post as it should be!'

'Mamma!' Diana was shocked, but Lady Blentham took no notice. She wrestled with the arms of her chair.

'To make a proper use of men for one's necessary purposes, discreetly and kindly of course, is one thing, is unavoidable – it's what one must *try* to do, within the limits of – of Christian marriage.'

'Mamma, please.'

'Do you know I could have married you to some man in need of good connections, some weak man,' said Angelina, 'if you had not done this? Don't you see? By this time, most people have forgotten the – the talk there was about Molloy, and he's dead, you could have married again!'

'Mother, I've no intention whatever of becoming anything more – anything but what I am!' Diana shouted.

They both took deep breaths.

'I don't want to see you,' said Angelina, backing her chair towards the grate. 'I don't understand, and I don't wish to see you . . . That man debauched you. I am extremely sorry for you.' She looked away, and seemed very old to her exhausted daughter.

'Which man are you talking about?'
'Please go.'
'*Which man?*'
'*It doesn't matter!*'
'I thought you'd understand,' said Diana on her feet. 'I truly thought you would – what a fool I was, wanting you. I'd forgotten. Well, we'll leave it at that: I am a *mercenary, common little whore*, and you can disown me if you like.'

'I shan't, I can't forgive you,' said Angelina, looking straight across the room with both hands in her lap. 'Naturally – I can't acknowledge you in public, or receive you, or call at your house, but I shan't *disown* you, whatever your faults, and I wonder at your thinking me capable of such melodramatic and – and unsuitable behaviour.'

Diana left the room quietly, and then ran. She nearly forgot to collect Alice, who had been given into the care of Angelina's maid after a brief re-introduction to her grandmother and the promise of tea with her later. Alice screamed at being carried away, but in fact it was her mother's icy face which upset her so much.

Lady Blentham sat without moving, and did not see the two of them hurrying down towards the Old Brompton Road and South Kensington station. The tears dribbled down her too-soft face as she supposed she need not be entirely cut off from the poor sinful dirty girl. Diana could come to the house veiled in a hackney when her mother was alone.

Poor thing, poor thing, thought Angelina, and tried to transfer all her rage from Diana to the man who had seduced her. I'm still in a state of shock, of course, she thought.

She had no difficulty in feeling charitably towards ordinary fallen women, the victims of men's coarseness and men's laws; laws which also supported Christian marriage, the one frail, disagreeable protection of women against universal rape. But if it had not been for the fact that the thing was done through sex, which she wondered at God for inventing, Angelina would have felt envy and admiration for the grand horizontals who ruined men and pulled off their masks of reason and authority.

Angelina remembered Cora Pearl and Catherine Walters, who had been the great whores of the sixties when she was young Mrs Blentham, and she knew that Diana would be just like them. The thought gave her a heart-attack, a minor one from which she soon recovered.

CHAPTER 15

A HALF-GROWN HARLOT

In the autumn of that year, the breaking out of war in South Africa coincided with Catriona Fitzclare's learning that her husband's mistress was his one-time betrothed, who had been such a scandalous beauty; and with Diana's first introduction to Mr Archibald Trefusis at the Empire Promenade.

Julian was walking with his arm round Diana's waist and as they talked together in low voices they acknowledged no greetings from people they knew. It was several months now since they had started to go out together, sometimes quietly, sometimes to raucous and brilliant places where Diana would never fit in. All discretion was at an end. Diana was trying to amuse herself and become like a real whore, because Lady Blentham had told her that was what she was.

She still felt much as she had done in the early secret days; for her cautious re-entrance into a kind of society had offered her remarkably little. It was curiously as though she were back in the schoolroom: wearing her hair down, trying to read seriously, fighting inexperience and isolation, and experimenting with sensual thoughts.

'You d-don't seem to understand that y-you're *d-different* f-from the others, t-to Catriona as w-well as to me! What with her and – ' Julian stopped.

'Yes, I know – you must give me up, and rejoin your regiment, and go and be killed out in the Transvaal – and preferably get a posthumous VC,' Diana interrupted. They had both been drinking a good deal of champagne.

'I should p-prefer to l-live to enjoy m-my VC.' Julian lifted his head, for Diana's 'give me up' had angered him.

'Your wife's outrage, my wickedness, and a nice little skirmish on the frontier providing a chance of escape for you from both of us,' said Diana. 'So very commonplace a story, don't you rather think?'

'I s-should have thought,' said Julian, 'that it was r-rather like the p-plot of a d-daring novel with p-pious overtones. It j-just happens I'm n-not religious, but it w-would be r-rather r-romantic if I were k-killed, eh?' He squeezed her waist, but this did not move her.

'As I said, commonplace. But you don't want to be killed?'

'I've got p-plenty to live for,' said Julian, looking across the room and starting slightly at the sight of his father's old acquaintance, the retired millionaire banker, Archibald Trefusis.

'Well, it's certainly not *romantic* to pass your mistress on to another man in cold blood.' Yesterday, Julian had angrily suggested that Diana accept the advances recently made to her by a friend of his called Charles Windlesham. 'A kindness in some circumstances, but romantic, no,' said Diana.

'D-damn you,' said Julian, releasing her and digging in his coat pocket for cigarettes. Diana took one from the gold case without asking him. 'D'you think I w-want you to be k-kept by another m-man?' His voice was quite loud.

'I think you rather do. Oh – I ruined myself, you didn't ruin me. Don't say, once more, that I'm accusing you.'

'Why d-don't you *enjoy* life!'

There was a long pause, full of other people's noise. They searched each other's face.

Diana and Julian had found it impossible ever since the start of their affair to forget what might have been. Memories had sometimes pulled them together, and made both think in their loneliness and wisdom that they were in love at last. More often, the past made the present intolerable. They were more at one now than they had been nine months ago, for both said privately: 'I would be able to love him, her, *now*, if it had not been for all that.' They were equals, bound together in irritation, and it was really quite unlikely that they would part in fact.

'Not much to enjoy, except reading, and writing,' said Diana. 'I used to enjoy making love, of course.'

'L-listen, D-diana, Charlie's a good f-fellow, and in any c-case, I didn't introduce h-him to you w-with any idea that he would try to g-get you for himself. I was d-disgusted, I m-must say, when you t-told me that! You women are the d-devil,' he added: 'never b-believe anything a m-man says!'

'Oh, dear.'

Mr Trefusis was making his way towards them. Julian took hold of Diana's arm and whispered: 'Now b-behave yourself. It's Trefusis – I told you about him. Knows my f-father – I told you how m-much influence and m-money he has. Got his eye on you, I c-can s-see!'

'Why do *we* need a person with influence and money, Julian?'

He ignored this.

'My f-father's always at B-ballynore now, h-he d-doesn't know about you b-because no one w-would d-dare t-tell him!'

'And this man would, would he?'

Diana saw an old man of sixty or so, who in spite of his white hair and stiff beard looked a little like the dead Prince Consort. His eyes were large and slightly bulbous, and his forehead was rounded like a billiard-ball. He had a straight nose, stern nostrils and full lips, and his skin was slightly mottled, wrinkled heavily only round the eyes. Diana guessed that his beard concealed dewlaps.

'Hullo, sir,' said Julian clearly. 'B-been to Ballynore lately, b-bought any more w-winners from us?'

You're not behaving, thought Diana, quite pleased.

'Julian,' the old man said, in a slightly foreign accent which surprised Diana. Mr Trefusis had had a French mother, and he spent a good deal of time in France. 'How are you, my boy?' A close look at Diana made his lips continue to move when he had finished speaking.

Diana, with her hair so simply brushed back and tied, was the most beautiful woman he had seen since he made the acquaintance of the quiet friend of the King of the Belgians, the celebrated Cléo de Mérode.

'Is life going splendidly?' he said to Julian.

'As you s-say, sir,' said Julian, smiling a little, 'S-splendidly, h-how could it b-be otherwise?'

'May I have an introduction to this lady?' Mr Trefusis knew who she was.

'Mrs Molloy,' said Diana. Both men looked a little taken aback at her speaking so plainly.

'This is Mr T-trefusis, D-diana.'

'Yes, you were saying so.'

There was a short pause.

'May I tell you, Mrs Molloy, what a very, very beautiful woman you are? Julian, you'll allow such an old friend of the family as myself to call on Mrs Molloy?'

'I can s-see no p-particular h-harm in that, sir,' said Julian solemnly. 'Mrs Molloy will – '

'But I might not like it,' said Diana, who could not be truly repelled by a man who was frank, like Michael, about other people's exact positions in life.

'Oh,' said Mr Trefusis. He turned. 'You should take Mrs Molloy to Paris, Julian, there's nothing in London to compare. London is no fit setting for her! How can you bring a lady – so charming – to such a place as this – it's mere glitter, mere glitter – no gold!' He waved his gold-topped cane at the company, and wheezed. Diana pitied him and smiled at him. 'Worse, if possible, than Marlborough House,' he said.

'I prefer glitter,' said Diana, for no particular reason.

'I m-must t-take you h-home.'

Mr Trefusis raised his hat to Diana, winked at Julian and, as he walked away said: 'I believe the address is Flask Walk, in Hampstead? I can't remember who told me that. Allow me at least to leave my card!'

He took the arm of a jewelled young courtesan with a bare bosom and a great loaded hat.

'Intolerable,' said Diana. She was blushing with anger only because Mr Trefusis already knew where she could be found.

'V-vile old man,' said Julian. 'But h-he's s-so rich he's

almost n-never been s-snubbed as he d-deserves to be.
D-degeneracy of m-modern times and the P-prince's influence,
as my f-father says, old h-hypocrite.'

'Was his grandfather a tin miner, or something like that?'
said Diana with interest.

Julian laughed. 'Oh, n-no one knows, except he's n-not
C-cornish, *that's* c-certain. H-his name's adopted. J-jew, probably, or h-half J-jew!'

'Very vile,' said Diana.

Bridget O'Shea had taken a dislike to Julian, and to show her
dislike she annoyed Diana by wearing a brown nursemaid's
uniform and leaving the room when he entered it. Julian
approved of this, but she was only waiting for the next bout of
ill fortune to discard her servant's costume and resume her
place as a substitute for Violet Montrose.

Bridget had crude ideas about the discarding of unwanted
mistresses, and she told Diana several times that they would
all three find themselves on the street again one day. 'I shall
take care of that, Bridget,' said Diana. 'Besides, we were not
literally on the street before.'

'Oh, he still wants you for the present, mam.'

'Don't you like this house, is that it?'

'It's never been anyone's home, a furnished house like this,
modern as it may be with electric light and all. And,' she
added, 'I'd have supposed so rich a man would have been able
to give you a fine place, with a garden, and French furniture,
and a satin bed like a sea-shell, 'twould be fitting. He's mean,
mam, and I let him know it. Oh, he does hate me, sure!'

Diana tried to be amused by Bridget. She thought perhaps
the nurse disliked Julian because he was an Anglo-Irish
Protestant, part of the ruinous Ascendancy; she would
probably think Diana was betraying her dead Fenian husband
merely by being polite to him. Diana knew that Michael
himself would have found this present love-affair hard to
forgive on this score quite as much as on others, but she
enjoyed arguing with Julian about Home Rule. Once her pro-
Irish and pro-husband feelings had made him angry enough to

leave her alone for a week in the middle of the London Season. It made her laugh.

'Never trust a man,' said Bridget.

'No, Bridget.' Life was very simple: Michael himself had effectively deceived and deserted her, therefore every other man was far worse than he. Nowadays, Diana did not put the case to herself quite so directly as that. She could not afford to. 'But leave me alone for a little while now. I did come upstairs for a rest.'

'I've not brushed your hair yet.'

'I'll brush it myself. Really, Bridget!'

Bridget sniffed and left Diana, in bed, smiling at the thought of how Bridget would sincerely admire some gimcrack palace of a kept-woman's house and of course think herself immoral for doing so.

Perhaps Bridget was right: even if one were not going to be happy in it, one might as well extract the most gaudy and expensive lodging from a lover and then make fun of it. This simple house in Flask Walk was not hers forever, and so Diana could not love it. In fact it made her sad, because Julian had chosen it with such very great care and regard for her taste.

Diana was determined one day to have enough money to buy a house of her own, in Bloomsbury, not Hampstead, not Camden Town. Although Julian paid her living expenses, and had only recently begun to grumble at her spending, his outright presents were not generous. It had not once occurred to him to present her with the freehold of the house. He did not give Diana jewels worth more than a few pounds, and he believed that she would find presents of straight cash deeply insulting.

When Mr Trefusis had offered her money for nothing, Diana had turned away.

Julian rejoined his regiment in November 1899, but he had not yet been sent out to fight the Boers when the new century began. Catriona was quiescent that winter, and meanwhile both Julian and Mr Trefusis believed that the former's attachment to Diana was unbreakable, however difficult. She was just a second wife, barely a mistress at all.

Diana herself believed that, very soon now, her lover would put an end to everything. He had always been slow about such things, out of kindliness and indecision; except when he first took her to bed almost exactly a year ago. It seemed to her much longer than that.

On the second of January, Trefusis came to dine with Diana and Julian, to whom he had lent a large sum of money to pay his debts and buy a farm. Julian had not yet repaid it. Diana knew nothing at all about this.

'My dear Julian,' said Trefusis, as the four-wheeler dropped them both at the top of the street, 'don't trouble yourself, eh? It was a gentleman's loan – no interest payable, and to be prolonged at your convenience! You're the son of an old friend, if I may call him so, a very old friend.'

'Damn this mud, and the w-wind,' said Julian, not looking at Trefusis. 'I've a g-good mind to take D-diana away, j-just for a l-little while. N-no one in Italy at this t-time of y-year.'

'Oh, an excellent idea. All I ask, my boy, is that you persuade dear Diana to invite me to call on her more often . . . and don't worry, don't worry, she's yours! At my age, you know, one doesn't . . . And besides, a *most* unworldly woman, content with so little when she might have so much. Oh, I knew when I first set eyes on her, my dear boy, it would be hopeless for any man to tempt her away from you! *I'm* not a handsome young devil of an officer, *I've* only got a couple of millions to offer her. And what would that be to such a woman as Diana?'

'Did you offer it to h-her?'

'No, no. My dear boy, when I joked with her – did offer it to her, you know, as a jest – she said she'd rather have her subscription to the London Library – but she wouldn't let me pay it, oh, no. She's very droll, very droll.'

Julian laughed, took out his latchkey and threw open the door.

'Hello!' he shouted, scowling, for it was silent in the house. Diana was rereading a letter from her mother:

194

. . . I spoke too harshly to you then. "Justly but mercilessly," a clergyman would say, or so I suppose. Roderick, at least, made that remark. But it was never my intention to be entirely divided from you, Diana.

I ask you to abandon your present life and come with me to live abroad. We could not, of course, continue together in London, but living quietly at Pau we should attract no attention. Everything you have done I at least can forgive at last. You are my dear daughter. Would peace, obscurity and my companionship be so very disagreeable to you, after your hideous experience of the past year? I think not.

I make this offer in affection and pity, but if you reject it, and above all if you cease to live as discreetly as I must be grateful that you have done till now, I think we cannot even meet.

This letter had made Diana hysterically angry. She had received another letter today, from Kitty, who had written only because last week Edward had come to visit her examine her minutely in the course of a acid, fascinating little talk. Diana had showed herself to him as a bitter, passionate, elegant feminist, a believer in the right of both sexes to love as they pleased or at least to be equally censured.

But as you seem to have discovered, Kitty wrote, *it is useless to rebel against the way of the world. As a believer in Women's Rights, could you not have chosen a less old-fashioned profession? I don't, of course, mean to mock you or cause you more pain than you must be suffering already! What an odd girl you always were – to think that a girl so well bred as you should have ended up no better, than many a pretty girl from the East End. And all through your own deliberate choice! That is what old Lady Blentham and Edward and I find so hard to forgive.*

So, thought Diana, throwing this into the fire, dear Mamma

and Kitty are very friendly now. How her style of writing has improved! Quite the lady she is! The corner of Diana's mouth was twitching uncontrollably though she had never suffered from a tic before.

She heard Julian's voice in the hall and closed her eyes.

'D-diana! I say.'

Of course, she thought, he doesn't give one warning, he doesn't ring the bell, he lets himself in as though this were his own house. She remembered then that Trefusis was coming.

'I'm not yet dressed,' she called over the banisters, running up from the drawing-room to the second floor. 'I'm still changing!'

In her bedroom Diana quickly unbuttoned her skirt, and called for Bridget to help her put on an amber silk evening dress trimmed with a little Valenciennes. It had no sleeves, and a modest decolletage. Diana was determined never to put her bosom on open display.

At dinner they were waited on by Molly, the young housemaid, whose skirt brushed the shedding Christmas tree and made it jangle each time she came into the room. The food was good, and conversation not difficult, for Julian and Trefusis talked politely about the war. Then they all discussed the past Christmas, and moved on to the wonderful fact of its now being nineteen-hundred. Diana and Trefusis had a mathematical argument about whether the twentieth century proper had begun, or whether it would start on 1 January 1901.

'Don't leave us, don't leave us, Diana!' said Trefusis as Diana prepared to go upstairs after the fruit. 'Julian tells me you can drink a glass of port and smoke a cigar with the best.'

'Perfectly true,' said Diana, and sat down again. Julian and Trefusis both offered her a cigar. Life's going to change, she thought, it will change, it will.

Julian considered proposing that they all visit the theatre, then thoughtlessly suggested instead that they have a game of baccarat, or whist.

'But we've no fourth!' exclaimed Trefusis. 'I suggest a show. I believe Eleanora Duse is playing in something, somewhere. Oh, she's a great beauty, but not to compare with you, Diana! You agree, Julian?'

'Bridget can make a fourth,' said Diana.

'No,' said Julian.

'Yes, she plays quite well. Only whist, nothing else.'

'Diana . . .'

Holding her cigar, Diana ran upstairs to warn Bridget, who protested but agreed when Diana said she wanted and needed her, did not want to be alone with the men.

The men looked rather glum when she returned to them and suggested they all move up to the drawing-room. Bridget was there, setting out the card table, and so was Alice in her dressing-gown. Two of the electric lights had failed, and the room looked dim in the light of the remaining bulb and four candles.

'N-nursery games?' said Julian, seeing Alice and setting his glass down.

'I couldn't sleep,' said Alice, with an Irish accent nearly as pronounced as Bridget's. 'Dethided to come dow'stairs.'

'Dethoided t'com' dowsteers, did ye!' said Trefusis, and laughed. The child stuck out her tongue at him, and he was silent.

'Alice can stay,' said Diana, as the men waited for her to send her daughter out of the room. 'You'll be quiet and just listen, won't you Alice?' Alice nodded.

'My good Alicky,' said Bridget, who had removed her cap and apron in order to play whist, and had also pushed up her sleeves as though for physical labour.

They sat down in silence, and Julian dealt the cards.

'We'll play for – shilling points,' said Diana.

'I'll not,' said Bridget.

'Oh, don't worry,' said Diana, meaning that she would pay her debts.

'Pound points? Five-pound points? said Trefusis.

'No, no,' said Diana, watching Alice climb over the sofa.

'We'll p-play for love,' said Julian. 'I w-won't p-pay D-diana's card d-debts, my own are b-bad enough!'

'Penny points,' said Diana, 'we can all of us afford that.'

'Very well,' said Julian.

The game began. Bridget, whose face was ill-tempered tonight, studied the sleek, deliberately composed faces of the other three.

'What an oddity you are, Diana,' said Trefusis five minutes later.

'Why, Trefusis?' she replied, glancing at Bridget.

Bridget spoke. 'He means, mam, that you will have your servants in to make up the numbers for a game, and your little girl watching a scene of vice, too!'

'This is not a scene of vice,' said Diana.

'My good young woman,' smiled Trefusis, 'I meant nothing of the kind.

Bridget yawned, imitating a favourite gesture of Diana's.

'Then what did you mean?' said Julian, taking no notice of Diana, or of her disgraceful maid.

Alice was on the floor now, sitting still and slowly fingering the curtains in the window as she watched the group. Hearing Bridget speak had made her listen. Diana thought about Michael, how she had sold her soul to him and put all her eggs in one basket, and how she loved his child.

'Oh,' said Trefusis, taking a trick, 'I meant that she could so easily be a rich woman, and doesn't choose to be.'

'An unoriginal remark of yours, you've made it before,' said Julian. His face was flushed because he was so thankful that tonight, at this moment, the stammer which had shamed him all his life was under his control. It always came back after a while, but each time he would imagine being free of it forever. 'All your life you've been an oddity, haven't you Diana?' he said, simply in order to practise his voice.

'Very true,' said Diana, so impressed by the absence of his stammer that she could not look at him. 'I'm very much an oddity.' She thought of Kitty the actress.

'But you won't come with me to Paris, will you?' said Trefusis.

'Are you inviting me?'

'Of course.'

'How much do you offer me?'

'As much as you care to have. My only demand on you is that you shall outshine them all.'

Diana glanced up and noticed suddenly that Trefusis's face was sweating. She looked away, and her heart thumped with embarrassment.

'Oh, be quiet, Trefusis,' Julian laughed. He was not in the least uneasy now, for this was too ridiculous.

'I'll go to Paris,' said Diana then. 'Yes, I think I will.' She put her cigar down on the felt of the card table and Bridget took it before it rolled off the edge. Diana looked at her cards, put them down, and was frank. 'After all, Julian, I may as well end our little affair before you do. You *are* planning to end it, seriously planning, aren't you? And you see – ' she looked at Alice, who was staring at her, and then looked away. 'It's the second time I've run away from you, I know. I'm sorry.' If she became a full-blown tart in Paris, Diana felt, she would escape becoming a shady gentlewoman in Pau. But of course, she thought then, some grand tarts must end up as precisely that. Some lived with their mothers, too. I'm not going to cry, she thought, I can't cry any more. She looked remarkably calm.

'Oh, my dear,' said Trefusis in confusion, stroking his temples.

Diana said: 'Yes, it should be rather pleasant.' She would learn to drive a motor-car through the Bois de Boulogne. Trefusis of course was repulsive.

Julian bit through his port glass, just like Lady Caroline Lamb. He had been holding it steady at his lips for nearly a minute. There was no blood.

Diana started to laugh, quite gently. Her daughter, wide-eyed, stirred the adults' dropped cards round and round the table.

199

CHAPTER 16

A GRAND HORIZONTAL,
PARIS 1900

Trefusis was impotent, and had been so for thirty years. He had developed a positive distaste for lovemaking, which added to the dizzy strangeness of Diana's time as his creature.

She soon learned that it was his life's ambition not to have a pretty mistress, but to launch a queen of courtesans upon her career, to be her discoverer and her beginning. Though he knew that Diana was not ideally suited to being the greatest of *grandes cocottes*, Trefusis did not regret or resent her for her beauty moved him too deeply. It was only her seeming inability to take other lovers which seriously displeased him. Diana found this hard to understand, until she realised that his worship of harlots was as simple as it was pure. His ambition had come upon him because his secret wish was not to be the protector of a great whore, but to be a great whore himself; and a courtesan must have many lovers.

Diana was far more beautiful at twenty-six than she had been at eighteen. Then, she had been a large handsome girl, but now her whole appearance was finer; though she was still, Trefusis told her, Juno and Minerva combined, rather than mere Venus. Her perfect nose was much admired, and a sketch of her appeared in the *Paris Herald* only a month after her arrival. Trefusis was in transports over it.

He made her order fabulous clothes, and liked her to change her dress three times a day. He loved to see her undress down to nudity, and very occasionally he would pat her thighs and bottom when he saw her thus. He never did more. To comb her magnificent hair and dress it when she was half-clothed was Trefusis's most exquisite indulgence. (He was

200

like the old gentleman Diana remembered from reading *Fanny Hill*, of which she no longer had a copy: the book was too much bound up with memories of Dunstanton and Violet.) He would spend hours at this, telling her meanwhile how both the Parisian *haute-monde* and the *demi-monde* were not what they had been in his youth under the Empire.

The harlots of the sixties were every one of them superior to those of today. Liane de Pougy could not compare with Cora Pearl or Giulia Barucci. A part of the miracle of those days had been the fact that nearly all the courtesans (save Countess Castiglione) had come from backgrounds so humble they could hardly be imagined.

'And now we have officers' daughters – and English peers' daughters – instead of bottle-washers and little *grisettes.*'

'Like Nana?' said Diana, but he did not understand.

She remembered Nana's dying to the words 'To Berlin! To Berlin! To Berlin!', and her bosom swelled. She thought that on the whole it would be better for Trefusis not to read the book. He would never do so now, of course, he was too keen an anti-Dreyfusard, and had in any case always considered Zola's novels immoral and badly written, which amused her.

Diana watched the ribbon-like veins pulsing in his old temples as, for the sixth time, Trefusis combed out her one particular, thick lock of hair, and laid it on her bosom whilst drawing back the rest, so that she looked like a painting after Lely.

Trefusis began to tell her another story – they were all very similar – of how a courtesan had ruined a young man of family in the most unkind and dishonest, but laughable way. He grew increasingly excited, and before he had finished it he suddenly said: 'Touch me. Touch me, Diana.'

She put a hand on his head: it took her a moment to grasp quite what he meant.

Bridget came in. 'Viscount Daymien is here, mam, playing with Alice, and shall I tell him you're engaged? Sure he's a very handsome gentleman!' she said crossly.

Diana did not laugh. 'Tell Monsieur d'Amiens I will come down shortly.'

Trefusis struggled with himself. 'I wish you would get rid of that – that Irish girl! You don't understand how much harm she can do.'

'If Bridget goes, I go, Trefusis.' She was behaving according to form, making outrageous demands. Bridget, she had told him, must have the right to come and go where and when she pleased.

'D'Amiens!' said Trefusis, getting to his feet. He frowned. 'Monsieur d'Amiens is a noted personage, Diana. And a man who actually tired of Caroline Otéro after a month.' He paused, and become dignified. 'You should try to attach him, my dear.'

'I have attached him. Here he is, after all.' She got up, and lifted her eyebrows. 'Really, Trefusis!'

'No, no, you can't say that, merely because he approached you at Maxim's! That girl said your daughter was with him, and you know, Diana – ' He stopped.

Diana adjusted the shoulders of her dress, and looked into one of the great self-reflecting mirrors which hung on the walls. She was like a child when it came to contemplating with fascination an infinity of receding Dianas and Trefusises.

'Nobody seems to have objected to Alice so far. They think she's an amusing little monkey.' She turned.

'It's her clothes, Diana my dear, and the questions she will ask.'

'Nonsense! It's amusing. Don't be such an Englishman, Trefusis.'

Presently, Diana went down to her salon. All the rooms in her house in the rue St Lazare were furnished alike, with photographs of herself, Aubusson carpets, real and imitation Louis Quinze furniture, real and copied Bouchers and Fragonards, bowls of hothouse flowers, screens, *portières* and nude figurines. There was a little courtyard with an atelier at the back, and there she kept some old clothes, two of Michael's paintings, and a typewriter.

M. d'Amiens got to his feet and kissed Diana's hand when she came in. She saw a box on the table, and told Alice, who was very dirty, to find Bridget for a moment. 'Un petit cadeau, Monsieur?' she said. Diana's French was imperfect, but easy, and she spoke with a good accent, having had a French governess when she was seventeen.

'Chère madame! On m'a dit que c'est votre anniversaire aujourd'hui. Mes félicitations!'

'Ce n'est pas vrai,' smiled Diana, and opened her present. 'Mais, merci!' Inside the box, there was a coach-and-four in gold, jewels and enamel, obviously made by Fabergé. Diana sighed, and decided to sleep with the man who had brought it. She had been in Paris five months now, it was the middle of May, and she had as yet made no move in spite of Trefusis's encouragement.

'Ce n'est pas mal, n'est-ce pas?' said M. d'Amiens.

'Pas mal du tout,' said Diana. The thought of taking more lovers unnerved her, though Trefusis sometimes managed to inflame desires which neither he nor she could satisfy alone. No one, she thought, would ever be able to. From her protector's conversation, she had learnt that even the most powerful whores were expected not only to make love in the common way, but to do all manner of other things. She felt her lack of experience and excess of delicacy, and was afraid she would blush, stammer, make excuses and look a fool.

Julian had been excessively straightforward, and so had Michael. He had merely awoken her passionate taste for a very little violence with laughter and tears, because ordinary love had never seemed to release quite enough of their energy, back in Camden Town.

Diana raised her eyes from the monstrous jewel to the man's full well-cut face. 'Alors, Monsieur,' she said, tapping her foot on the carpet, 'je suis enchantée de vous voir! C'est dommage que Monsieur Trefusis est encore chez moi. Mais vous avez envie de moi?' She paused throatily, moved her eyelashes, and wondered what on earth he would expect her to do. M. d'Amiens shrugged and smiled.

Talking French, Diana felt herself to be almost unreal, an amusing monkey like Alice. 'J'espère qu'il prendra son congé, monsieur, quand cela nous sera convenable. Mais asseyez-vous, attendez un petit moment. Il ne nous dérangera pas aujourd'hui.'

The man took out a cigarette. 'Madame, vous êtes si gentille.'

She thought she would tease with a little polite conversation. 'Dîtes-moi, est-ce que vous êtes un bon Dreyfusard, monsieur? Et que pensez-vous de la victoire de Mafeking, et de la guerre en l'Afrique du Sud?'

Diana had no friends in Paris, and Trefusis told her that if she meant female friends, no *grande coquette* had any. Diana, who had three men to sleep with by the beginning of July, and sometimes forgot to charge them, tried not to be disgusted with his stories of their ostentatious rivalry. She could observe the signs of it for herself, in the Bois, at the Opéra and Comédie Française, at races at Longchamps and fashionable restaurants. They were no different from any other men.

She wanted a woman to write to and describe her life, but she corresponded only with Arthur Cornwallis, who seemed to enjoy writing to her about himself more than reading her letters. His only comment on them was that he had always followed her most extraordinary career with devout and absorbing interest. Cornwallis was Diana's only contact with England; and she had never been able to be fond of him. He was simply the person who, by accident, had been the most steadily present in her life since she was eighteen.

Occasionally, Diana thought of making friends with Maud, who was slightly scandalous herself in her dowdy way, and had expressed only mild disgust at her younger sister's conduct. But far more often, she thought of a woman who had recognised her in the London Library two days before she came over to France. The woman's name was Clementina Wood, and she was an old acquaintance, who had met Diana in Camden Town in 1896. Soon afterwards, she and her husband Augustus had gone to live in Italy, but they had returned to London a fortnight before Diana quitted it.

The two women had spent a long time murmuring together in one of the brown, grid-floored tunnels on the fourth storey. Clementina Wood, who was also a poet, was as plain and good as Diana was beautiful and wicked. Diana had found herself telling Clementina the exact truth about Michael's death and all that had happened since, and Clementina had nodded in a most interested way, and asked Diana to call on her when she came back from Paris. She had also asked her to write if she felt like it, but having confided in her, Diana was too shy to do so.

Diana remembered the shrewd placid kindness of the other woman's face, the ache in her own lower back, the light sucked in by book-backs, and the dry shabby warmth. 'Very like a womb for grown women,' Clementina had said. That dark afternoon among the fat volumes would always be a precious memory of solid life without enchantment, enchantment of any kind.

Diana believed she must not think of things like the London Library and London fog, wet rosy summers, proper food, and the odd Clementina and all she meant. But one day, she thought, I'll simply say 'I'm homesick', and I shall go. This was a fantasy; she did not believe she would ever go back.

In the meantime she was very rich, and she did not dislike it though she could not grow used to it. Diana had all the possessions and loaned objects she had supposed she would have as a courtesan, but they came to her in ways and in quantities which she had not imagined.

Her little Dion-Bouton motor-car had been delivered to the rue St Lazare one morning in a gigantic pink-and-white case, round as a hat-box and tied up with two dress-lengths of crimson satin. When Trefusis told Diana what the commotion in the street was, he had pushed her out onto the sunlit balcony and made her watch it being unpacked amongst a crowd of staring, crowing, whispering Parisians. When Diana came out, the people looked up at her, and some grinned, and for the first time in her life Diana had swayed and nearly fainted. She laughed just in time, as she wondered whether this piece of extravagance was an original idea, or Trefusis's copy of some other man's.

If she wanted another dress, it made no difference to

‍‌‍‍‍‌‌‌‌‌‍‌

‍‌‌

‍‌‌

Trefusis whether she ordered muslin or taffeta, one frock or ten. She might have bought houses in just the same way, and once she commented on this to Trefusis. Her lover asked her whether this was not marvellous, but Diana only said she would prefer a large but fixed annuity and moderate presents beside. She called the money which ran through her hands, fairy gold: but though her first comment had made Trefusis scowl, this second one produced a smile. He knew nothing of fairy tales, and believed his money to be absolutely sound.

'Did you keep your other mistresses in this style?' said Diana, one autumn day in the Bois de Boulogne. They had just returned from a visit to Deauville, and were soon to go on to the Riviera, where they would stay until Christmas.

'No,' said Trefusis, and continued: 'I used to be something of a miser. No question of what you're suggesting, my dear Diana, I was too much of a miser, until I – found you. Despite what you may have thought, supposed. I was well known for it, surely you've discovered that by now!' he exclaimed.

'I'm afraid I don't listen enough,' murmured Diana. She did not believe him, she remembered what Julian had told her about Trefusis and his race-horses, his yachts and picture collection.

After a pause, Trefusis said suddenly and rather pompously: 'I trust you, Diana.'

She understood then that he had not spent his fortune on any of the great established courtesans because he was terrified of their discovering his impotence. Perhaps it was her good birth which had made him take the risk of launching her as a *cocotte*, rather than any other; perhaps he thought of her as a highly intelligent woman of principle, and a kind person too, in spite of everything.

'You can trust me,' Diana said, and her voice was tender. 'Don't worry, Trefusis.' Oh dear, they must think him such a fool! she thought. I must remember to pay more attention to gossip.

'As a young man,' said Trefusis, swinging his cane, 'I was only moderately rich. Too, too moderately, that was my trouble.'

It would be a terrible strain, she reflected: preventing him from discovering that he had become ridiculous.

It was January again, and too cold to use the unheated atelier at the back of the courtyard in rue St Lazare. Diana's comfortable clothes and her typewriter had been moved into an upper bedroom, and she was sitting there now, typing out a caustic poem about Paris in the spring. She had called it 'Blue City with Shuttered Eyes'. Chestnut trees, she thought, crowded pavements, beggars, river wider than the Thames and all the pigeons thinner than in London. There was a cigarette gripped between her teeth.

Bridget came in and threw the door shut.

'Bridget!' said Diana, jumping in her chair.

'Diana,' the other said, using her name as she often did when things were very serious, 'mam, there's the new Duke come, don't you remember telling him you'd be in this morning? And Mr Cornwallis has come from London, and there they are, together in the salon!'

'Oh, my God,' said Diana. 'I quite forgot about him, why didn't you remind me earlier? And – and you say *Arthur*'s here, Arthur Cornwallis?'

'And how should I be remembering every sinful appointment of yours?'

'Oh, be quiet!'

'Well, mam, what are we to do, then?'

Diana got up. She was wearing a flannel nightdress and a dressing-gown from Whiteleys', and her hair was roughly pinned up at the back of her head.

'I must dress. Tell Jean to tell the duke I'll join him, and – and you must tell Arthur to go – in front of the duke – but tell him *privately* to come up, no, come back tomorrow.'

'You're frightened,' said Bridget quickly.

'I'm not. Come and help me get dressed.'

The two of them left the room. As they clattered downstairs to the second-floor bedroom, Bridget said loudly: 'There's too many men in this house, that's what it is!'

'Yes, yes, yes!' As she said this, Diana ran straight into

Arthur Cornwallis on the half-landing. She gasped, and Bridget came tumbling behind her.

'Diana!' Cornwallis said.

'What are you doing here, in my house?' she said, stepping backwards, remembering irrelevantly that he was now a widower, because Julian's sister was dead. 'Why did you come upstairs? Who gave you permission?'

'I escaped from your solicitious servants!' he said. Cornwallis was bald and rather wrinkled now, and he looked far less the wise and prissy owl than he had in 1890. 'Mayn't one pay a friendly call? Do you know, you don't look – at all – as I had imagined. How are you?'

'I am going to change,' said Diana.

They looked at each other, and their chests moved quickly up and down. Bridget kept a close watch.

'And so how is Julian?' she said.

'Quite recovered from his wound, one might say, although he did lose an arm, do you remember? I wrote to you. Well,' Cornwallis said, 'the Frenchman downstairs – whom I imagine to be a most valuable acquaintance, Diana, can poor old Trefusis quite approve? – obviously wishes me other-where, and so do you. I have to go on to Biarritz tomorrow, and then home, and so, alas – I don't think I shall see you until you come back to London.'

'No,' said Diana. 'Goodness me, you're very like Trefusis.'

'This is quite a magnificent *hôtel particulier*,' he replied, taking one step down and gazing at the staircase ceiling. He was speaking very fast, as though he were shy. 'How magnificently unreal it all is! But I can't be mistaken – that's a genuine, a very real Watteau, isn't it?'

'Get out,' she said. 'How *could* you not warn me you meant to come?'

He turned round, and quickly patted her hand on the banister, then kissed it and said: 'Don't cry, my dear Diana. Don't, I'm sure there's nothing to cry about.' He paused. 'In your – glorious situation, the only real immorality would be not to enjoy it – and not to be beautiful.'

Diana took a deep breath. 'Goodbye for the present,

Arthur,' she replied, and entered her rooms. She did not see Cornwallis go.

Half an hour later, when she was perfectly dressed, Diana entered her salon and told the plump young duke in the crudest way that she would do nothing for less than two million francs.

The duke was quite taken aback. Diana had a reputation for easiness, sexual naiveté and civilised behaviour, and her shouting at Cornwallis had made him very hopeful.

She looked ugly as she refused to bargain; her mind was all the time on Cornwallis's intrusion, and on how men should never be allowed to be part of a household. All these men were beginning to advance much too far, they were forever disturbing the peace made by herself, Bridget and Alice. Diana felt that she and her friend and her daughter were no longer able to combine against the clients and, powerless as they seemed to be, exclude them from their real lives. Once, she had thought they were able to do that.

'Touts *les plaisirs de l'amour* je déteste,' she told the duke, who spluttered. 'Alors donc, Monsieur le Duc, je dis: pour moi deux millions. Deux, trois millions me donnera tant de plaisir, et vous si peu de peine!'

As she had expected, he turned her down and tried to laugh.

When he was gone Diana remembered that, as Bridget had told her, she had been frightened an hour ago. She had irrationally imagined that this man would see her for what she was, and would hold her in contempt because of it. But she had changed, she had learned something from her interview with him, and she was not in the least bit afraid now.

She must become fiercer, more demanding and ill-tempered, and thus attract masochists. That might make her corruptly happy. But I can't manage it, surely, she thought. Diana went slowly back upstairs to her sea-green boudoir, let down her hair again and watched herself in the glass.

She could see Paris, framed by the windows, reflected in the mirrors behind her head. It was the 20th January, and on the high black roofs snow lay, like a shaking of flour on dark marble in a pantry. The snow was old and it was not melting, it was merely being eroded away in the streets by endless feet and wheels. The sky was whiter than frost and its light turned Diana's skin almost to blue.

It was true that she now hated sex, hated everything she had had to do with a man in the last year and had learned quickly and carefully how to do: but she noticed as she looked in the mirror that she seemed to thrive on it all the same. Her health and her looks were better than ever, she would grow more and more physically admirable until she burst with it.

Diana turned aside and began to undress. When she was back in one of her better negligées, she rang the bell and asked the housemaid to tell Alice to come to her. The child arrived after what seemed a long time and said: 'Well, Mamma?'

Diana looked at her. 'You're not going to be a beauty, Alice, are you, but at least you're going to be interesting. Little *jolie-laide*, then! You look so nice in your sealskin hat, it's so ridiculous.'

'Are we goin' out in the motor, then?'

'No,' said Diana, and picked her up and carried her over to the window. It was so convenient, she thought, that Trefusis was away with friends. 'We've got to stay in for a while yet, Alice.'

'Beautiful,' said Alice, who was remarkably contented, and did not seem to mind having two half-mothers and a series of men in the house. Alice understood reasonably well what they were there for. Diana knew with absolute certainty that she was right to allow Alice to grow up as fast as possible, to conceal no knowledge from her, so that the girl would never make the mistakes her mother had made through rebellious ignorance of the world. She knew that few people who made mistakes ended up half so well as she, Diana Blentham, had done.

'I want to go in the motor, Mamma, and wear me sealskin.'

Diana spent the night of the 21st struggling with morality in her large and empty bed.

One telegram had been sent to Arthur Cornwallis in Half

Moon Street, another to Clementina Wood in Gorden Square, and a third to a comfortable hotel in Bloomsbury Way. Nearly all the packing was finished, and the other arrangements made. But Diana could not decide whether she had a right to a fortune with which to start life in London, or next to nothing at all. She would certainly have to explain everything to Trefusis in a letter, which must be left on her dressing-table, and she felt this to be rather degrading in itself. In it, she supposed she would include the various press cuttings about herself from the *Paris Herald*, *Le Journal* and *Gil Blas*.

I am so used to running away, thought Diana: from home to Michael, from poverty, from Julian, and now this. Each time she deserted, she felt joyful and strong. It was said, of course, to be weak and bad to run away. Diana wondered what the servants would do and say, when she and Bridget and Alice turned up in the hall in travelling clothes, and ordered two fiacres to be sent for to take them and their luggage to the Gare du Nord. Probably they would think she was in trouble with the police, or had run up unpayable debts. Yet she was only leaving because she did not want to be immoral, and because she wanted friends.

Diana got out of bed and turned on the electric light. She went into her secondary boudoir and took out both her jewel-cases from their satin-covered safe. Returning to her bedroom, she sat down and tipped them out on to the pillows for counting, like a miser. She scattered them over the bed.

There was a bracelet of black pearls, diamonds and black enamel, two identical bracelets of gold and sapphire, about fifteen different rings, a tiara, brooches, earrings, headbands, more bracelets, and necklaces. Diana counted seven necklaces, five of which had been paid for by Trefusis. One matched the black-pearl bracelet, another mixed rubies, jet and emerald to make a collar of jewel poppies, and one was a heavy chain of interlaced diamonds. Diana sighed. Among them was the only piece her mother would consider fit for a lady: a three-row choker of very fine pearls with a clasp containing one yellow diamond.

She made her decision. She would take her simpler dresses from Worth (Bridget had already packed them), all the loose cash in the safe and in her dressing-table, and the big pearl choker. There must be about a hundred thousand francs in the house, thought Diana.

The rest of the jewellery, and everything else of value, she would leave. She would allow Trefusis to give it all to his next mistress. It was as though she, Diana, were the widow of a landed gentleman, obliged to hand the family jewels over to her son's wife. As for the other men who had given her charming presents, Diana pictured them fighting over what she had abandoned so easily.

By the evening of the 22nd, Diana, Bridget and Alice were at Boulogne, waiting for the ferry to take them to England. It was stormy, and it seemed they would have to wait some time.

As she watched Bridget and Alice playing Snap in the corner of the palm-filled hotel lounge, Diana thought how simple it had all been in the end though travelling was, of course, always exhausting. Paris seemed very far away, and as she tried to see the dark Channel through the window, she imagined that there, in the Bois, it was summer.

Within twenty-four hours they should be in London, settled in their hotel, and ready to look for a house in Bloomsbury for whose freehold Diana would pay cash. Diana felt sea-sick already; but wild and nervous and brilliant as a young girl set suddenly free from schoolroom constraints. No doubt, she thought, tears were close to the surface, as they usually were with her.

None of the family slept well that night in the over-heated yet draughty hotel. Diana was kept awake because she could not stop the words of one Kitty's favourite songs from *Iolanthe* running through her head. Even Lady Blentham had enjoyed *Iolanthe*.

For you dream you are crossing
The Channel and tossing

About in a steamer from Harwich,
Which is something between
A large bathing machine
And a very small second-class carriage.
And you're giving a treat –

However hard she tried, Diana could not remember the next few words, which came before 'to a party of friends and relations'.

She felt unwell the next morning, but the weather was better, and they were told that the ferries would be able to set out for Folkestone. Diana, Bridget and Alice left to catch their boat in a comfortable hurry.

It was not until they had reached the quayside, where they saw a hungry boy selling newspapers, that they learned the tidings which had reached Boulogne the night before. Diana stared at the black-edged English papers before she bought one; and she read it in amazement, because she had not thought of such matters for months.

'Who'd have thought it, poor old lady, God rest her soul, and her in Ireland only last year!' said Bridget, crossing herself as she stared over the boat's side at the French coast. Everyone in England would be dressed in black, because Queen Victoria had died.

Diana put the paper down at last on the deck of the ferry, and lit a cigarette, which spoiled the respectable picture she made of a pretty English widow travelling with her servant and child.